Steven Hamburg will donate all royalties he receives from the sale of Introspection to organizations that help our planet, people, and animals. The donations will be made in honor of his mother, his Uncle Fred, John Wagner, Jim Kopka, and David Snow.

INTROSPECTION
Transformation

Introspection: Transformation

Steven Hamburg

PRODIGY GOLD BOOKS

PHILADELPHIA * LOS ANGELES

PRODIGY
GOLDBOOKS

INTROSPECTION: Transformation

A Prodigy Gold Book

Prodigy Gold E-book edition / October 2018

Prodigy Gold Paperback edition / October 2018

Copyright (c) 2018 by Steven Hamburg

Library of Congress Catalog Card Number: 2018958693

Website: https://www.prodigygoldbooks.com

Author's e-mail: steve@introspection-novel.com

ISBN 978-1-939665-94-2

Published simultaneously in the US and Canada

PRINTED IN THE UNITED STATES OF AMERICA

ACKNOWLEDGEMENTS

My daughter Allie

Among my three children, Allie provided the most vocal support throughout my writing this novel. Additionally, while focusing on her coursework in college, she performed a very thorough edit of *Introspection: Transformation* One of the most difficult things Allie did during her editing process was to provide critique. I am very thankful for her honesty, and this novel would not be in its current state without her selfless support.

Dylan Horwitz

Dylan, an extremely avid reader of novels encompassing diverse genres, is the son of a good friend of mine. While he was a senior in high school, he offered to read and critique an earlier draft of this novel. Once done, we coordinated a date and time to discuss his assessment of the novel, and he arrived at our meeting with eight pages of notes. I mean, what senior in high school takes the time to comprehensively critique a novel drafted by a friend of his father? I cannot thank Dylan enough since his comments and suggestions enabled me not only to make this novel appealing to readers of all ages, but to ensure it particularly appeals and is relevant to young adults.

My brother Mike

Mike has been a very avid reader of novels encompassing many genres for as long as I remember. Through his extensive reading activities, and through all of the television shows and movies he has watched, this guy has seen just about everything anyone could possibly imagine. Mike read my novel and provided invaluable feedback that helped me incorporate unique elements that he has never seen before, which he thought readers would find stimulating and refreshing. He also expressed how proud he was of me for exerting the effort and demonstrating the creativity necessary to write this novel.

Chris Biles

Chris took the time to read a very early draft of this novel and provide feedback. The feedback he provided was invaluable, and enabled me to improve the quality of my work. Additionally, the encouragement he provided me throughout the creative writing process was instrumental in motivating me to complete *Introspection: Transformation.*

Many other friends and family members

Once I began writing *Introspection: Transformation*, the notion of conjuring up names for the characters was very daunting. However, I came up with the idea of using my friends' and family members' names, and all of a sudden, the character naming process became much simpler and much more enjoyable. All I ask of my friends and family members is to understand that there is no intended relationship between your attributes and the attributes of the fictional characters that are named after you!

<u>DEDICATION</u>

Introspection: Transformation is dedicated to the following people who have had a profound impact on my life.

My Mother

My mother passed away in December 2016. For my entire life, she was my biggest fan, and she will always remain my greatest hero. Despite enduring many hardships with her health, she always had a positive outlook on life. And regardless of how irrational or large my goals and aspirations may have been, she incessantly supported and encouraged me to reach for the stars.

My Uncle Fred

Doctor Fred Hamburg lost a miraculous and long-standing battle with cancer. Uncle Fred was one of the most brilliant people I knew. Perhaps more important and notable than his intellect is he was by far the most humble person I have ever known. He was the first person to read this novel. At that time, it was the first draft that I had completed. Despite the physical, emotional, and psychological hardships he was experiencing at that time, he made reading *Introspection: Transformation* a top priority. He completed reading the novel in three days and provided me invaluable suggestions for improving my work. Most importantly, Uncle Fred instilled the confidence necessary to motivate me to continue the writing and refinement processes so that *Introspection: Transformation* would emerge as a novel I could be proud of.

John Wagner

Like my uncle Fred, John lost a miraculous and long-standing battle with cancer. John lived across the street from my wife and me while we lived in Louisville, Kentucky nearly 20 years ago. John was like a second brother and a second father to me. What I loved most about John is as reflexively as I breathe, I could not help but cast a huge smile from my face every time he greeted me. Despite the hardships he experienced in life, and despite his illness, his love for his family, friends, and life itself has been immeasurably inspirational to me.

Jim "Jimmy K" Kopka and David Snow

Jimmy K and David were two of my closest friends. Both Jimmy K and David passed away much too soon. David was always very supportive of me, and his belief in me never wavered regardless of how ambitious my goals were. I will also never forget him helping me purchase my first two suits after I graduated from college. Jimmy K was the glue in our community. Everyone gravitated towards him and he was always capable of making me laugh regardless of what was on my mind at the time. I know both Jimmy K and David would be proud of me for completing more than a 30-year journey in order to write this novel.

INTROSPECTION
Transformation

Chapter 1
Transformation

June 2146

On his way to chemistry class, Jake was confronted with an onslaught of students' and faculty's trite greetings:

"Hey, Jake."

"How's it going, Jake?"

"What's up, Jake?"

Jake was numb to the attention because it happened whenever he was on school grounds no matter where he was. He wished things were the way they were before the incident when he was only visible to the people he cared about and vice versa. While he suspected these acts were an acknowledgment of his heroism and regret for what he had endured, the incident was merely something he tried to forget until each anniversary.

However, the walls riddled with campaign posters were a good distraction, especially since Jake found the girl running for class president to be beautiful. Additionally, he had wireless earbuds in his ears. Even though most times he wasn't listening to music, he pretended he was to minimize interaction with other students.

The next thing he knew, Jake was on the verge of falling asleep, with his head on his desk in his seventh-period advanced placement chemistry class, and a stream of highly viscous drool hanging down from his lips. His long hair was nearly covering the entire surface of his desk. Moments before falling asleep, Jake barely heard the words, "Today we're going to revisit the topic of entropy," from Joel Plonsker, his chemistry teacher.

"Jake, what is entropy?" Mr. Plonsker asked as a tactic to awaken Jake, although he was typically the only student either capable of or interested in answering any of the teacher's questions anyway.

In typical fashion, Mr. Plonsker had his hands inserted between his pants and tucked-in shirt, with his enormous belly overhanging the waist of his dress pants while pacing the classroom. Immediately bolting upright as if shocked by lightning, Jake answered, "Entropy is the amount of disorder, or randomness, in a system."

"And what does that mean?" Mr. Plonsker probed, transitioning Jake away from relying on his photographic memory and toward translating the complex concept into terms that his classmates could understand. The teacher absent-mindedly messed with the part in his greasy dark hair while he waited for the answer, a feeble attempt to conceal his baldness.

"Entropy is as a measure of how close a system is to equilibrium, and represents the amount of the disorder in the system."

"Excellent, Jake. Very good." Jake looked around to see his classmates rolling their eyes in disgust. He was not only Mr. Plonsker's favorite student but also all of the other teachers'. Anger abruptly displaced his uneasy feelings as he felt a spitball hit an exposed area on the back of his neck between clumps of unkempt, light blonde hair. The ball was moistened with the perfect amount of spit to affix itself to his neck until he peeled it off of his skin.

Mr. Plonsker transitioned into his lecture, and all Jake thought about was the uncertainty of his relationship with Julie Loren. They had been schoolmates since the second grade and began a romantic relationship earlier this school year. They were juniors. Jake reflected upon Julie's long, sandy blonde hair, six-foot-tall frame, and beautiful face, making him feel more upset.

"Jake, what is absolute zero?" Mr. Plonsker asked him after noticing he was distracted.

After a moment of silence, the teacher repeated the question in a sarcastic, high-pitched tone, "Ohhhhhhh Jake? What is absolute zero?"

Jake snapped out of his trance and responded, "Absolute zero occurs at zero entropy."

"Meaning?"

Jake was visibly frustrated by the attention, and said, "Meaning that no system can exist at absolute zero. I mean, life as we know it cannot exist at absolute zero."

"Very good." Again, the teacher's praise was followed by barely audible moans among Jake's classmates.

Given that class was nearing its end, and in light of his angst regarding the current state of his relationship with Julie, Jake blurted out, "I need to go to the bathroom." He stormed out of class and scrambled to his car, parked in the high school student parking lot.

Deciding to skip his eighth-period advanced placement biology, Jake drove his car to Cherokee Park in Louisville, Kentucky. He always went there when he was troubled. He parked and went into the deeply wooded area.

I'm such an idiot. What's my problem? Jake berated himself as he skipped a rock into a creek.

Not knowing what was straining his relationship with Julie, he assumed it was his fault. *Why did I ask her to be my girlfriend? I should have just kept things as friends. Hell, we're both going to college in a year and a half, and at that point, our relationship will have no chance of surviving. Guys will eat her alive in college. What was I thinking?*

Watching the rocks skip in the water and the ripples they created was soothing to Jake. The sun was unobstructed above the clouds and trees, creating a gold, glittery canvas on the water. Its reflection was nearly as bright as it would be if one were to look directly into the sun itself. The downside of the observation was it provided Jake with a visible reminder of the acne on his face and his six-foot-four-inch tall, chunky build.

Just as he was regaining his composure, Jake was startled by a noise he heard in a nearby bush.

"Who's there?" he yelled after picking up a flimsy stick and rock from the ground. There was no response, and Jake started to feel inexplicably dizzy. Suddenly, Jake detected an overpowering odor that smelled like flowers. He was perplexed since there were no flowers in bloom and only trees and bushes for many feet in all directions.

"Whooze thur?" he repeated in a slurred voice.

Just then, an elderly woman emerged from behind the bush. She was pale and appeared to be using all of her strength to make her way toward Jake slowly. She must have been close to one-hundred-years-old; she was nearly completely bald, with sparse and very long strands of white hair hanging down from her scalp, which was covered with brown age spots of various sizes. As she approached Jake by crawling along the grass, trying to avoid exposed tree roots, he found himself feeling drawn to her by force similar to what drives two droplets of water to reunite after being spilled on an impervious surface.

"Whoo ahh youuu? Whatz wong width youuu?" Jake's slurred speech continued.

The elderly woman uttered no words but continued crawling closer to Jake until she was near enough to grasp his hand. Immediately following contact, the elderly woman transformed into a light blue gas. Jake felt a jolt of electricity, became unconscious, and then collapsed to the ground.

Chapter 2
Discovery

January 2146

"I don't mean to appear insensitive, but why is Luallen convening a closed urgent-action meeting, in the Pentagon of all places, regarding the commercial airliner crash last week?" Senior Master Sergeant Kent Jacobsen said as he was rushing to catch a taxi.

Kent was more concerned for his job security than he was about the purpose behind Chief Master Sergeant Greg Luallen convening the meeting itself. Luallen was a real hard-ass; he was one of the leading contributors to the attrition of FBI agents, and Kent did not want to become another addition to Luallen's growing list of casualties.

"I have no idea, but I'm sure he has a damn good reason," Senior Master Sergeant Emily Tyson responded nervously, as she, too, was concerned for her longevity in the FBI. "He's not one to coordinate these meetings just to see attendees' pretty faces," Emily continued.

"Couldn't he have picked another day for this meeting? It's pouring outside, and I'm buried in fieldwork," Kent said, trying to convince himself that whatever reason Luallen had for calling the meeting paled in comparison to his continuously growing inventory of commitments.

Emily did not respond to Kent's rhetorical question. She was uncomfortable discussing it with him even though she shared Kent's concern regarding the meeting that Luallen had organized. Emily did not want to intensify the stress from which Kent was already suffering.

Luallen was not known for coordinating closed urgent-action meetings, let alone ones that occurred at the Pentagon. He had only convened three of these meetings—none of them at the Pentagon—during his ten-year tenure with the United States Air Force and two-years as the Secretary of Defense.

"Hey, wake up. What the hell's wrong with you?" Kent shouted at the driver.

Kent knew the driver was tired because of the cab slightly swerving.

"We're on a schedule here, and today is not a good day to die," Kent continued.

As if lightning had struck the cab, the driver became alert, and all issues were eliminated.

"I'm so sorry," the driver responded. "I'm new to this tandem-driving technology; understanding these cars have been available for years, I only recently was able to afford one."

Numerous advances had been achieved in neurotechnology during the past twenty years. This particular cab, although not equipped with the latest technology, was powered and controlled by the driver's brain and physiology. This, and other alternatives needed to be formulated because of increasing radiation interfering with satellite-controlled self-driving vehicles.

"Take it easy, Kent. I'm sure he hasn't slept for days," Emily interjected, sympathizing with the cab driver.

Kent didn't acknowledge Emily. He was buried in the process of self-inventorying in his mind all of the facts he could recall from the crash.

I N T R O S P E C T I O N: TRANSFORMATION

Boeing 777-200 aircraft with two Pratt & Whitney PW4070/4090 turbofan engines, three-hundred twenty-six passengers, of which twelve were Tranquility Airlines crew members. No act of terrorism currently suspected due to reliable preliminary findings indicating the flawed integrity of the metal comprising one of the wings of the aircraft, causing the formation of fatigue cracks leading to wing failure. Review of the audio and video flight recorders did not reveal anything suspicious within the plane or related to any communications between the aircraft pilots and air traffic control.

Emily put her hand on Kent's hand, which was equipped with long and chubby fingers.

"We're here," she uttered in a tone similar to one that would be used when entering a theater in which a movie was underway.

Kent's entire bulky body quivered as if he had just reacted to a frightening scene in a horror movie. Notwithstanding his inventorying process had been interrupted, he was convinced there was no foul play involved regarding the crashed airliner. He was convinced that the plane crash was unfortunately attributed to a manufacturing or human error. Still, he was very concerned about Luallen's reason for coordinating this meeting.

Kent and Emily left the cab and proceeded to get drenched by the rain as they entered into the Pentagon.

"I hate this place. I always feel like I'm at a cemetery when I'm here," Kent said as he began shaking the rain off his clothes and swiping the rain from his light brown hair.

"You are so high-maintenance, Kent. Sometimes I think you're the woman in our partnership," Emily wittingly responded.

"This way, please," a security guard commanded.

"OK, take it easy. Can't I dry myself off first?" Kent directed toward the security guard, more out of embarrassment from Emily's comment and his inability to effectively formulate and vocalize an effective retort than from real displeasure.

After drying himself off and patting his ever-growing belly with both of his hands, the security guard led them through the main lobby, a security checkpoint, and then into a corridor. The corridor led to a series of elevators requiring rare security clearance that both Kent and Emily had been granted so they could attend the urgent-action meeting convened by Luallen. With an expressionless face, the security guard gestured Kent and Emily to enter the elevator.

"Level 12-C? Levels 12-A through 12-E? I've never seen *that* before," Emily expressed after focusing her attention on the digital elevator panel. "It's always just been 'level 12' from what I've seen," she continued. "You know…"

She was cut off by the tone that sounded, the elevator indicating that the level of interest had been reached. The security guard inserted a device into a jack that only became visible to Kent and Emily once the device was close to the elevator panel. Upon entering the device into the jack, the elevator doors opened. The security guard left the elevator, placing his back to the chamber within which the retractable elevator door receded, and he motioned Kent and Emily forward.

"It's pitch dark in here," Kent said as he left the elevator. "I can't see my handsome reflection along the walls."

"Yeah right, Kent. Luckily for you, you don't have a visual reminder that you can stand to lose a good thirty pounds, and you continue to disable your BioSense implant, you fat ass," Emily said, poking Kent in his gut overhanging the waistline of his pants.

"Forgive me," the security guard responded.

A quick succession of three ringing tones sounded from his mobile device, and lights illuminated throughout the area. Kent's eyes were met with a long, sterile corridor. Several hallways extended on either side of him and Emily as they walked through the hall.

"Ah, yes. There I am," Kent said proudly, accentuating the part in his straight hair and improving the posture of his six-foot frame.

Kent's stomach sank, and his tall stature shrank once he noticed a heavily guarded door. He assumed that was where Luallen's urgent-action meeting was located. Sure enough, as they approached the protected area, two security guards opened the door.

INTROSPECTION: TRANSFORMATION

Upon entering through the door, Luallen greeted Kent and Emily sarcastically. "Pleased you two could join us."

Rather than establishing eye contact with Luallen in response, the first person Kent and Emily saw upon entering the room was the President of the United States, who was sitting at the far end of a multi-purpose table facing them.

"What in the hell is she doing here?" Kent said softly to Emily.

"I'm the President of the United States. I believe that affords me the clearance to be wherever the hell I want to be at any point in time, does it not?" President Elyse Claring responded.

President Claring could have pierced a hole through Kent's chest with her intimidating glare. Her brown hair hung down over her shoulders and was uncharacteristically disheveled.

"Please forgive me, Ms. President," Kent replied, his head down in shame as he reaffirmed that this was going to be a very long and bad day.

"Are you going to sit down, or are you going to continue delaying our meeting with your tails between your legs?" Luallen asked rhetorically in a raised voice.

As they navigated their way to two vacant seats at the table, Emily and Kent could not help but notice President Claring's expression. It was reasonable for anyone present to assume that President Claring was upset with Kent's remark. However, she appeared to be visibly troubled by something else. Although it seemed she was looking directly at Emily and Kent as they made their way to their assigned seats, President Claring was in a daze, absently looking right through them to some random point on the wall.

"This isn't going to be good," Kent muttered under his breath to Emily. They proceeded to the places at the dark brown stained mahogany table with placards bearing their respective names.

Both Kent and Emily were not only surprised by President Claring's presence but also by the fact that all five of the United States armed service branches were represented in person by their respective senior ranking officials, something Kent himself did not recall ever previously occurring.

"I'm sure all of you have pressing questions." Luallen's voice cracked during this statement. His face was severely scarred and nearly entirely callused, ridden with gashes. His fierce look was complemented by his chiseled chin and two partial ears. He was tall, muscular, and slender at the waist—a very intimidating person who always commanded a dominating presence.

"Luallen demonstrating signs of shock? Weakness? Unprecedented," Kent whispered to Emily. "Is this happening?"

"Shut up. This isn't the time to talk. You're distracting me and embarrassing us," Emily responded.

Anyone who had served with Luallen, and all who knew him, were acutely aware of his fearlessness. Statistics would indicate that he should have been killed in action at least sixteen times over. Tour after tour, when nearly all fellow pilots and soldiers died around him, Luallen had inexplicably found ways to survive. Considering prisoners of war do not typically live to walk once again on United States soil, Luallen had done so on three separate occasions.

None of his subordinates ever questioned his judgment, as they knew second-hand from understanding Luallen's history that being assigned under his command yielded their best chances for survival. Further, none who served under his command ever saw him succumb to, acknowledge, or express any fear whatsoever. Even though neither Kent nor Emily had ever served under Luallen's direction, they knew plenty about him because he was the most decorated African American in the military: a living legend. This understanding of Luallen's history and the respect he garnered from all who knew him made his audible fear that much more disconcerting.

"I am sure many of you are wondering why I have asked you to attend this closed urgent-action meeting. By way of explanation, I ask each of you to watch this video carefully." Perspiration accumulated just above Luallen's brow.

INTROSPECTION: TRANSFORMATION

There was dead silence that seemed to linger for days, though only a matter of seconds had elapsed.

"Greg," President Claring said at a heightened volume, leaning forward with her shoulders on the table and hands clamped.

"Yes, Ms. President." Luallen's response was barely audible. He seemed to shake himself out of a haunted trance and continued more loudly. "This video was captured from the audio-video flight recorder located in the front of the aircraft, which was facing the passengers."

In result of the high frequency of airline crashes drastically increasing from 2120 through 2135, the Federal Aviation Administration had sanctioned the design, manufacturing, and placement of flight recorders that could capture video in addition to audio throughout the fuselage and cockpits of all commercial airliners. Prototypes were designed in 2136, and the Federal Aviation Administration approved the first audio-video flight recorder in 2137.

"The video began approximately 45 seconds before something noticeably went awry with the trajectory of the plane. Based upon the sounds made by the aircraft itself, the plane appeared to experience a series of abrupt and violent jolts. After analyzing data received from the flight recorder, it had been determined that the aircraft was at an altitude of approximately 37,000 feet at this point in the recording," Luallen continued.

Screams could be heard. Luallen fast-forwarded the recording to twenty-one minutes following the first occurrence of the jolts and passengers' initial screams. Shortly after resuming, visible images could finally be seen on the recording. Passengers could be seen screaming, bracing themselves in their seats, and crying hysterically as the plane was utterly rotating about its length approximately every five seconds.

Many passengers who did not have their seat belts fastened before the plane beginning its spinning could be seen unconscious, their bloody, distorted bodies violently colliding with seats, other passengers, the floor, and the inner ceiling throughout the aircraft.

Sounds of bones and ligaments being crushed and further disintegrated each time a passenger's limp body impacted a surface nearly outweighed the cries of the remaining living passengers.

The entire interior of the aircraft was engulfed in streaks of blood. In each subsequent instant, the number and volume of cries from the passengers decreased as, one-by-one, they were rendered unconscious. Sensing that everyone watching the video was more focused on the horrifying sounds captured on the recording than on what had been visibly recorded, President Claring addressed the group.

"Did everyone see what just happened in this video?" she asked. Her piercing blue eyes met Emily's hazel-green ones.

Emily looked down at her lap out of intimidation. Luallen had already watched the video dozens of times and was not watching it now, though he appeared visibly disturbed.

"I apologize, Ms. President, but I didn't see anything of particular significance other than the horrible pain, suffering, and deaths among the passengers," Kent said, still wondering why the closed urgent-action meeting had been convened.

"Rewind the video ten seconds," President Claring directed the FBI data analyst who took over operating the controls of the audio-video recording from Luallen as she stood up from her chair and leveraged her nearly six-foot athletic build to take command of the meeting.

"Pay close attention to these two areas of the screen," President Claring instructed, pointing to the screen with her laser pointer.

What happened within those ten seconds was inexplicable. The FBI data analyst transitioned the video to slow motion. Caused by the spinning and violent jolting of the aircraft, the line of sight of the video camera changed, and new images appeared in the video at the two areas of interest identified by President Claring. In an instant, what appeared to be some gas could be seen within the aircraft. The gas was immobile, contained within a rather small area, and bright blue.

INTROSPECTION: TRANSFORMATION

One minute and twenty-two seconds later, they heard the chilling sound of the impact of the aircraft into the ground. The silence was deafening as the projected image became still and lifeless. Within moments, all that could be seen were the bodies and other contents of the plane becoming engulfed by flames. The video was replaced by a still image containing the two areas inhabited by blue gas.

"We have confirmed that the crash resulted from the flawed integrity of the metal comprising one of the wings of the aircraft, causing the formation of fatigue cracks, and leading to wing failure, as has been reported to the public," Luallen said with a blank face. "We have also confirmed that the gas contained in the aircraft, as may be seen in this image, played no role whatsoever in the failure of the wing. No terrorist activity is suspected to have occurred. Dr. Agon, please take it from here."

"At the time my team of scientists arrived at the scene of the wreckage, what may be seen in this image as blue gas had changed into a viscous blue liquid, as you can see here," Dr. Yash Agon, Nobel Peace Prize-winning Indian Chemist and former Harvard University professor of Science, said with intrigue and insatiable curiosity in his voice as he transitioned from one image to the other.

"The recovered liquid consists of materials that could not be identified, possesses a pungent metallic odor, and did not appear to be affected by the heat from the fire that was ablaze soon after impact," Dr. Agon said, holding up a transparent glass vial containing the foreign blue liquid. It made a harsh contrast to Dr. Agon's dark complexion and black hair.

"What do you mean the materials cannot be identified?" Kent asked dismissively.

"Um, elements comprising the liquid are not in our periodic table," Dr. Agon responded after a moment of uncomfortable hesitation and silence.

Everyone at the table looked at each other, not understanding what Dr. Agon had just explained.

"We believe this liquid is of extraterrestrial origin," President Claring uttered faintly.

Chapter 3
Imminent Exodus

June 2145

"Key elements of our atmosphere are disintegrating because of Shangten's ever-increasing proximity to its sister suns. I estimate we have three solar eclipses before our planet is no longer able to sustain life." Gralp perceived that his superiors were not acknowledging the severity of the situation. "Further, it is difficult to know whether the depletion of our planet's resources will outpace the survival of the planet itself." Gralp turned toward Jarga, the ruthless ruler of Shangten.

Gralp's anger and frustration were visible as an increased brightness and intensity to his orange-colored, amorphous body. He stood alone while communicating his concerns to Jarga in the ruler's military quarters. The facility was sterile and monotonous, comprised solely of shiny silver-colored alien metal.

"We understand your concerns, Gralp, considering this is the sixth time you have shared this with us in as many days," Jarga responded in his usual condescending manner.

Then why are you not..., Gralp's thought was interrupted. He suddenly felt as though he was being suffocated. Even worse than experiencing the sensation of suffocation, Jarga implanted an image of Gralp dying into his mind. Gralp's previously bright orange body transitioned to a flickering pale orange.

"That will be all, Gralp. Your stink disgusts me. Leave us." Jarga released his psychical hold over Gralp as he uttered his last few words. He turned away dismissively, as if Gralp was no longer present and of no more value to him than a morsel of trash.

Gralp was relieved that the last thing he saw before dying would not be the increased intensity of Jarga's emerald green body.

"On second thought, wait," Jarga insisted. "Just how much time will three solar eclipses afford us?"

"Approximately three years," Gralp replied.

All inhabitants of Shangten that had survived its largest ever genocide, which had occurred in Earth year 1956, communicated telepathically, possessed psychical abilities and completed activities via telekinesis. Those species that couldn't were deemed by Jarga to be unworthy of life and were mercilessly eradicated.

Jarga, an Ungden, had orchestrated this action against the other races. He was the most powerful among all inhabitants of Shangten due to his unsurpassable telepathic, psychical, and telekinetic abilities. Perceiving companionship and friendship as weaknesses had consciously left him without companions and friends, so Jarga was a dictator who used his mind to exercise his will.

Following the merciless killings, only four of twelve previous races remained. The Grunats, Sellinians, Ungdens, and Flares existed in a caste system dictated by their respective intellectual capabilities. The Sellinians were the lowest members of the society, followed by the Flares and then the Grunats, with the Ungdens possessing the most significant intellectual skills.

In spite of the tension that existed between the Grunats and the Ungdens, the Grunats' telepathic and telekinetic abilities were no match for the Ungdens'. The Ungdens considered the Grunats as subservients that should assume remedial tasks too demanding for the Sellenians and Flares. Generally, the Sellenians and Flares accepted their place in society.

"What is your reaction to Gralp's claims, Leese?" Jarga inquired.

Leese was the closest thing to a friend to Jarga and the only one he would acknowledge individually among all inhabitants of Shangten.

"Unfortunately, they come with great accuracy, Jarga. We should respond to his assessment with appropriate urgency," Leese replied.

Jarga could sense the sincerity of Leese's sentiments given the chaotic variations his emerald green body was undergoing and the steadiness of the density of his gascous body.

"Very well then. Assemble and deploy a sufficient number of survey parties to consist primarily of Sellinians and Flares, considering their expendability. Relay the expectation that planets on which we may sustain life are to be confirmed and identified to me within fifteen-and-a-half months," Jarga demanded. After considering Leese's psychic energy for a moment and noticing variances in the density of his typically dense Ungden body, Jarga continued, "I sense your doubt, Leese. We are not afforded the luxury of doubt. Either one of our survey parties is successful, or life as we know it will cease to exist. We are not equipped to wander aimlessly and indefinitely in space. We need to migrate to a host planet, so we can explore galaxies currently too far from our purview. Do not disappoint me."

Leese sensed Jarga's urgency, both telepathically and by witnessing the intensity of the color of Jarga's body; its color was brighter and more intense than Leese had ever seen.

Seeing the variances in the density of Leese's body reminded Jarga of a painful memory involving his father in November 2015.

"Why do we have to leave here, Father?" Jarga asked.

"Because, my innocent son, our ruler only wants more for herself. Nothing is enough for her."

"I don't understand. I like it here. Why can't we stay here and let her leave?"

"That is not an option. We must follow Qarta's will."

"Why are you so weak, Father? If you don't want to leave, you shouldn't leave. What are you doing, Father? Stop it, you're hurting me," Jarga said. He was in agonizing pain.

"You will not question my judgment, and you will never disrespect me again."

"Dad, stop it. Stop. Stop."

Leese left Jarga's military quarters only to find Gralp staring down the corridor formed by a seemingly endless succession of transparent glass walls. The glass corridor looked out upon a massive magenta body of water so clear that reflections of Shangten's three moons and two suns could be seen with crystal clarity. Gralp commonly marveled at the sheer coarseness of his planet's terrain, which was riddled with spike-like rock formations of varying heights that could easily be mistaken as random arrangements of swords and knives. Gralp found beauty in the terrain, even though most inhabitants were either threatened by its visible harshness or bored by its consistency and abundance.

"I sense both from your thoughts and your reduced density that being forced to find a new host planet is not the only thing that is troubling you, Gralp," Leese relayed telepathically.

"I love Shangten. This planet has been good to us. And our way of showing our gratitude is by killing it?"

"You are far too sentimental, Gralp. Planets are but vessels with the sole purpose of sustaining life. There is no shortage of planets, and relocation keeps us sharp, alert, and resourceful," Leese responded.

"There may be many planets, but finding one inherently capable of enabling us to survive is becoming increasingly difficult. As intelligent as Jarga thinks we are, our transient history is nothing to be commended."

I N T R O S P E C T I O N: TRANSFORMATION

Leese's impatience with Gralp was intensifying. "Remaining dormant indefinitely on a planet does us no good. Dependence and complacency grow and vulnerability to hostiles increases. Further, we deserve all that we desire in consideration of our intellectual superiority over all other beings we have encountered." Leese's intentions of bringing this conversation with Gralp to a quick conclusion were obvious.

"That may be true, but what entitles us to exploit our intellects by purging subsequent host planets of their current inhabitants?"

"We require no entitlement. This has been the way of our people since the beginning of time, as coexistence has proven suboptimal."

"'Suboptimal'? Do you not mean 'inconvenient'?" Gralp spoke with resentment and disgust. The luminous intensity of his orange body was nearly blinding.

"Perhaps you would like me to put you out of your misery, so you need not suffer anymore?"

Gralp intellectually retreated with a pause before responding, "No, that will not be necessary."

"You cannot suppress your thoughts from me, Gralp. I know of your intentions," Leese stated while scanning Gralp's non-vocalized thoughts. "Either you show support for our way of life, or the privilege of living will be taken from you."

Gralp was overwhelmed with distaste toward Leese, Jarga, and all of those who blindly upheld Jarga's bidding. Acknowledging defeat amidst his powerlessness, he turned away and headed for his living quarters.

Chapter 4
Fear

March 2146

"Thank you so much for spending time with my family, Yash," Sangeeta said graciously.

"Our children always love seeing you," Sangeeta's husband, Raj, added.

"It has been long overdue. Please do not mistake my scarcity as an expression of disinterest or lack of love for you and your family. I love all of you very much. You know me. My work consumes me," Dr. Agon responded, sounding a bit ashamed.

"You don't need to apologize, Yash. I completely understand." Sangeeta embraced her brother around the waist.

It was a beautiful day. The sun was shining, unobscured by clouds. The sky was pale blue. It was warm enough to dress in short-sleeved shirts and shorts, yet cool enough not to break much of a sweat when engaging in physical activity. Days like these were scarce in number. Most days were either excessively warm, excessively cold, engulfed by clouds, or showered by relentless rain.

INTROSPECTION: TRANSFORMATION

"Uncle Yash, will you push me on the swing?" his six-year-old niece asked.

"Me too. Me too," his two nephews, one eight-years-old and the other four, pleaded in unison.

"Daaahhh wheeey shooogeeee flum," Dr. Agon interpreted this as a plea to be pushed on the baby swing by his ten-month-old niece.

"OK, OK. Here I come," he responded, feeling regret for neglecting his sister and her family for so long.

The truth was that Dr. Agon could not get enough of them. Although his relationship with Sangeeta was not quite as close as it had been when they grew up together in Bangalore, India, it was still strong. They both knew that each would do anything for the other. It was just the two of them in their immediate family, aside from their parents, and they shared a unique bond.

"Whee," Dr. Agon cried as his eight year-old nephew was on the verge of reaching a height where his bottom would lift from the swing seat, and he would enter that brief moment of weightlessness.

With the grace of agility at his disposal, Dr. Agon pushed his other nephew and two nieces in succession. "Whee," he continued.

The children's giggles were the only sounds Dr. Agon, his sister, and Raj could hear. They were filled with pure joy, not suffering from a single worry in life. Dr. Agon could not remember the last time when he was so happy. He was in a trance that he hoped would never end, the burden of his job and his relentless pursuit of purpose temporarily forgotten.

"Lunch is served." Raj had arranged a picnic lunch for them on a blanket sprawled on the vast lawn at Rock Creek Park in Washington, D.C.

Before Dr. Agon could say a word, both nephews, Mark and Johnny, and his six-year-old niece, Pubali, were aloft from their swings and scrambling toward the food. Responding to her cries, Dr. Agon lifted his niece, Miriam, from the baby swing and jogged over to the picnic site while repetitively throwing her up in the air and catching her. Miriam's cries transitioned to giggles as she felt like a rocket being shot into the sky.

"Wow, this looks amazing, Raj," Dr. Agon said with genuine praise and amazement as he joined the others on the blanket.

"You should open a restaurant, seriously." He threw a grape up in the air and caught it in his mouth.

Dr. Agon, Raj, and Sangeeta enjoyed each other's company while appreciating their surroundings along the Carter Barron Amphitheatre and playing with the children.

"Uncle Yash, catch," Pubali said, right after she threw and hit Dr. Agon in the face with a grape.

Her laughter, along with everyone else's, filled the air.

After finishing lunch, Dr. Agon played a game of tag with his two nephews and Pubali. Raj and Sangeeta were pampering Miriam. As he was running around chasing after his nephews, he heard shrieking in the distance, which appeared to be coming from Sangeeta. He grabbed and carried his nephews over each shoulder, with Pubali at his side, running back to Sangeeta as she continued to scream for him.

"What's the matter, Sangeeta?" Dr. Agon was alarmed as he looked down to see Miriam violently convulsing in her lap.

Just as he began tending to Miriam, Raj collapsed to the ground and started convulsing similarly. Suddenly, Miriam transitioned into an eerie state of stillness.

Without warning, and in a matter of only a few seconds, Miriam's body transformed into a pool of blue liquid, similar to ice melting in an extremely hot skillet. Dr. Agon began to panic. Before he had time to react, Raj, too, transformed into a pool of blue liquid. He and Sangeeta were crying hysterically at the same time Mark, Johnny, and Pubali were screaming in terror.

"I don't know what to do, Sangeeta." Dr. Agon cried out through tears.

All of a sudden, silence overwhelmed them; the other three children were no longer crying.

INTROSPECTION: TRANSFORMATION

As Dr. Agon turned to check on his nephews and niece, Sangeeta cried, "No," and then she was reduced to violent crying in a fetal position.

His once lively and beautiful nieces, nephews, and brother-in-law had all been reduced to nothing but small pools of blue liquid.

All Dr. Agon heard was a high-pitched sound similar to what was heard in close proximity of an explosion. Trying to ease himself of his pain, he turned back around to console Sangeeta but found that she had also become a pool of blue liquid on the ground.

"Don't worry. We will not hurt you. You are too important to us. There is a purpose you must serve," a voice uttered behind him.

Turning around, Dr. Agon was confronted by a group of blue-colored aliens. Each was approximately eight feet tall, with sheer blue skin that had the appearance of flowing water. The appearance of the aliens instantly tempered the severe shock of losing his entire family.

"What in the hell have you done? What do you want from me? Why did you have to kill my only family? Where are you—" Suddenly, everything began to go dark, and Dr. Agon collapsed.

When he regained consciousness, he was vertical, bound by a blue adhesive material against a metal wall. He was naked and noticed blue and green discolorations on his feet and legs. No aliens were in the room with him, and his thoughts were more consumed by the loss of his family than fear for his wellbeing. He was shivering violently and realized that the room was freezing.

He attempted to free himself from the bindings, and each time he did so, his flesh ripped off his bones. Three times, he tried to free himself. However, regardless of the extent to which he could release portions of his body from the wall, he was immediately reattached by the alien adhesive material. He quickly realized his efforts were futile, the pain was unbearable, and he ceased his escape attempts.

"We apologize for the shock of the loss that we have inflicted upon you. We find our human subjects are more focused and reliable without familial attachments," an alien said as his body slowly emerged from what appeared to be a pitch black corridor located in front of Dr. Agon.

"Attachments? That's how you refer to my family? I'll never be of use to you." Dr. Agon suddenly became concerned for his wellbeing as he got a good look at the grotesque alien. It had a huge, glossy head. There was no hair anywhere on its body. Its five eyes were elliptical, and each was a different size, uniquely oriented, and bright yellow. A substance that appeared to be similar in consistency to human saliva was continually oozing out of the alien's mouth and other orifices.

It had no teeth but was equipped with a very long, snake-like tongue. Various unidentifiable appendages were extending from its torso, and it was supported by what appeared to be two wide legs bent at the knees. Since the alien was facing Dr. Agon, he was unable to see its rear. Similar to the aliens he'd encountered at the park, this one was also approximately eight feet tall, with sheer blue skin that had the appearance of flowing water.

"Your response is not uncommon. Once the transformation is complete, your thoughts will not be your own. They will be what we want them to be. And worry not, the pain from which you are currently suffering will soon be no more."

Dr. Agon was overcome by excruciating pain as he heard deafening crunching noises from within his body. The sounds originated from his entire endoskeleton. All of his bones and cartilage were contorting and transforming into another substance and form. His body was becoming gelatinous, consisting solely of flesh and blood. The pain was unbearable.

"Ah." He cried as he found himself awakened from sleep, covered in sweat in his bed. Because of how vivid the nightmare had been, he decided to call Sangeeta later in the morning to confirm that she and her family were well.

Chapter 5
Mystery

March 2146

"OK, so what anomalies have been identified? What in the hell is it? Give me something," Kent yelled at his Special Task Force, specifically assembled to investigate further the alien substance found among the remains of the crashed airliner.

Kent had been appointed by Luallen to assemble the Special Task Force and lead the investigation for the United States Air Force, and more broadly, on behalf of the United States and the entire world. Even though only two weeks had elapsed since the airliner crash had occurred, Kent was feeling the pressure from his boss, as Luallen was seeking some intelligence that he could provide to his peers and superiors. At this point, Luallen had nothing, and his credibility was beginning to be questioned.

"Just last evening, we were able to identify and correlate the remains of all deceased passengers to the passenger manifest, and we have confirmed what may explain the presence of the two blue masses." Dr. Agon broke the deafening silence in the room. His voice cracked when he spoke, and sweat rolled down his temples. He shared in the pressure felt by everyone on the Special Task Force, and the fact that he felt uncomfortable in the presence of groups did not help his situation.

"Well, what's the explanation, Agon?" Kent insisted impatiently.

"Take it easy, for god's sake. I'm doing the best I can, considering the situation at hand," Dr. Agon snapped in response, which was a shock to everyone in the room who knew him. He had always been a soft-spoken and mild-mannered person.

"Forgive me, Agon. I know we're all doing the best we can," Kent spoke more calmly.

"After correlating the remains of all of the deceased passengers to the manifest, no remains could be located for two people on the list, which is consistent with the two blue masses seen in the video flight recorder. This appears to be no coincidence."

"That doesn't make sense. Why would the manifest indicate that these two passengers boarded the plane. . ."

Kent cut Emily off before she could finish her question. "What are the names of the passengers whose remains were not located?"

"Stacey Smith and Jennifer Cole."

"Those are very generic names. It is suspicious to me that the two individuals whose remains cannot be located have the last names of 'Smith' and 'Cole'." Luallen directed his comment toward Kent, who gave him a blank look. "Emily?" Luallen tried.

"Yes, very generic," both Dr. Agon and Emily responded in unison.

"Tyson, I need you to learn everything you can about these two passengers. Did they ever board the aircraft? Is it just a coincidence that two people's remains could not be located and two blue masses were seen via the video recorder? We have too many fundamental questions unanswered; we need to achieve some progress here, or I am going to begin questioning my own, and this Special Task Force's, ability to address the task at hand," Luallen said to Emily in a harsh and elevated tone before leaving the conference room.

Kent was exhausted and frustrated. He couldn't remember whether he had slept at all during the previous 72 hours. It was noticeable that his faculties were becoming compromised even though he was still performing commendably. He was unbathed, his hair was greasy and unkempt, lacking its traditional and distinctive part, dark stubs of hair were forming sporadically on his chin and cheeks, and he had a strong resemblance to what a mad scientist may look like.

"Agon, do you have any more information regarding the blue substance?" Emily requested a Hail Mary at this point.

"Nothing. I'm sorry," Dr. Agon responded, hanging his head. "But I assure you that Hendrix and I are doing everything we can to —"

"Hendrix," Kent said to himself, trying to recall why she looked so familiar. "You were present during the closed urgent-action meeting in the Pentagon a couple of weeks ago?" he inquired of her.

"Yes, that's me," she responded.

"I appreciate your service on our task force. Your help is greatly needed and appreciated."

Kent turned to Emily, "OK. I need some coffee. Let's get out of here."

Emily and Kent left the conference room that had been established as the Special Task Force hub and went to a nearby break room.

"Who is this Hendrix?" Kent discretely asked of Emily. "And why is it that she is the only person Luallen appointed to my Special Task Force?"

"I don't know, but I'll look into it. On to more important matters; acknowledging you are a superior ranking officer, with all due respect, I'd be remiss if I didn't tell you that you look like hell. Despite still having your wits about you, you're not operating at 100%. Not even close."

Kent and Emily had been assigned to multiple initiatives together during the previous five years and had grown to respect each other both personally and professionally. She had not realized it, but her growing affection for him was distracting her from performing at her maximum potential. She was steadily working on building enough courage to express the feelings she had for Kent. Styling her long hair in different ways, coloring it, wearing it down instead of always up in a bun or ponytail, and donning what some may consider as slightly provocative clothing at social events to accentuate her attractive figure were all weak signals she'd previously broadcasted to Kent. She was reflecting on this very topic when Kent's rough voice snapped her out of her trance.

"Luallen is breathing down my neck in his special way, and he has every right to, Emily. I'm no closer to finding any answers than when we first saw the video from the flight recorder. It's been nearly three weeks. I didn't want this damn assignment. I'm lost here. Aliens on earth? What the hell is going on? Luallen wants an update at 0700."

Kent was frantic, actually speaking to himself rather than to Emily. She cut him off. "You need to get some rest. You're no good to anyone in your current condition. More importantly, you're no good to this country right now. What is your implant telling you?"

"Nothing."

"Yeah, I know. It's because it's never activated. Activate the damn thing now."

"It's worthless. All it does is tell me I'm overweight and not taking care of myself."

"Exactly, activate it now."

"OK. OK. Sheesh."

Kent activated the government-issued BioSense implant that were issued to all FBI field agents by using a pairing application installed on his mobile phone. After a few moments, the implant was fully operational.

Noticing Kent's right eye slightly flickering, which was a common occurrence when activating the implant, Emily inquired in a harsh tone, "OK, so tell me what it says."

INTROSPECTION: TRANSFORMATION

"I need to lose thirty-eight pounds. I'm severely sleep deprived. My blood sugar is dangerously low. My brain is operating at 66.38% capacity—"

"OK, you get my point," Emily interjected.

Kent's demeanor and expression abruptly transformed. His sole purpose in life was to serve his country and to do everything possible to preserve its freedoms and the safety and wellbeing of its citizens. He processed Emily's words and the output from his implant as if he was just injected with a powerful sedative that induced calmness and mental clarity. "You're right. I need to get some rest. Hold down the fort for me. I'll see you at 0500. Hopefully, we'll be able to provide Luallen with something encouraging in the way of progress during our update. Oh, and yes, someday I'll lose some weight."

Chapter 6
Exploration

June 2145

"I have assembled the survey parties you requested," Gralp presented nervously to Leese and Jarga. "I have formed a total of 132 survey parties, one for each potentially viable host planet I have been able to identify within a distance that will afford us sufficient time for travel, exploration, and eventual migration. Based on my understanding of the composition of its atmosphere, planet Earth in the Galma region appears to possess an atmosphere most similar to our own. As such, if you approve, I will lead that survey party."

"Proceed. Since we will not have the means to communicate during these expeditions, direct all survey parties to return to Shangten in fifteen months. This will leave us slightly more than fifteen months to confirm which planet we will migrate to and afford us sufficient time to formulate an assimilation strategy."

"We could save precious time if we were not required to meet together physically. We need every moment we can get in support of this effort," Gralp responded primarily out of frustration and stress.

I N T R O S P E C T I O N: TRANSFORMATION

"Careful, Gralp, my patience for you is nearly entirely depleted," Jarga quickly responded. However, regardless of Gralp's powerlessness and subservience to Jarga, Gralp was correct. Physically versus telepathically meeting with Jarga or anyone else for that matter was unnecessary due to their telepathic communication abilities. However, Jarga required his subordinates' physical presence to demonstrate his dominance over everyone else further, and to instill anger and frustration as a tactic to compromise the full potential of their psychical abilities during interactions.

Gralp performed necessary preparations and congregated all survey parties at the primary military base located just below and alongside Jarga's living quarters. The ruler could peer out of his window and observe Gralp's interactions with the survey parties. The dispersion of the azure, electric blue, chartreuse, emerald green, yellow, orange, and tangerine colors of the gaseous life forms of the Sellinians, Flares, Grunats, and Ungdens was quite a spectacle from Jarga's vantage point. The arrangement of the colors was chaotic, although beautiful.

Such a fool am I to entrust the future of our race in him, a petty Grunat. So easily controlled, like a pawn in chess. Pathetic. Jarga was not in any way distracted by the appealing arrangement of the survey parties in the military base.

The juxtaposition of the colors of his congregated subordinates in the military base reminded Jarga of a vital turning point in his life that involved Qarta, his predecessor. Unlike all other Ungdens Jarga has ever seen, Qarta's body consisted of several colors, including emerald green, orange, and a slight amount of blue.

"I will not stop until I know you have learned right from wrong, that you have learned your lesson, and . . ." Jarga's father's telepathic communication abruptly ceased. In the flash of a moment, he fell lifeless to the floor.

Unbeknownst to Jarga, Qarta was silently observing in his living quarters.

"You were right to do as you did, Jarga, to will the death of your father," *Qarta relayed in a consoling manner. "He does not understand the way of our people. I will teach you if you allow me."*

Jarga did not respond; he was overwhelmed by grief. "I'm sorry, Father. I did not mean for this to happen. It was an accident."

"Come with me, Jarga, I will take care of you now."

Jarga had no confidence in Gralp's abilities but accepted the reality that his assessment of their situation was accurate. Although their inability to find a new host planet would be the most significant failure ever recorded in Ungden history, Jarga found consolation in the fact that there would be no one left alive to record his profound failure.

Gralp was afforded more control than he'd expected from Jarga to assemble his survey parties. However, Jarga still had a hand in the process. Jarga required the inclusion of particular individuals to participate primarily in the survey party Gralp would be leading when on Earth. Gralp accepted these conditions recognizing they were required so he would be permitted to conduct the surveying process despite the concern Jarga's act instilled in him.

"You are all aware of our dire situation regarding the impending implosion of our planet," Gralp telepathically communicated to all survey party members. "As you know, we will be incapable of communicating with each other during our respective expeditions due to the vast distances that will be between us. Take nothing for granted, overlook nothing, and ensure complete recall of everything you encounter. Covertly integrate with each society you encounter as you deem fit. Conduct yourselves in such a way as to not attract unwanted attention. Common sense will prevail in all situations; do not cause disruption. All survey parties are to return here exactly fifteen months from today. Account for the travel time required to return in your own itineraries—you must return on time."

Gralp himself felt his efforts were futile. Two years' time, which included the four-and-a-half month round-trip travel time to visit

INTROSPECTION: TRANSFORMATION

Earth, to identify another inhabitable planet was severely insufficient. The "heranlu," which is the aliens' equivalent to what humans consider to be a lead engineer, staffed at the military base confirmed for Gralp, to the fullest extent possible, that their cloaking technology would mask all ships from being detected by various screening mechanisms known to be used across all of the planets that the survey parties would be visiting.

Further, to eliminate remaining doubt, Gralp was instructed by the heranlu to inform each survey party leader to telepathically monitor and manipulate encountered surveillance technologies so their presence would not be detected. Even though the stakes were high regarding the importance of being capable of entering and leaving the visited planets completely undetected, the essence of time required him to rely on the heranlu's efforts and assessment.

The survey parties boarded their respective ships, which were spherical and varied in size. Metals were abundant on Shangten, and as such, the exteriors of all of the ships were constructed of metals which were more resilient to force, heat, pressure, and natural elements than any other metal the aliens were aware existed elsewhere. The ships were silver, and the manner in which the metal was treated made it so bright you would swear when looking at objects reflected from the ships' surfaces that you were looking directly upon the original objects themselves.

After all of the survey parties boarded their respective ships, the ships slowly hovered above the military hangar floor. In an instant, like bubbles being blown from a wand, they departed from the military base, shrinking in size until the darkness of space swallowed them.

Chapter 7
Enlightenment

April 2141

"I can't wait to go to the zoo," Jake's younger sister, Allie, said as she imitated various animal sounds.

"Roar." It was an imitation of lions, Allie's favorite animal because she felt her golden blonde hair resembled their manes.

"Shut up, Allie," Jake's younger brother, Gabriel, said. His patience was depleted.

"Gabriel, don't you dare talk to your sister that way. Apologize and nicely ask her to be quiet," Jake's mother, Amy, insisted.

"Please be quiet," Gabriel said in a sarcastic tone, squinting his entire face in an attempt to scare Allie.

After turning away, only to observe his mother's eyes peering at him through the rearview mirror with laser-like focus, Gabriel faced Allie. He found her sticking her tongue out at him, a huge grin on her face.

To garner additional approval from his mother, Gabriel made another, more respectful, attempt. "I'm sorry, Allie. Would you please be quiet?"

"OK. Oh, I'm so excited. Are we there yet, Mom?" Allie asked.

INTROSPECTION: TRANSFORMATION

"I know you're excited, Allie. We'll be there soon. I promise," Jake said, sharing in Gabriel's growing impatience and frustration with her.

Jake was excited although his friends did not think it was cool to go to the zoo. Jake did not believe he was too old, at eleven, to still enjoy it. Although Jake was the eldest of his parents' three children, he wanted to remain close and relevant to his siblings by sharing common interests with them.

"Let's all play I Spy," Jake suggested, in an attempt to distract both Allie and Gabriel from the drive, which seemed to be taking an eternity.

"I spy something that is white," Allie responded promptly, granting herself the first turn in one of her favorite games.

Gabriel was a huge fan of I Spy, demonstrated by his immediate guess, "It's the speed limit sign right there." He pointed toward the sign they would soon pass on the right side of the street.

"Nope." Allie was proud of herself.

"The inside of the gum wrapper in Mom's ashtray." Gabriel was sure he had it right.

"Nope." Allie began giggling.

The truth was, Allie had a habit of changing the objects she had spied if others correctly guessed them within a timeframe she considered too short.

"Are you cheating, Allie?" Jake asked, while in this instance not suspecting it because she hadn't wrinkled her nose, which was her "tell." He merely wanted to tease her a bit.

"Nooooowuh," Allie replied.

Without warning, Jake heard a loud crash, and then everything went dark. He realized he had been unconscious when he found himself in an inverted position with blood dripping down from his forehead. He was deafened by a constant and very high-pitched sound in his ears. He slowly felt around his body as he regained consciousness, and after recognizing he was not experiencing any pain, he realized it was not his own blood. He then transitioned attention from himself and his wellbeing to looking around the car. It all finally made sense to him; they had just experienced a severe car accident.

Gabriel, Allie, and his mother, Amy, were all unconscious. As he became more alert, his senses began to return to normal. Just then, a strong scent of gasoline crossed his nostrils. He started feeling pain, which steadily increased in intensity. Looking down, he noticed the seat belt was tightly wrapped around his ribs. The rear portion of the car was contorted in such a way that the seat belt was supporting his entire weight. He concluded he'd likely broken some ribs.

I need to get out of here. I need to get my family out of here.

Gabriel, Allie, and Jake were all in the rear row of seats, and Amy was alone and unconscious in the driver's seat. Since Allie was in the center of the back seat, nestled in her car seat, and closest in proximity to him, Jake decided to remove her from the car first. The fastener of Jake's seat belt was dented during the collision, and he was unable to unlatch it. Fortunately, he remembered he'd brought his Case pocket knife that his great-grandfather Kurt had given him. Just before Jake had cut entirely through the width of the seat belt, it snapped apart, and the back of Jake's neck hit the inner roof of the car.

Just after he rotated his body ninety degrees to get into a better position to free Allie from her car seat, he caught a glimpse of his mother. Numerous shards of glass of various shapes and sizes had pierced her entire body, with the most noticeable one protruding from the bridge of her nose. The safety foam that was deployed by the car to reduce the severity of the impact on his mother's body had already dissolved and been reduced to a white, chalk-like substance that covered her from her face to the tips of her shoes.

"Mom," Jake shrieked, as tears began to flood his eyes and rain down his dark red cheeks. He froze for a moment and focused on regaining his composure.

I need to get out of here. I need to get my family out of here. This is what I need to do. OK, OK…OK.

Jake turned his attention to Allie and began unlatching the car seat's straps. He placed his hand under her neck while cupping her head into his chest, pushed her body upward to relieve the stress on the car seat's straps, and removed them from around her arms. Allie slowly descended, Jake's chest absorbing most of the impact as his back was pressed against the inner roof of the car. He hadn't realized how heavy she was.

Even though the window area of the rear car door closest to Jake had compressed due to impact against the ground, there was still just enough room for him to slide out first and then pull Allie out. Fortunately, she was still unconscious, which made removing her from the car much less complicated than if she had been awake.

INTROSPECTION: **TRANSFORMATION**

As Jake picked her up and carried her in his arms, as a parent would their newborn baby, he noticed they were close to railroad tracks. Despite Jake considering his proximity to the railroad tracks as being odd, he stuck to his task, placing Allie on the grass and turning back toward the car. Suddenly, he felt a sharp and severe piercing pain in his ribs, and he fell to the ground. Looking down at his chest, he noticed a growing blood stain and holes in his shirt from glass shards.

Ignoring own situation, he returned to his feet and began walking toward the car. He started hearing sirens in the distance. As he began to kneel down to re-enter the rear portion of the vehicle, he felt intense heat, and then once again, everything went dark.

"Where am I? Where am I?" Jake yelled in delirium as he sat himself up from a reclined position.

He looked around and noticed that he was in a hospital bed. Overcome by pain in his mid-section, he collapsed back down into the bed.

"Dad?" Jake's father sat in a chair nearby, crying, the palms of his hands covering his eyes.

"H-hey b-buddy. Are you OK?" his father, Glenn, replied as he wiped tears from his eyes and pushed his long light brown hair out of his face.

"Yeah, I'm fine. How's Allie?"

"You're a hero. You saved her life."

"Mom? Gabriel?" A long, awkward, and uncomfortable silence followed.

"Dad?"

"They didn't make it, Jake. I'm so sorry," Glenn replied, trying to maintain strong composure, although his hazel eyes swelled, visibly conveying complete devastation. Jake had never before seen his father, who he considered an unwavering giant of a man, so upset and crying.

Jake quietly began crying. "I don't understand. I got Allie out of the car and was just about to get Gabriel out—"

"The car's gas tank exploded just as you were going back to the car to get Gabriel. It's a miracle you're alive considering how close you were to the explosion. At least that's what the firefighter told me at the crash site."

"They're dead?"

"Yes. The railroad crossing gates didn't work." Glenn was spiraling in grief, regret, and disbelief.

"You mean we were hit by a train?" Jake asked, breaking Glenn out of his trance.

"Yeah. It's a miracle that you and Allie are alive."

Jake turned away from Glenn, moved onto his side and into a fetal position, and cried himself to sleep.

June 2146

Jake heard faint barking and stomping noises that seemed to be right above his face. He opened his eyes, and although he could see the sun in the sky above, it was heavily distorted and contorted. He was engulfed by a sensation similar to when one gets goosebumps—he felt chilled but was not cold. Upon completely regaining his senses, he realized that he was fully encased in ice.

Why am I not cold? Ice surrounds me.

Just as he wondered how he would escape his ice prison, all of it turned into water. Not acknowledging this marvel, he looked around for the elderly woman, the last thing he'd seen before losing consciousness in the park.

While he was unable to find her, he did notice a small puddle of blue liquid near his feet. Although most people would likely see it, suspect it was yogurt or nothing notable, and walk by it, Jake was drawn to it. He was compelled to reach down and touch the liquid. As he began kneeling and reaching for it, he was overwhelmed by the incessant cries and movements of animals around him, though he could not actually see, or even hear them.

Regaining his composure, he touched the blue liquid to get some on his fingers so that he could examine it more closely with his eyes and nose. But it was all instantaneously absorbed into his body, similar to the way a paper towel absorbs a pool of liquid on an impervious countertop. Suddenly, the animal cries and movements ceased.

Jake did not understand what had just happened to him. He also did not know whether absorbing the liquid would have a detrimental impact on his health. He began to panic, which was accompanied by excessive sweating throughout his body.

What has happened to me? What has happened to me? What am I going to do? I don't know what to do.

Animal noises and people's voices resumed. This activity was deafening. *How can I hear all of this when I don't see anything around me? I need to get out of here.*

Jake sprinted for his car to drive home.

Stop. Stop. Make these sounds and voices stop.

Finally, in an instant, everything became silent. Jake started his car and drove home.

"Now where has he been? Is he OK?" Jake's stepmother, Debbie, said as he pulled into the driveway located beside his house.

"I'm right here, Debbie, and I'm fine. Why are you referring to me as if I'm not here?" Jake responded, still in his car.

What the hell? Debbie isn't even here. He was neither in the house yet nor in his stepmother's presence. *This doesn't make sense. What has happened to me?*

He parked the car in the driveway, walked to the house, and opened the front door, only to see Debbie standing in the foyer waiting to greet him. Her dark brown hair was in shambles, some of it frazzled and stood eight inches straight up in the air as if lightning had stricken her.

"Where have you been? Why are you covered in leaves and dirt? Are you OK?" Debbie inquired frantically, her bloodshot blue eyes consumed with concern.

Jake felt a sense of déjà vu.

"I went to Starbucks with Julie, Ori, David, and Jed right after school, and then we hung out at Cherokee Park. I lost track of time. I'm sorry, Debbie."

Jake was observing Debbie, and there was no change in her demeanor or expression. It was as if she could not hear him.

"I went to Starbucks with Julie, Ori, David, and Jed right after school, and then we hung out at Cherokee Park. I lost track of time. I'm sorry, Debbie." He repeated his explanation and apology with a rising voice and more profound emotion.

His stepmother shouted, "Are you going to keep me in suspense all night? Say something, will you?"

"Are you deaf? I told you twice that I went to Starbucks and then to Cherokee Park with some friends." Jake did not realize he'd subconsciously attempted to communicate with Debbie telepathically.

"Don't talk to me like that. I've been worried sick about you. It's ten o'clock, and you're usually home at four thirty. And no, I'm not deaf. It's hard to hear someone when they aren't speaking. What's the matter with you?"

Debbie was both concerned for and infuriated with Jake. And to make matters worse, she was exhausted and severely disheveled.

Perplexed, Jake sprinted upstairs and into his bedroom. Debbie followed immediately behind him. Hearing the commotion from his bedroom, Glenn intercepted Debbie just before she opened Jake's door.

"What's the matter with you?" Debbie asked again through the door, tears meandering down her cheeks and onto her chin.

Suddenly, like robots directed by their masters, Debbie and Glenn turned their backs to Jake's bedroom door and went into their room.

What the hell? Jake's parents had just done exactly what he had hoped they would do. What he had willed them to do.

Chapter 8
Perilous Surveys

June 2145 - August 2145

Survey of Planet Carpul in the Farna Region

Umal, assigned by Gralp to lead the survey party on planet Carpul in the Farna region, directed the pilot to land the vessel in a massive crater that was visible during their descent after entering the planet's atmosphere. Even though Carpul was among the smallest of the planets that were being surveyed, it was still large enough to sustain life for the current and projected populations of the Grunats, Sellinians, Flares, and Ungdens.

Nearly 90% of its surface was covered with vegetation. Based upon their research, it didn't appear that any intelligent life inhabited the planet. Carpul neither contained trees, bushes, nor other vegetation in forms previously familiar to the aliens. The primary type of vegetation was gelatinous and consisted of different variations of orange, red, brown, and grey colors. It left the surface of the planet wet and too slippery for anyone to walk upon.

"Our vessel is secured, and we are ready to commence deployment of our survey party at your command, Umal," Beele reported, anxious to commence the survey.

"Convene everyone just outside of the vessel so that I may remind them of the surveying process we will employ," Umal directed as he gathered the thoughts he needed to share with the survey party. "Gralp informed me that this planet, Carpul, based upon his research and analysis, is ranked third on the list of potential host planets for us, behind only Earth in the Galma region and Louse in the Zamma region, in that order. As such, this survey is critical to secure our future.

"Carpul has a surface area of seventy million square miles, which is approximately ten percent of Louse's surface area. We have one-hundred-ten members in our survey party. We will break up into groups of four. I will defer to you to determine your groups. There will be one group that will consist of six members, which will include Beele and me. I will choose which group of four Beele and I will join once all other groups have been assembled.

"Since we do not believe there to be intelligent life on this planet, we are to reconvene at our vessel in four months. Once we have reunited, we will perform a mind integration so that we may all share our respective experiences with one another. I have overlaid a virtual grid upon the entire surface of Carpul. Each square of the grid represents approximately one-hundred square miles, totaling nearly 700,000 squares comprising the grid.

"We will be exploring areas contained in only two-hundred-seventy of these squares—ten squares per survey party. Areas designated for exploration are in yellow on the grid. Since we will only be evaluating 27,000 square miles, not even one-tenth of one percent of Carpul's surface area, once again, capturing all relevant details during your respective expeditions is of utmost importance."

"Why so short a stay? I estimate we could spend twelve months here surveying the planet, which would enable us to survey three times more surface area," one of the survey party members relayed to all others and directed the question to Umal.

"I already conceived and reflected upon your intelligent thought, Halm. We do not know how Carpul will fare among the other candidate host planets. We need to afford ourselves time in the event Gralp wishes us to survey planets in addition to Carpul," Umal relayed in response.

"We will return to the vessel and perform a brief mind integration so that we may all understand and confirm who will comprise each group and which areas each group will survey. Rest will follow and then we will begin our expeditions. Finally, be cognizant of this environment. I am currently violet in color, not my typical yellow Grunat self as I am when at Shangten. Chemical reactions are occurring with our bodies, and we do not yet know if and how such reactions may affect us."

They all returned to the vessel. Before initiating the mind integration, Umal and Beele relayed relevant parameters regarding the impending surveys to the crew of five that would remain behind to protect and preserve operations of the vessel. The mind integration was completed, and all survey party members went to their respective living quarters to rest for several hours and prepare for their upcoming surveys.

Instead of resting, Umal was overwhelmed by the weight of the future of his race that rested upon his shoulders. He looked out of an observatory window from within his ship upon what could eventually become his new home. The sky was aqua green; the color was visible by light cast by a distant sun. There was no concept of either days or nights on Carpul. The color and appearance of the sky and the light cast upon the planet were constant. Considering it being seemingly monotonous, the aqua green color had a calming effect and was beautiful.

As far as Umal could see, the terrain was smooth and uniform. Other than the crater in which they'd landed their vessel, the ground was flat. Umal found it challenging to believe prior research performed indicated that no intelligent life inhabited Carpul. Still, none of the vessel's crew, including Umal, sensed any surveilling devices or thoughts originating from any beings on Carpul. They did not detect any life whatsoever.

"Our crew is rested and ready to leave," Beele relayed to Umal, and in doing so, abruptly interrupted the meditative state Umal had entered as he peered blankly out of the vessel.

"Very well, Beele. On our way, then."

Umal, Beele, and the four other members of their survey party began their exploration in the area closest in proximity to the vessel. Umal suspected they were left there because the other survey party members wanted to explore portions of Carpul that they had not yet seen. Umal's survey party members split up so that they could effectively observe the first one-hundred of a total of 1,000 square miles in approximately one and a half weeks.

Because of their gaseous life forms, Umal and the others hovered above the ground while traveling, and their levitation was a profound benefit given Carpul's slippery surface.

The first thing Umal wanted to do was better understand the materials that comprised the soil. He extracted material from the ground in the form of a sphere whose diameter was approximately twelve inches and watched as it instantly changed from its orange in situ color to burgundy. This perplexed Umal.

To better understand its properties, Umal telekinetically applied pressure to the material. As he did so, it began decomposing as it concurrently emitted a liquid. This explained why Umal had not seen any bodies of water here. The ground was very moist, and whatever liquid may be needed to survive could easily be extracted from it.

As Umal released his grasp on the soil, he noticed a burgundy discoloration approximately ten feet wide on the ground; the center of its discoloration was where he had extracted his soil sample. The recess created by the material he removed was also burgundy. The land surrounding the discolored area remained its natural orange color.

INTROSPECTION: TRANSFORMATION

Resuming motion away from the vessel, Umal traveled due east. The terrain was much the same for nearly six miles until he encountered what he surmised was some form of vegetation that emerged from the ground. Umal saw dark red, cup-shaped organisms that looked like jellyfish hoods all over the ground for as far as he could see.

Probing the organism, Umal determined that it was safe to consume and that it contained nutrients that could sustain life for all inhabitants of Shangten. Umal found the abundance of this organism very encouraging. As he continued his journey, he began feeling fatigued and rested himself on a nearby bed of dark gray rock.

Shortly after he decided to rest, Umal felt a shock in his brain, causing him to wake up. His consciousness was suddenly filled with death, illness, and relentless suffering.

"I do not understand what is happening," Beele relayed to Umal. "I thought Carpul was one of the most promising potential host planets. Despite the atmospheric conditions appearing to be extremely similar to Shangten's, all members of our survey party are feeling increasingly uncomfortable, and I have received updates from crew members that remained at the vessel that the materials comprising our ship are slowly but steadily decaying."

"Why are you only just now providing me this update, Beele?"

"They indicated they have been attempting to contact you directly for nearly twelve hours with no response."

Umal did not understand how this was possible. After regaining his composure, he realized that they had landed on Carpul nearly two weeks ago and that he must have been unconscious for twelve days. His thoughts were incoherent, and his cognitive abilities were severely compromised.

"Instruct all survey party members to return to the ship. I am unable to do so myself, as I have somehow been compromised by this environment," Umal exclaimed after he assessed his condition.

He noticed that a majority of his formerly bold violet color had changed to teal, and he was feeling a sensation that his body and mind were in the process of disintegrating.

Umal received no response, which was an immediate indication to him that Beele was likely dead and that he would reach the same fate if he did not return to the vessel as quickly as possible. Mustering as much energy as he could extract from himself, Umal miraculously made it back to the ship with extremely limited energy to spare. Upon entering the vessel, he noticed the visible, yet fortunately moderate, disintegration of its fuselage.

"Close the bay door. We need to return to Shangten," Umal instructed in a deranged manner.

Realizing the dire situation they were in, the vessel's crew obeyed Umal's wishes and set a course for Shangten. Without issue, the vessel took flight and began its return.

Umal nearly lost consciousness just as the vessel became airborne. He could sense the concern among the crew and survey party members. "I am fine. I am returning to my normal state rapidly now," Umal shared with everyone on the ship as he evaluated himself. He was very relieved to see that his body had returned to its original yellow color.

"Are you certain you are well, Umal?" a concerned crew member inquired. "You were not yourself when you entered the vessel."

"I assure you, I am fine. I am steadily recovering. And yes, I was greatly compromised. It is obvious we are incompatible with Carpul's environment. Whether it is its atmosphere or the organisms on its surface, we must eliminate Carpul as a candidate host planet. Because I am still healing, please inform all surviving survey party members that we will need to perform a mind integration in three hours."

From Umal's perspective, the time elapsed in an instant. He suspected this was attributable to his mind and body focusing all of its resources on recovery. He proceeded to establish mental links and was alarmed to sense that only thirty-one survey party members were still alive. Beele was not among them.

INTROSPECTION: TRANSFORMATION

"The terrible loss that we have experienced brings me great sadness. I can sense that many of you feel regret for leaving our comrades behind. No one feels more remorse than I. However, if they were not dead before our departure, I assure you that their time was limited, and death was likely imminent. I know this, as I nearly died myself."

Still not at full strength, Umal had to pause for a moment before continuing.

"Gralp made us aware of the risks when we embarked upon this mission. These risks were necessary so we could secure a prosperous future for us all. Although it is obvious that Carpul is not equipped to serve as a viable host planet for us, performing a mind integration will still be useful so that we may collectively obtain a greater understanding of the causes behind the demise of our comrades. Further, we will need to relay all details of our experiences to Gralp and, ultimately, to Jarga."

As all thirty-two of them engaged in a mind integration, each was overwhelmed by the death, pain, and suffering the others had endured. Of the thirty-one survivors, other than Umal, twenty-three of them were in no way adversely affected by the environment. All twenty-three were Sellenians, and it became evident that this was due to unique attributes of their chemical composition. It was no surprise that each Flare and Grunat member of the survey party reacted similarly to Carpul's environment as did Umal since there were known biochemical similarities between their races.

Like Umal, Beele was a Grunat. Of the thirty-eight total Grunat survey party members, only Umal and two others had survived. Because none of the Sellenians had being detrimentally affected by Carpul's environment, Umal shared that his disposition regarding whether Carpul could serve as a host planet had changed. It was agreed among them that if Carpul were to emerge as their next host planet, the Flares and Grunats would need to determine a means of manipulating their chemical compositions to more closely match that of the Sellenians. Additionally, research would need to be performed to determine whether or not Ungdens would experience incompatibilities with Carpul's environment.

Grief consumed Umal over the extensive loss of life that had occurred within his survey party. He was especially upset by the loss of his closest friend, Beele, who had befriended Umal when they were very young. Umal was always intrigued by Beele's hickory brown color. He had been the only Grunat on Shangten who was not yellow.

This needs to change, Umal thought. *Whichever planet becomes our new home must remain our home indefinitely. Migrating from planet to planet brings with it too much unnecessary risk and loss. Beele's death was completely unnecessary, and now I am left without my closest friend. Without my brother.*

Survey of Planet Salunda in the Talgari Region

"I do not understand how they could have possibly detected us," Baj relayed to the pilot and other crew members as their vessel was under heavy attack by the Salundans. "Surveying Salunda was presumed by Gralp to be a formality, among the least likely to cause any casualties."

"They must have a protocol where they send out their military when any of their surveillance equipment does not operate correctly. Our tampering with it must have issued some alarm," the pilot relayed to Baj.

"That makes sense. However, how are they able to detect our vessel? And why are our efforts to manipulate them ineffective?"

"Our cloaking technology and telepathic tactics are ineffective on the Salundans," the pilot retorted.

"Our intelligence was flawed, and now we are likely going to die for our mistake," Baj relayed to everyone in the vessel.

As Baj prepared for death, the vessel's shields were compromised. Seconds later, the spherical metallic vessel combusted. The giant ball of flames disappeared in an instant like it had been sucked into a vacuum, and all traces of the vessel and its crew of 320 were gone.

INTROSPECTION: TRANSFORMATION

Survey of Planet Louse in the Zamma Region

"There is a reason this planet is named Louse," Pang relayed to his four-hundred-fifty survey party members. "It is infested with tens of thousands of species of creatures and was assigned its name in acknowledgment of parasites on planet Earth. Still, from the research our scientists have conducted, none other than the Tungstrae, Phlemangne, and Illioxjay are known to be harmful. However, the research could be flawed; proceed very cautiously. Further, it has been determined that some of the liquids on Louse's surface are toxic and extremely harmful."

The survey party split into groups of fifteen with the understanding that they would return to the vessel in twelve months. Nearly eighty-five percent of Louse's surface was covered with liquids of varying compositions. Visible fluids were primarily fluorescent pink, yellow, cyan, and green.

Louse was covered with trees, plants, and other vegetation. As abundant as Louse was with liquid, trees, and plants, it appeared there were more creatures than the planet could sustain. The survey party confirmed this as they observed frequent occurrences of creatures consuming each other.

Suddenly, screeching cries filled the minds of all fifteen members of one of the survey parties. They hadn't detected the vapors emitted from a body of liquid below them since they were hovering well above Louse's surface. Before they could react, a deadly chemical reaction ensued. In an instant, they were dead. The vapor completely disintegrated them, leaving no traces of their remains.

The remaining thirty-four survey parties sensed this group's demise but were unaware of the cause. This motivated them to proceed even more cautiously than before. Eleven other groups met a similar fate from other bodies of liquid within five minutes of each other. Sensing what was occurring, Pang realized a horrible flaw in how he'd organized his groups. Failure to require more detailed and frequent accounts of each group's locations and what they were about to encounter was costing too many lives.

In response, Pang relayed these new instructions to his group and the remaining twenty-two groups still among the living. He also emphasized how important it was to mask their appearances by projecting themselves as creatures identical to the many different species that inhabited Louse. As a survey group was observing plants and trees, some of the group members were attacked by Phlemangne, the only of the three Lousian species known to be harmful to them that could fly.

Phlemangnes were hideous creatures, equipped with three pairs of wings. Their entire abdomens and thoraxes were covered by setae that looked like dark black needles. They had two pairs of antennae extending from their heads. Each Phlemangne was approximately thirteen-inches long and three inches wide.

The Phlemangnes attacked seven of the group members. The remaining nine astutely recognized that all seven that were being attacked were projecting themselves as Illioxjays. It was evident that Illioxjays were vehement enemies of Phlemangnes. Before they could aid the survey group members that were being attacked, a fluid regurgitated by the Phlemangnes shut down the victims' brains. They were all suddenly brain dead, and they collapsed to the ground. The creatures rapidly consumed their remains. The surviving survey group members relayed this intelligence to the other groups.

Acknowledging that there were too many risks associated with their expedition, Pang ordered all remaining survivors to return to the vessel. After having been in the ship for nearly five hours, Pang deduced that those that had not yet returned were likely dead. Of the four-hundred-fifty survey party members, only one-hundred twenty-eight had survived. This had all transpired in less than a single day. Pang and the crew began their return to Shangten.

Survey of Planet Earth in the Galma Region

INTROSPECTION: TRANSFORMATION

Gralp landed his ship undetected in Mborokua, an uninhabited, jungle-covered volcanic island located approximately 1,500 miles southeast of New Guinea. He had selected this location based upon the fact that, other than occasional visits conducted primarily by fishermen, the island had no inhabitants. Knowing that humans lived on Earth, Gralp wanted to gradually ease into interaction with them to the fullest extent possible.

Through telekinesis, Gralp bored a hole into the ground and buried the ship so that it would not be found. He and his survey party remained at Mborokua for nearly three weeks. During that time, they focused on recording attributes of the environment and making preliminary determinations regarding whether they could sustain life in that region of Earth.

The year-round high temperatures at Mborokua revolve around freezing, and the year-round low temperatures hover around 24 degrees Fahrenheit. By humans' standards, such temperatures are considered rather cold, but by Gralp's and all inhabitants of Shangten's standards, they were hot. Gralp's party was able to survey and mentally document everything of interest in less than four days because of the tiny size of Mborokua Island, which was one-and-a-half square miles. Because it was a jungle-covered volcanic island, there were some creatures the survey party members had encountered for the first time, and the geographic environment, in particular, was of great interest.

Gralp was highly confident that Earth would be a viable planet to enable habitation by all on Shangten. The results of his analyses of the air, atmosphere, soil, biological composition of the various creatures native to Mborokua, and other environmental components were all favorable. He decided to assign one of his survey party members to remain behind to ensure fishermen didn't discover their ship while he and the others left for a nearby island, Vangunu. Gralp chose Vangunu as their next destination because he sensed the presence of human beings there.

"There are humans on this island. Control their thoughts accordingly, and withhold your presence from them," he directed the others as they were approaching Vangunu. "We need to conceal ourselves since, in light of their small population, they would likely become alarmed if they saw people they did not recognize."

Gralp and his survey party reached Vangunu undetected. They were all hovering above the surface of the water of the Solomon Sea. They followed the sounds and thoughts of the natives to observe them closely. Once they were within sight, they manipulated all natives in proximity to perceive them as open space, that is, invisible.

Gralp instructed his party to engage in telepathic experimentation with the natives so they could understand the extent to which they could control humans' actions. They were able to direct the natives to sleep, run in any desired direction, walk into the sea, inflict harm upon themselves, and perform several other actions.

"A weak species, easily manipulated," a survey party member relayed to Gralp.

No different than us Grunats compared to Jarga and his fellow Ungdens: puppets are we, Gralp thought. *Enough of this. We need to continue our journey by relocating to a more populated area and continue our research.*

Chapter 9

Investigation

March 2146

"All we know at this point, sir, is that there were two passengers on the manifest, a Stacey Smith, and a Jennifer Cole, whose remains have not yet been located among the aircraft's wreckage. Considering the two blue masses seen from the video recorder, we do not believe this is a coincidence," Kent reported.

"What have you learned about these two women?" Luallen inquired.

"They do not appear to have known each other. They have no criminal records, and they have limited data profiles. Any interaction from either of them with social media outlets is non-existent. Ms. Smith was twenty-six-years-old, and Ms. Cole was twenty-three. We suspected potential foul play taking into account the generic nature of their names and not being able to account for their remains, but what little we've been able to learn of them indicates they're clean."

"No apparent terrorist ties?" Luallen retorted in disbelief.

"None," Kent replied, cringing a bit to Luallen's dissatisfied and questioning tone.

"If they weren't on the aircraft, why were their names on the passenger manifest?" Luallen continued his questioning.

"We haven't ruled out the possibility of them having been on the aircraft. If they were aliens and died, or if they are aliens and currently alive, we are unaware of their capabilities. We cannot ignore the fact that there are two bodies unaccounted for, and that these two bodies, per the passenger manifest, were assigned the two seats over which we saw the two blue masses in the video from the flight recorder. Their remains could be the blue liquid we recovered from the crash site, or they could have found a means to exit the aircraft before impact. Or, once again, they may not have ever been in the aircraft."

"You're beginning to sound like a science fiction novel, Jacobsen. We need answers, not a fantastical plot."

"I assure you that my team and I are approaching this matter with utmost priority, urgency, and seriousness, sir. We're dealing with numerous unknowns and apparent confirmation of alien life forms on our planet. With all due respect, sir, this is unchartered territory." Kent's patience and stamina were wearing thin.

"Indeed it is, Jacobsen," Luallen said, nearly inaudibly. "Indeed it is," he mumbled again as he trailed into deep thought. He ran various scenarios in his mind.

Several minutes elapsed before Kent blurted, "Chief Master Sergeant Luallen?" in an attempt to jar his superior from his thoughts.

Luallen stirred. "Dr. Agon, what have you and Lead Analyst Hendrix been able to discern from the alien substance?"

"It contains elements familiar to us, such as carbon and nitrogen, in addition to other elements found that are completely alien—I mean foreign—to us," Dr. Agon responded, sweat streaming down his temples.

"Any notable properties of interest?" Kent inquired. An awkward silence followed. "Agon?" Kent prompted.

INTROSPECTION: TRANSFORMATION

"Um...I'm sorry. I've been immersed in researching the alien remains. Not much sleep. Ah. Um, I sincerely apologize. It is possible this substance was at one point a living organism, and that—"

"The blue substance must, therefore, be tied to the aliens, proving that aliens were on the aircraft at some point during the flight," Luallen blurted out, suggesting a conclusion that he felt should have been presented to him at the onset of the update meeting.

"Um, yes sir," Dr. Agon uttered, looking down at the floor. Kent glared at Agon. This was the first he had heard of this conclusion.

"Jacobsen, why didn't you bring this to my attention sooner? Are you not effectively managing communication among your Special Task Force team members?"

"It's my fault, sir," Hendrix cut in. "We only discovered this shortly before this meeting, sir."

"Very well." Luallen appeared unexpectedly satisfied with her response. "I want to know how these aliens were able to board the aircraft undetected and how they passed as the two women on the passenger manifest. I want to know how far back their records go."

"The airline staff working the gate and administering the boarding process for that flight have been flown in for questioning, and we will be meeting with them at 0900 tomorrow morning. We'll get more answers, sir," Kent said, sensing that this was likely what Luallen wanted to hear.

"Good work, Jacobsen. We will convene for another update meeting at 1300 tomorrow. I would hope four hours would afford you sufficient time to glean essential information from the airline personnel."

Praise from Luallen? Unprecedented, Kent thought, as Luallen did not have a reputation for expressing satisfaction to anyone. *I'll take it.*

"Well done, Kent," Emily whispered in his ear, jabbing him in the ribs with her elbow just after Luallen walked out of the meeting room.

"Those gate agents better have answers. This isn't about keeping Luallen happy, Emily. These, or other, aliens could have downed that plane. We don't know how long they have been among us, and we don't know how many there currently are. I fear we are in grave danger."

Chapter 10
"Civil" War

"What are we doing? This is no contest, and they have done nothing wrong."

"Continue complying with Jarga's bidding or you risk endangering our lives, as well as the preservation of our fellow Grunats," Gralp directed. "We need to unwaveringly demonstrate our allegiance to Jarga."

"But—"

"Enough. Do it, Kamen," Gralp insisted.

Millions of lives were taken in a matter of days, each life exterminated in an instant, like an ignited match extinguished by water. It was a mass genocide. All Sellinians, Grunats, and Flares executing Jarga's orders were directed to extract all thoughts and memories from each targeted member of their society before ending their life.

"We need to mine the thoughts of all current and former members of our society, particularly those of the Flares," Jarga relayed to Leese as all surviving Sellinians, Grunats, and Flares congregated in the main military hangar.

"The Flares?" Leese inquired.

"Yes, the Flares. It is no mystery that they are unhappy with my current reign and the favoritism I afford my fellow Ungdens. We will survey their intentions, along with those of the Sellinians and Grunats, while we mine all of the memories they have gathered from the other races that we have eradicated during this cleansing process."

"My esteemed citizens," Jarga opened as everyone was finalizing their congregation into the hangar. "The past four days embody the unfortunate consequence of hatred and malicious intentions. Our wellbeing, and that of our planet was severely endangered by a civil war that the Argas, Estens, Lumars, and other eradicated races were plotting. Acknowledging today is a sad day, it also marks a new beginning," Jarga continued while he, Leese, and their Ungdens lieutenants were probing and mining thoughts and memories from all who were present.

The Sellinians, Grunats, and Flares genuinely resonated with Jarga's words and intentions. They had demonstrated their authenticity when they had extracted the memories and thoughts of those they had killed. This was all part of Jarga's scheme to increase their allegiance to him.

"I will not hide behind lies. As many of you know, it was my bidding to remove these races from our planet. They were of no value to us and did nothing to sustain the wellbeing of Shangten. They were incapable of achieving anything that would yield meaningful contributions to our society. The weak have been purged, and we have now begun to forge a more secure future for us, the victorious Grunats, Sellinians, Flares, and Ungdens," Jarga concluded.

After extracting the desired information and sensing overwhelming support from all that were present at the rally, Jarga lost interest in continuing his charade.

"As you all were," Leese followed.

Jarga, Leese, and other high-ranking officials then receded into their private meeting quarters.

INTROSPECTION: TRANSFORMATION

"Our future is secured. So many fewer pests to manage now," Jarga relayed to Leese before returning to his quarters.

June 2146

"That elderly woman was a Lumar," Jake screamed as he awoke from a deep sleep while in his bed.

She...Langi must have been special since Jarga believed that he had killed all Lumars on Shangten.

Not only was Jake amazed at Langi's ability to conceal her true race from Jarga, but he was also shocked that she was willing to perform such deceit given the penalty for doing so was death. Due to the intellectual abilities of all aliens, it was simple for them to fabricate images, thoughts, identities, and many other things and implant them into others' minds. Since mind-tampering would result in chaos, Jarga's enforcement personnel were directed to constantly scan for instances of implantation of false items into others' minds. Confirmation of each instance of mind-tampering resulted in the killing of the offending alien. Since the stakes were so high, aliens committing the act of mind-tampering was rare.

And man, Jarga is an asshole.

Jake then fixated on Jarga and became overwhelmed with fear. *My God, he murdered entire races of his people, thousands of people. What if he finds me? How can I possibly defend myself against someone who effortlessly demanded the killing of thousands of people?*

Noticing his blanket was affixed to his body by thick layers of ice which extended down to the floor was just the distraction Jake needed to escape his frenzy of fear. Jake then refocused his thoughts on Langi.

She was no woman at all. She was an alien from Shangten.

Jake was unaware that Langi's life had ended immediately after physically contacting him. He was also unaware that, by contacting Langi, he would have complete recollection of all of her personal and inherited memories and experiences, somewhat similar to the human condition of hyperthymesia.

"Aliens are here on Earth. I am no longer human," Jake softly said.

My god, I have an alien inside of me. I'm an alien. I'm a freak. And Jarga is going to hunt me down and kill me.

His backpack on his desk, the holographic monitors on his walls, and the curtains hanging over his bedroom windows began shaking. Jake was hysterical.

My God, I have an alien inside of me. I'm an alien. I'm a freak. My god, I have an alien inside of me. I'm an alien. I'm a freak.

His bedding, backpack, hand-held minicomputer, and mobile device began to hover in the air. Jake frantically and repetitively surveyed his entire room from left to right, then right to left, and then left to right again. He was scared of his inherited telekinetic abilities, and that he could not control them.

"What was that? Go check on the kids, Glenn," Debbie whispered to Glenn in their bedroom.

It was at this moment he realized he was telepathic, and that with practice he could likely master this new ability. He understood that he'd obtained these abilities from Langi, the alien he had encountered in the woods.

Oh shit, he's coming.

Everything levitating in the air abruptly dropped and returned to near their original locations and orientations.

Jake frantically jumped out of bed, chaotically shook and contorted his body to remove all of the ice from it, and then sprinted for the bedroom door. Lucky for Jake, Glenn was peeking in Allie's bedroom first, since Jake's room was at the opposite end of the hallway from where his parents' bedroom was located. Just before Glenn touched the doorknob of Jake's bedroom door, Jake popped out of his room like a banana being squeezed from its peel.

"What are you doing up at this hour, Jake?" Glenn asked.

"I'm sorry, Dad. I had a bad nightmare. It seemed so real," Jake responded. "I must have been swatting at something with my hands and knocked a few things off of my nightstand."

INTROSPECTION: TRANSFORMATION

Jake was freaking out. He was terrified about the possibility of his dad wanting to go into his bedroom and then seeing the inexplicable presence of melting ice.

What am I going to do? Jake thought. *Just go back to bed, Dad. You and Mom go back to sleep.*

As if in a trance, Glenn turned around and returned to his bedroom. Jake went to his parents' bedroom a couple of minutes after Glenn left him. He quietly opened the door just enough to peer in and see Debbie lying on her back with her wavy brown hair covering her entire face and Glenn already deeply asleep.

Jesus Christ. What have I done? This isn't happening. This isn't happening. This isn't happening.

OK. OK. I need to cool down.

After several minutes of concentration, Jake regained his composure.

This has to stop. I can't manipulate people. I can't manipulate my parents. If I'm not careful, I'll start treating people like they are my puppets, and then I'll become no better than Jarga.

Chapter 11
Agent Hendrix

March 2146

"I wanted to get back to you regarding FBI Analyst Sherri Hendrix," Emily said to Kent. "I think you will find my discoveries," Emily suddenly became visibly uncomfortable, "quite disturbing."

"What's the matter?" Kent asked, genuinely concerned about Emily.

"Do you remember Agent James Parks, if that's even his name?"

"He's a legend. One of the best field agents to have ever served in the FBI. It's a shame how he died—his son shot him."

"Well…" Emily once again lost her train of thought and was disturbed by Kent's comments.

"Well what, Emily? What's the matter?"

"Agent Hendrix used to be a field agent. One thought by the FBI to have a bright future ahead of her."

"I had no idea. This is the first I've heard of someone transitioning from being an active field agent to an analyst. Shocking, in light of what you said about her potential as a field agent."

"She waaaas raa…," Emily could not get the words out, and her speech became incoherent. She appeared as if she was on the verge of passing out although she had her strength about her. Kent took her hand and put his arm around her.

"Do you want to sit down?"

"No." Emily leveraged the readings from her implant to help regain her composure. Emily's entire demeanor and stance changed. She searched within herself to find a surge of strength to enable her to get through this challenging moment, just as a marathon runner does when approaching the finish line.

"She was raped. That son of a bitch raped her, and the FBI covered it up."

"What are you talking about? From where? From whom did you receive this intelligence? If the wrong people heard your claims, you'd likely be terminated from the Bureau."

"My source is reliable. I saw the documents to substantiate the claims with my own two eyes. Parks was showing Hendrix the ropes. It was one of her first field assignments after graduating from Quantico. He gave her a bit of a covert tour of a massive multi-layered drug cartel. He drove her to multiple locations and pointed out things that should be of interest to her. Once they were well into the twilight hours, he took her to a diner to get something to eat."

Emily became silent and froze, tears forming in her eyes. An expression of rage overcame her, her brows furrowed, and her tan complexion becoming increasingly replaced by red.

"It's OK. Let's get this out in the open," Kent said as he took Emily's hand after she had previously abruptly pushed him away from her.

"Hendrix testified that she suspected he put something in her drink when they were eating together in the diner. The next thing she remembered after eating some food at the diner was him…"

"Take your time, Emily," Kent said, staring into her eyes and moving her sandy blonde hair away from her face. He put a hand on each of her shoulders.

"He was inside her, from behind, in his car under Key Bridge. The son of a bitch blocked off an access road to his location to ensure no one would see what he was doing. To his surprise, Hendrix regained consciousness during the act and did all she could to get him off of her. He proceeded to beat the hell out of her. She got her firearm and shot him repeatedly until she ran out of rounds."

Kent was shocked, not only by what Parks had done but also by how this horrible incident had been covered up by the FBI. Serving the Bureau to help make the world a safer place for society was Kent's mission in life. This was in his blood and was exhaled through every one of his breaths.

"I can't believe this. His son is rotting in prison for a crime he didn't commit, to preserve Parks's revered reputation, not to blemish the FBI," he said as he walked away from Emily in disgust, sorting out his thoughts and trying to regain composure.

"Hendrix hasn't been comfortable working in the field since, which is why she requested to be transitioned to becoming an FBI Analyst. It all makes sense. This is why, in hindsight, she's always in the presence of at least four FBI personnel."

Kent felt like he'd had the wind knocked out of him. An agency that he had believed unconditionally stood upon unwavering integrity had engaged in this disgusting, dark, and unethical act of deception.

What else have they done that I don't know about?

"I modeled my entire career after that asshole. I wanted to be him. Jesus. One day, I'd hoped I would receive a compliment from him. How could I have so poorly misjudged his character?" Kent said to Emily.

She knelt down and put her hands on his face. "There was no way you could have known. You never even met him. Listen to me. No organization is free of corruption. As unforgivable as this is, it's obvious the FBI has their reasons for concealing the truth."

"It just doesn't make sense: concealing Parks's horrible act, the secret Hendrix is keeping, and the horrible experience I'm sure she relives at least once every day. Her coping with the FBI withholding the truth and Parks's son rotting away in prison for a fabricated crime he didn't commit. What am I doing? How can I continue to—"

INTROSPECTION: TRANSFORMATION

"Listen to me, Kent, we have a job to do, one more important than any other. We both need to regroup and get ourselves back together."

"I'm going to get to the bottom of this, Emily."

"No, you can't. Remove that from your mind. Neither of us can let anyone know what we know."

"You can't ask me to do nothing. How can you ask this of me?"

Emily grabbed hold of Kent's arm firmly, and her demeanor once again transformed into complete calmness and strength. "Kent, you know I'm right," she said softly and compassionately while looking directly into his eyes. "We'll get through this together, OK?"

That which defined Kent as a human being—honesty, integrity, valor, respect, character, and humanity—had been shattered. Not knowing what else to do or say, he replied, "OK…and here I thought I was going to console you. Thanks, Emily."

Kent kissed Emily on the cheek and hugged her as a physical expression of his gratitude toward her. They stood facing each other until they felt comfortable relocating into an open area within the facility.

Chapter 12
A Leader Emerging

October 2145—April 2146

"Human populations will be much greater than what we encountered here. We do not yet know the capacity of our telepathic abilities; therefore, we must plan accordingly. Begin by covertly placing yourselves in smaller populations, and gradually increase your exposure to larger populations. Decide upon a human physical appearance you wish to assume—take no detail of your appearance for granted—and remain consistent with that appearance throughout the remaining duration of our time here. This will be your new physical identity." Gralp relayed these instructions to his entire survey party.

Deciding to leave his ship behind, Gralp and his survey party split up so they could penetrate and research nine distinct geographic locations, each with varying populations of humans, climatic conditions, and geographic regions. Gralp and twenty other members of his survey party targeted Washington, D.C. because of its strong military and legislative activity and the presence of the United States' FBI headquarters facility.

I N T R O S P E C T I O N: TRANSFORMATION

Knowing that the United States possessed a dominant military presence on Earth, Gralp dedicated three of the remaining eight sub-groups of his survey party to Chicago, Illinois, Belmont, Maine, and Cottonwood, Utah. The remaining sub-groups were assigned to Bolivia, Zambia, Austria, Thailand, and Russia. Each survey party was afforded discretion to explore other areas within the United States as time permitted.

The members of Gralp's crew that were embarking upon surveys disbanded into their respective groups and departed to reach their assigned destinations.

"We will station ourselves here initially," Gralp instructed his survey party as he pointed toward the center of the Greenbelt Forest Preserve, located near Washington, D.C., from far above.

"Earth is showing great potential. I am not experiencing any detectable detrimental side effects from exposure," Langi shared among the other survey party members.

"Agreed, it is encouraging. We need to assimilate the inter-workings of human society as well as inject safeguards to insulate our presence here covertly. We need to remain undetected for another four Earth months and continue to gather as much intelligence as possible. Jarga will confirm for himself that we have left no detail unexplored," Gralp relayed to all survey party members.

All survey party members, except Langi, transitioned into a state of mental stasis to regenerate for the following day. This was how Sellenians, Grunats, Flares, and Ungdens rested. Given their highly elevated levels of intelligence as compared to humans and the extent to which their brains were used, insufficient rest frequently resulted in death. At least one of their survey party members needed to remain alert at all times in the event human encounters occurred. Langi volunteered to fulfill this role that evening.

Approximately two hours elapsed. It was early morning. Gralp was ready to deploy his survey party. "Remain within a 100-mile radius of this location, which is well within our ability to maintain communication with each other, and explore. Under no circumstances are you to harm anyone. We will all reconvene here in four Earth days," he commanded.

I sense humans' intellects here are more advanced than those at our previous location, Mangar thought, relaying it to the other survey party members. "I am going to absorb some humans' archives and will glean to what extent my will may control them," Mangar continued.

"Proceed delicately," Gralp responded. "These are appropriate and prudent actions for all of us to employ accordingly. Once again, inflict no harm upon the human subjects with whom you interact."

Mangar gathered five adults ranging in age from 26 through 81 Earth years and relocated them to a remote area within Battery Kemble Park. Upon initially gaining possession of these people, Mangar instilled visions in surrounding peoples' minds that each person continued walking along their original course, subsequently forcing each person in proximity to forget about their presence subconsciously. Mangar and the people she had abducted were made invisible to others. Sensing the initial discomfort among the humans, she eradicated their fears and convinced each of them that they knew each other and were continuing toward their intended destinations.

Mangar continued making herself and the people she had taken invisible to others. Concurrently, Mangar telepathically surveilled the area for the presence of other humans. She was also telekinetically hovering each person in a confined grouping approximately twenty feet above the ground to avoid other people potentially walking into them. She began extracting, absorbing, and processing each person's archives, that is, all of their memories and experiences, similar to the manner in which they would be transferred from a dying Sellenian, Grunat, Flare, or Ungden to another. Mangar was surprised to learn of the minimal extent to which each person was aware of their respective family's histories, as well as their upbringings and life experiences.

How can their society expect to advance and evolve at a sufficient pace, and to an adequate extent, when they exert minimal effort to retain and frequently recall their history? Careless and stupid.

INTROSPECTION: TRANSFORMATION

"Two of these humans could be useful to us. The others are useless," she relayed to the others in her survey party.

Mangar then applied her mental dominance to each human to learn to what extent they could be controlled. She had each person run, walk, dig, and eat grass. Unfortunately for the humans she'd abducted, Mangar was unaware that humans did not eat grass. She and other inhabitants of Shangten frequently consumed what resembled Earth's grass.

Mangar also had each person jump into Maddox Branch, a stream off of the Potomac River, sleep, and then bow as if they consciously acknowledged their inferiority to her.

Pathetic. I'm done with you pitiful subjects.

Mangar completed her evaluation of the humans she'd abducted and returned them to the original locations from where each person was extracted.

Mangar then navigated herself throughout downtown Washington, D.C. and selectively picked humans she felt demonstrated potentially greater intellects than the others. This time, she captured sixteen humans and returned to the same location in Battery Kemble Park. It did not take her long with this group of people to recognize that her first group of humans were likely representative of the entire human race. Mangar's patience with humans was quickly deteriorating, and it was only her second day of observation in Washington, D.C.

She returned the second group of humans to the points from which she had taken them and then submerged herself 60 feet deep within the Three Sisters to rest.

Survey Party in Leoben, Austria

This is very disappointing, yet favorable, as it will be no challenge eliminating humans should Earth be our next habitat, Caman, a Flare thought after completing his fifth day of observation in Leoben, Austria. *That is if they do not kill themselves.*

Caman, along with all of the other survey party members on Earth, had been informed by Gralp of humans' propensity to kill each other. Caman and other survey party members were able to deduce this realization themselves upon extracting life experiences and other memories from the people they abducted, because humans had endured many wars and other violent conflicts.

Caman's thoughts were shared by most of the survey group members dispersed throughout Earth at Gralp's command. Also common among the majority of the survey party members was a growing disrespect for humans, and to varying extents, a strong disregard for human life. A desire to eradicate the human race was growing within them.

Survey Party in Washington, D.C.

Each of Gralp's survey party members convened at their point of origin in Washington, D.C. and engaged in a mind integration to circulate all thoughts and experiences that were gleaned from each of the humans they had temporarily acquired as well as their first-hand thoughts and experiences. They were intrigued by several insights they had extracted from humans. Two items of great interest were the concept of love and how humans reproduced.

Love was more a mystery than a curiosity for them since it was merely something none of the aliens had ever experienced. Contrary to humans, where reproduction is a product of sexual intercourse, which, among humans, is an expression of affection, reproduction among the inhabitants of Shangten occurred via chemical reactions and was performed to sustain their culture, history, and existence. Only aliens of the same race could reproduce, and the reproductive process was not dependent upon the genders of those involved.

All aliens were capable of reproduction only twice in their lifetime, once when they reach an age representing a quarter of their life expectancy, and the other when they reach three-quarters of their life span. Knowing exactly how long they would live was considered an invaluable insight versus a burden. The indicator of each reproductive phase was an increased concentration of mobleteum, a chemical present in every alien typically at much lower concentrations. When mobleteum was at higher concentrations, all aliens in sufficient proximity intertwine with the alien experiencing high concentrations of mobleteum.

Upon the intertwining of the aliens, a chemical reaction occurs only between the reproductive alien and precisely one other alien. The result of the physical intertwining of the aliens is the production of a new gaseous mass, which is the offspring. Only one offspring was created in result of each reproductive process, and the aliens consider it a privilege to know their life expectancy upon initiation of their first reproductive process. Unlike humans, the inhabitants of Shangten do not experience love for their offspring. Reproduction was an obligation they fulfill so they may preserve their people.

The mind integration continued traditionally until Gralp broke his link, disrupting the process for all of his remaining survey party members. Before the others had time to react, they sensed severe displeasure and anger from Gralp.

"What are you doing, Gralp?" Mangar inquired, alarmed.

He was applying fatal pressure to Mangar's brain, in a rage. Though she tried to suppress memories of killing one of the humans she'd acquired from the survey party, Gralp's superior telepathic abilities were able to extract the direct violation of his primary directive not to harm any humans.

"It is obvious to me that your cruel act was a senseless redirection of hostility toward Jarga and his fellow Ungdens, as well as a primal distaste toward humans. However, there are no excuses for directly disobeying my order," Gralp relayed not only to Mangar but also to the other survey party members.

"Humans are worthless. There is no need to consider cohabitating with these mindless primates. We should spare our brethren on Shangten the effort and eradicate the entire human race since we are already here," Mangar responded.

Moments later, Gralp extracted the last remaining experiences and thoughts within Mangar's archives, and she immediately transformed from her gaseous form into a viscous liquid, falling lifelessly to the ground.

"I can sense it in each of you. You must fight your instincts that desire killing—senselessly and mercilessly murdering these humans. I am aware of how you reacted to our 'civil' war, the war that was orchestrated by Jarga. We will not repeat the eradication of entire races, that is, in this specific instance, the human race, in Jarga's shadow. I know this is not what you want."

All of Gralp's survey party members conveyed concurrence, as his understanding of their sentiments was acutely accurate, or so Gralp thought. As feeble as humans were, there were morals about them that tempered the urge to inflict harm upon humans. Further, as Gralp reminded the survey party members, they had not yet confirmed that Earth would be their next host planet.

In the back of his mind, though, Gralp knew that, should Earth be chosen as their next home, Jarga would insist upon a merciless annihilation of all humans before his arrival.

Chapter 13
Obsession

January 2146

Dr. Agon continued his strictly regimented and in-depth analysis of the alien contents of the liquid remains recovered from the commercial airliner crash site. He subjected samples of the liquid to varying temperatures. It neither showed any indications of change in molecular structure when exposed to frigid temperatures, nor became gaseous, nor changed phases when exposed to scorching temperatures.

He subjected the liquid to various chemicals amidst varying environmental conditions for days, causing no changes whatsoever from the liquid's original state. In time, Dr. Agon transitioned his interest from attempting to change the properties of the liquid in any way to trying to isolate the alien items from those that existed on Earth. His efforts proved futile, and frustration was growing within him.

This doesn't make sense. I don't know what to do.

He was performing all of the work by himself, and the more time he immersed himself into his work, the more detached he became from his everyday behavior. He was losing himself and his connection with society.

Chapter 14
Human Suspects

March 2146

"Hendrix, start with your updates for Chief Master Sergeant Luallen," Kent directed in a confident tone that had been absent from him since he was appointed to lead his Special Task Force. Considering what he'd learned about Hendrix, he felt good about assigning her the opening of the session. He figured doing so was the least he could do, and that she'd earned the right to distinguish herself among her colleagues to the fullest extent possible.

Perhaps attributed to being slightly overweight and suffering from dermatologic issues, Hendrix did not embrace opportunities to be the center of attention. She was startled when Kent called upon her at the onset of this Special Task Force session. However, fulfilling her sense of duty, she mustered enough courage to respond to his prompt.

"I accompanied Agents Jacobsen and Tyson to the meeting with the gate agents who facilitated the boarding process for the Tranquility Airlines flight number 2122. One of the gate agents accurately recalled the appearances of both Stacey Smith and Jennifer Cole."

Luallen interrupted Hendrix, "You're telling me this gate agent is capable of recalling the physical appearances of every person that boards every flight for which she is the gate agent?"

"Hendrix's account so far is accurate, sir," Emily interjected, receiving a non-approving glare from Kent. While Emily had a heightened sensitivity to disrespect being directed toward females from male military personnel, especially considering the traumatic and tragic situation that had befallen Hendrix, she knew Kent had a right to be disappointed with her actions toward Luallen.

"Continue, Hendrix," Luallen directed, ignoring Emily.

"The gate agent confirmed that both women boarded the aircraft and remained on it, at a minimum, through its departure. Bearing in mind that we suspect both of these women are aliens, it would be prudent to believe anything is possible regarding their abilities."

"What are you getting at, Hendrix?" Luallen pressed.

"We cannot rule out the possibility that they exited the aircraft before it crashed," Hendrix responded.

"Just as we should not ignore the possibility that the aliens remained on the aircraft through the crash, leaving their blue liquid remains behind," Emily interjected, knowing that she expressed what Kent was thinking but could not express himself because he did not want Luallen to suspect that, once again, Kent and Hendrix were not in sync with each other.

"That's all well and good," Hendrix said in a heightened voice, "but there is one hole in your theory, Emily. Stacey Smith and Jennifer Cole were not aliens."

Kent put his face into his hands, as this was another indication that sufficient communication was not occurring among all members of his Special Task Force. *Luallen is going to eat me for breakfast and throw my remains to his dogs for dinner. This is a shit show.*

"How in the hell did you draw that conclusion, Hendrix?" Luallen inquired.

INTROSPECTION: TRANSFORMATION

"After we met with the gate agents, I returned to the Bureau and consulted with colleagues specializing in forensic profiling. We learned that, on the surface, Smith's and Cole's backgrounds were anything but extraordinary. However, we recovered Muslim jewelry referring to the *Ayat Al Kursi* from Cole's purse, indicating a potential tie to Middle Eastern life. The *Ayat Al Kursi* refers to a verse in the Quran that speaks about how nothing and nobody is regarded to be comparable to God, that is, Allah. The Quran is the central religious text of Islam, which Muslims believe to be a revelation from God."

"Are you aware of the recruitment practices employed by various Middle Eastern terrorist cells involving the kidnapping of children aged four to eight years that are not of Middle Eastern descent?" Kent asked.

"No, I'm not," Luallen answered.

"We have reason to believe that Stacey Smith and Jennifer Cole were kidnapped at a young age when visiting Israel with their families. However, if we are correct, their original names were changed after they were kidnapped," Emily explained.

"This is quite a stretch, especially because their remains were not found in the wreckage. How can you possibly draw such a conclusion?" Luallen inquired, seeming prepared to reject any explanation that would follow from Hendrix.

"We can address that later. Acknowledging their potential Middle Eastern terrorist cell ties, we extracted all actions captured by the aircraft management system. We learned that the landing gear was engaged when the aircraft was at an altitude of approximately 14,000 feet."

"Middle Eastern terrorists downed a United States airliner on United States soil? This hasn't happened since 9/11. Our intelligence suggested all Middle Eastern terrorist cells were effectively contained or eradicated." A long stretch of silence followed Luallen's comments. "I need to speak with the President." Luallen left the meeting room with urgency.

Chapter 15
Breakup

July 2146

What am I going to do with all of this ice? Jake thought as he returned to his bedroom. Before giving the matter a second thought, his thoughts became actions.

Three empty two-liter bottles of Mountain Dew relocated to the center of Jake's bed. All of the ice rose to just below the ceiling of his bedroom. Instead of telekinetically unscrewing the caps from the bottles, they were screwing tighter, causing them to warp.

No, the other way.

The caps briefly stopped moving, changed rotation, and then unscrewed. The ice then turned into vapor.

No, I want it to be liquid.

The vapor quickly changed its phase to liquid, and the melted ice flowed into the bottles. Because there was too much to fit into the bottles, Jake successfully routed the remaining water into a large bowl partially filled with stale popcorn.

What am I going to do? I'm no longer human, and I can make whatever I want to happen. I also make mistakes, which could hurt or kill people. Jake sat on his bed, his forehead resting in the palms of his hands. *My god, I'm a freak...as if I weren't already enough of a freak.* He telekinetically screwed the tops back onto the Mountain Dew bottles.

Jake had lost his composure. The best idea he could come up with was to sit at his desk and try to calm down. Hours passed, the sun rose, and it was time for Jake to get ready for school. Conducting himself as if nothing out of the ordinary had occurred, he stuck to his traditional morning routine and headed downstairs for breakfast.

After getting a bowl, a packet of Lucky Charms cereal, and milk, Jake turned around to make his way to the kitchen table, only to be confronted by Debbie and Glenn staring at him from the entryway into the kitchen.

"Rough night last night. I had the strangest nightmare where I was a marshmallow in hell," Jake said anecdotally in hopes of breaking the tension. "Where is Allie?" he continued, hoping to convince his parents to latch onto a topic other than what he knew they wanted to discuss.

"Are you OK?" Glenn asked.

"Are you doing drugs?"

"Debbie, really?" Glenn scoffed.

"Yes, really, Glenn. Not only has he been behaving oddly, but he's also lost a lot of weight. And have you noticed that the acne on his face is nearly completely gone? And all of the sudden he's been smelling like lavender. And why did he push his sister off of her bed while she was sleeping last night? Drugs certainly aren't out of the damn question."

My God. I must have inadvertently telekinetically knocked Allie off of her bed last night.

"I'm OK, guys. Everything is fine. I promise," Jake responded deceivingly calmly while thoughts of concern raced through his mind. "I had a rough day with Julie yesterday. We've been friends forever. I made a mistake. I should have never asked her to take our relationship beyond being just friends. I don't think things are going to work out. And no, I'm not doing drugs, Debbie." Jake could barely get his final words out without chuckling, further trying to make light of the situation.

"That's good," Debbie said with an audible sigh of relief. "But this still doesn't explain all of your weight loss and your clear complexion," she continued.

"Wow, Debbie, you're on a roll, and the day has only just begun. You're focusing on Jake's complexion? And you're worried because he smells like lavender? I'm sorry, Jake. I know this must be extremely difficult for you," Glenn said, putting his arm around Jake's neck and resting it on his shoulders.

Lavender? Why is Debbie saying I smell like lavender? After spending a few seconds tracing some of his recent experiences, Jake recalled an intense odor that smelled like flowers just before his encounter with Langi. *I must have permanently assumed her odor to some extent*, he concluded. *I'll have to play it off as if I'm using a new soap.*

"Julie is my only true friend. We've been through a lot together, and she was my only true friend when I was younger and constantly bullied. I should have kept things as just friends; she's so much more important to me as a friend than she is as a girlfriend. This 'love' stuff only complicates things. It sucks," Jake said as his eyes welled up with tears.

"Relationships are only temporary. Couples break up all the time in school," Debbie said as she walked toward Jake. "You two have a very long history. I'm sure you'll be able to work through this. It's going to be OK. You'll feel better after you eat some Lucky Charms. 'They're magically delicious,' don't you know?" Debbie giggled and then kissed Jake on his forehead before heading upstairs to change out of her pajamas.

"You sure you're not on drugs?" Glenn sarcastically asked Jake with a smile and a wink as he followed Debbie upstairs.

His parents had helped him feel better, although realizing how emotional he had become since his encounter with Langi was causing him concern. He could not recall the last time he'd cried since the tragic car accident had occurred, and including this morning, he estimated it had only been eight times in his life. He did not know whether the crying was a product of his inherited enhanced maturity, intellect, and wisdom, or if subconsciously, it was an indication of still being overwhelmed with his new abilities.

Jake reflecting upon his recent recurrences of crying prompted a vivid memory involving his mother.

Mom always enjoyed watching Gabriel and Jake playing in the backyard through the kitchen window while washing the dishes after dinner. Allie wasn't born yet. In this particular instance, Jake was drawing designs on their wooden picnic table using sidewalk chalk, and Gabriel was playing on the tire swing. Just as Jake had nearly completed scribbling his final design, he heard a faint thump in the distance.

Jake instantly rose from where he was sitting and walked toward the source of the sound, near the foot of the driveway where it transitioned into the lip of the cul-de-sac on the street. As he neared the end of the driveway, he saw movement on the ground. As Jake was getting closer, it became obvious to him that it was a bird, quivering sporadically.

Just as he realized that it had fallen out of a tree, the bird died. Picking it up, Jake petted it gently, as if it had long been a member of his family, like a pet dog or cat. Then suddenly, without warning, Jake began to cry, moderately at first and increasing in intensity as time went on.

Jake heard the pattering of his mother's steps. She rushed to him when she heard him crying. Not turning around to greet her, Jake continued caressing and consoling the poor bird. Just after her steps stopped, he told his mother what happened, crying hysterically. She then walked around him, knelt down on her knees while facing him, and joined Jake in petting the bird.

"What happened?" she asked.

"I'm not sure. I think she fell out of the tree."

"She sure is a pretty bird," His mother said, trying to console Jake by understanding the impact the bird's death had on him.

"It's just a stupid bird. Why do I have to be such a cry-baby? I didn't even know it," Jake said as tears were pouring down his cheeks.

"Jake, look at me," his mother said in her beautiful, peaceful voice as she placed the bird on the driveway and took both of his hands.

"You're crying because you feel love for this bird. Like people, moments ago, this bird was full of life, but then she was gone. No one, nothing, lives forever. This is all the more reason why we need to cherish the time we have by living life to the fullest. I mean, to have as much fun as possible," she continued, pinching the end of his nose.

"It's stupid that I have to cry about every little thing."

"Crying is a gift. It can be a release. It can be an expression of compassion and sympathy. It can be both at the same time. It is also a cleansing process. It cleanses your body and your conscience. I mean, what you're thinking. It can be so many different things. Most importantly, it shows that you are strong. Most people are too afraid to cry, especially handsome boys like yourself."

"Afraid to cry? Why would anyone be afraid to cry?"

"Well, why do you feel stupid crying?"

"Because I don't even know this bird. There is no reason for me to be crying."

"Is that the actual reason?"

Jake took a few minutes to reflect on his mother's question. Proud of the answer he formulated to her question, he said, "No, it's because it makes me look like a sissy."

"Exactly," she said. "Put differently, you think it makes you look weak, don't you?"

"Yes, I do."

"That's why many people are afraid to cry. However, crying demonstrates just the opposite—strength and maturity. And you know what else?"

"What?"

INTROSPECTION: TRANSFORMATION

"Who cares what other people think? You do what you need to do when you need to do it."

Jake giggled because the quick succession of her words sounded so funny to him. He didn't understand what they meant at the time.

Jake told her he loved her and then he gave her a long, tight hug. She had a way of making him feel better, regardless of the situation.

"Let's create a final resting place for this beautiful and amazing bird. What do you say?"

A flicker of light from the stained glass wind chime hanging outside the kitchen caught Jake's eye, causing him to abruptly disconnect himself from this long-lost memory that had occurred when he was only seven years old. He could not recall ever reflecting upon this memory before. He had completely forgotten it. Recognizing that this was not a trivial occurrence, he surmised that it must have been another enhancement inherited from his alien encounter.

In addition to telepathic and telekinetic abilities, and absorbing and processing memories from Langi, I must have also inherited a heightened ability to recall memories from throughout my entire life.

"Oh, man, disgusting," he scoffed as he looked down to find Lucky Charms soup in his cereal bowl. The cereal had been sitting in the milk for so long that it had increased in size fourfold.

Been there, done that, he thought. He emptied the bowl into the sink, grabbed his backpack, left the house, hopped into his vintage 2072 Honda Excelsior LX, and drove to school.

Jake was in a bit of a daze until he saw Julie in his third period advanced calculus BC course. She was already in the classroom when he arrived.

"When are you going to grow up?"

"I didn't think you even knew I was here," Jake blurted sarcastically in response to Julie's question. Everyone already seated at their desks in the classroom and others making way to their chairs all turned their heads toward Jake. It was just then that he realized Julie had not said anything out loud.

83

My God, I can also read people's minds? How am I supposed to tell the difference between someone's memories and knowledge, when they're currently in the act of thinking, and when I'm not looking at someone when they're talking? Jake wondered as many of his classmates aimed glares in his direction. *I remember learning something about the conscious versus the preconscious in sophomore advanced placement psychology, but that didn't make any sense to me. I guess I should have paid more attention in that class.*

"Stop giving me shit and just forget all of this happened," Jake blurted towards his classmates.

In response, everyone turned around, shocked at Jake's very uncharacteristic behavior. The students who hadn't yet been in the classroom to hear Jake's faux pas found their seats and sat down, oblivious to what had just transpired. As everyone was getting settled, Ms. Cheryl Ross arrived at the classroom.

"Why does everyone look so depressed? My class hasn't even started yet." Ms. Ross nervously chuckled. "Wow, tough crowd," she continued, noticing that not even a single student was laughing or even cracking a smile.

"Um, anyway, today we're going to learn the fundamentals of integration with a single variable. Most of you excelled at learning how to perform derivatives, so I'm sure you're going to enjoy what I'm going to show you today."

Ms. Ross's words were the last words, the last sounds, the last of anything Jake heard for the remainder of his calculus class, other than his thoughts. The teacher deduced that something was bothering Jake because he was not responding to her calculus-related questions. As was the case in most of Jake's classes, he was often the teacher's last resort to provide answers to most of the questions when no one else either volunteered or was capable of answering them. Since Jake was excelling in the class and was usually so helpful in enabling her to maintain a consistent pace of teaching, Ms. Ross decided to leave him alone.

As much as it hurt him, Jake decided that he needed to distance himself from Julie. Too much confusion, fear, and doubt were monopolizing his thoughts. He was adamant that he was no longer human. Further, he was unable to control his new abilities, and most of all, he did not want to risk harming Julie in any way. Just after the moment he feared for Julie's safety, Jake inexplicably achieved clarity in his thoughts. Immediately thereafter, the annoying tone sounded, indicating the end of his calculus class.

Julie was the first person to leave the classroom. Jake telepathically forced her to stop by the nearby lockers until he caught up with her. "I know you're pissed at me, and you have every right to be. I'm sorry, Julie." Jake expressed genuine regret just as Julie herself was preparing to break her silence.

"It's OK, Jake. I've been too hard on you," she responded.

"You have? I mean, no. No. The problem is with me, Julie. I know this isn't going to make sense to you, but I've changed. I'm different, and I think it's best we don't date anymore. I need some time on my own to figure things out."

Julie looked like the wind had been knocked out of her. She looked shocked. Before she could think of something to say, Jake was already halfway down the hallway.

Chapter 16
Soul Searching

June 2146

"There has been yet another shooting involving an African American police officer and an adolescent white male. My guess is the officer didn't use his firearm sensor in time to confirm the offender was carrying. This is the third such incident of this kind in two weeks, all of which occurred in eastern Louisville, Kentucky. However, contrary to the prior two incidents, as you can see from the video captured by Louisville native Michael Heald, the currently unidentified white male shot and killed the police officer, who has not yet been identified to afford the deceased officer's family much-deserved privacy and time to grieve." Jake listened to the newscaster as he was eating his favorite ice cream, pralines and cream, at his favorite ice cream shop.

This shit has got to stop. Whites killing blacks, blacks killing whites. What does it take for people to get a friggin' clue and recognize color is only skin deep? Both the shooters and their victims keep getting younger. Kids are killing adults and adults are killing kids just because of opposing colors of their skin. This shit just has got to stop.

Jake was enraged.

INTROSPECTION: TRANSFORMATION

Racial tensions were mounting between whites and African Americans. It was as if all that had been accomplished by the late Dr. Martin Luther King Jr. and other impactful civil rights leaders and activists had been all but erased from U. S. history. Violence between the races was escalating at a steady pace throughout the continental U. S. even though conditions were not quite as severe or as prevalent as they were in Dr. King's era. Once again, humanity was perpetuating tragic events with consequences and implications that had several times before become readily understood from historical events. This dark history was once again in the process of being repeated, rearing its hideous head.

Why can't we learn from history and not repeat what shouldn't be repeated? It's just not that complicated, Jake thought.

In an unfiltered, unadulterated fury, Jake's emotions dictated his actions, and he decided to drive to the area in which the shooting had occurred. He drove there to determine whether he could locate the shooter by using his new, and mostly untapped, telepathic abilities. Upon leaving his car, he could detect what he assumed to be the thoughts of numerous people in proximity to his current location since he could not hear any voices. He reasoned he was hearing all of the peoples' thoughts since he was consciously trying to locate the shooter as he was concurrently compiling prior attributes associated with his current location.

He was walking down Brownsboro Road toward Interstate 365 when he sensed the following: "Mom, the police slug was harassing me...questioning why I was where I was and what I had in my backpack. I didn't do anything. I was coming back home from Stephen Horwitz's house. The asshole pinned me down on the ground." Unbeknownst to him, a nearby convenience store had been robbed under gunpoint, and anyone fitting his description would have been identified as a suspect of interest by law enforcement officers.

Jake telepathically instructed this person to meet him at his current location. The speaking in his mind ceased, and within minutes, a boy was within sight.

Holy shit, it worked.

Jake began walking toward the boy, and they both stopped when their tennis shoes nearly touched.

"Are you the one who shot the cop last night?" Jake asked, despite being confident he already knew the answer. *He's the one, I know it.*

"What in the hell am I doing here?" the boy asked, not acknowledging Jake's question.

"Answer my question. Did you shoot a cop last night?" Jake insisted.

The boy stood there silently. He wondered why he was there in the first place.

Jake deduced that he must have been unsuccessfully attempting to speak with the boy telepathically. Frustrated at his continued inability to effectively control and execute his new abilities, he shouted, "Did you shoot a cop last night?"

"Chill, man. Where do you get off asking me such a dumb-ass question? Step off, and don't yell at me," he responded.

Blood began running from the boy's left nostril. "What the hell?" the boy said in alarm, rubbing his upper lip and finding blood on his left index finger.

"Listen to me. I'm not messing around. Answer the damn question."

Jake was still distraught that both his friendship and relationship with Julie was over, more so than he was upset regarding his inability to use his new abilities effectively. Blood now streamed out of the boy's right nostril, while the intensity of the flowing stream of blood increased from his left nostril.

"What are you doing to me? I can't breathe." He was more alarmed by the maniacal expression on Jake's face than he was about the fact that he could not breathe.

INTROSPECTION: TRANSFORMATION

Jake's expression personified hatred and anger. Jake was lost. The adolescent boy fell to the ground, gasping for air. He tried to speak, but his inability to breathe prevented him from doing so.

The boy then rose his hand as a form of concession, and moments later, he lost consciousness. Jake could sense he was soon going to die. The fact that this did not concern Jake was what forced him to relinquish his hold over the boy. Jake broke his self-induced trance as the boy began to cough and regain consciousness.

"I shot him. I shot him. Now let me go."

"How old are you?"

"Thirteen, now let me go."

"What's your name?"

"Dylan Pickel. What do you want from me?"

"I'm not letting you go," Jake responded in a monotone voice. "You are going to turn yourself in."

"Turn myself in? Yo, you're fuc—"

Jake stripped Dylan of his voice. The boy attempted to speak, but no sound was leaving his mouth. Concurrently, Jake delved into a meditative state and extracted numerous instances of Dylan's life experiences in only a matter of a few minutes.

I understand, and I'm very sorry Dylan, Jake thought. *You're just another statistic, a product of the incompetent upbringing of your prejudiced, spiteful, and resentful single mother. So much promise, with the rest of your life ahead of you.*

What am I saying? That isn't me. Who am I? What the hell am I?

Dylan returned to his feet, alarmed at the blank expression on Jake's face.

This is Langi. Somehow she is manipulating my thoughts. But she's dead. Get the hell out of my head. Get out of here.

"Fine, I'll leave."

"No, wait, you're not going anywhere," Jake shouted to Dylan, realizing he had vocalized what he assumed had been his silent thoughts. Jake was beginning to understand and appreciate the incomprehensible wisdom he'd inherited from Langi in addition to his new telepathic and telekinetic abilities.

Unlike this kid and countless other people in this world, I will not repeat the dark history that haunts us, and I will not allow others to do the same. For such wise and capable aliens, I fail to understand why they were unable to draw the same conclusion.

Ahhh. Stop it, Langi. Let me think for myself.

In a trance, Dylan walked with a designated destination Jake had implanted into his mind, nearly two miles, to the nearest police station.

"May I help you?" the receptionist asked Dylan, observing him standing motionless, with his body pressing against the reception desk and a "deer in the headlights" expression on his face.

"Hello?" the receptionist said inquisitively as she snapped her fingers in an attempt to elicit a response from Dylan.

"Sergeant, I need you to come out here," the receptionist spoke nervously into the internal intercom system.

"What seems to be the problem?" Sergeant Lam inquired of Dylan after seeing the blank expression on his face.

Dylan's trance broke when he realized he was in the presence of a sufficiently ranked police officer. "I shot Officer Russell Kopka." Before they could react, Dylan placed the firearm he'd used to shoot and kill him on the receptionist desk.

"Run this firearm through ballistics, process him, and place him in a cell," Sargeant Lam instructed one of his staff police officers. "What are we going to do with kids these days? It's damn depressing."

Jake returned to his car and drove to Cherokee Park. He left his vehicle and returned to the same location in the forest where he'd had his encounter with Langi. He was exhausted and realized he was losing himself.

I could have killed that kid. I wanted to kill him. He was only thirteen-years-old. What the hell is wrong with me? What am I going to do? I need to... Wait Oh my god.

INTROSPECTION: TRANSFORMATION

Jake collapsed.

Chapter 17
Return to Shangten

May 2146

"We have what we need here. All of our data indicates Earth will be a viable host planet for us. It is time for us to convene with the others at our starting point," Gralp relayed to his survey party members.

The other members of Gralp's survey party were motionless, confused, and hesitant to leave. Before any of them had an opportunity to speak, Gralp inquired about Langi's whereabouts. No one was aware of her current location. His most recent account of Langi was five days prior when she had extended her survey to Louisville, Kentucky after completing her original assignment in Chicago, Illinois and then surveying humans in various parts of Indiana.

"Mairia and Vingu, return to Mborokua via Papua, New Guinea, and inform the others that we are searching for Langi and that we will soon arrive. Everyone else, we leave now to find Langi," Gralp instructed, already hovering in the sky.

"We need to be swift since we need to begin our return to Shangten within three Earth days," Gralp instructed, already beginning his journey to Louisville.

INTROSPECTION: TRANSFORMATION

Langi was very special to Gralp, and he was the only one who knew that she was a Lumar. When at Shangten, he'd exerted all of his energy to ensure that no one else became aware of Langi's true race, since Lumars were thought by Jarga to be extinct after the civil war he'd orchestrated. But Langi could carry her weight because she possessed far superior intellectual skills for a Lumar. Understandably, no one, including Jarga, thought a Lumar could possess such intellectual abilities. Gralp experienced great pleasure witnessing Jarga's and other Ungdens' egos impeding them from realizing this effectively concealed the truth.

Once Gralp and his survey party had crossed the border from North Carolina to Tennessee, Gralp instructed everyone in his survey party to focus on telepathically locating Langi. None of the members of his survey party, including Gralp himself, could detect her consciousness. Suspecting that it was potentially Earth's environmental conditions interfering with their inherent telepathic abilities, Gralp instructed the survey party to continue toward their destination.

Having reached Louisville, Kentucky and returned to the ground, none of them could detect Langi's presence. They were also unable to identify any traces of the observation path she had taken when she was in Louisville.

"This can only mean one thing. Langi must have overexerted herself and expired," Gralp solemnly relayed to his survey party.

"But what of her remains? Why are we unable to detect and locate them?" one of the survey party members inquired.

"Our inability to do so must be a property associated with Earth's atmosphere and other environmental factors," Gralp mournfully responded.

He and Langi were extremely close and had known each other for nearly their entire lives. This was an extraordinarily difficult loss for Gralp. However, he knew Langi would agree that finding a future home for their people was more important than her own life.

"We need to leave. We will continue projecting human forms until we return to the country in which our starting point is located," Gralp instructed.

They went directly to Louisville's Standiford Field airport and purchased tickets to fly to Papua, New Guinea since that was the only way they would be able to return to their ship in sufficient time to begin their return journey to Shangten. Transporting themselves through their means would consume another eight days, approximately the same amount of time that was required when they first traveled to Washington, D.C.

They entered the airport and telepathically provided their fabricated credentials and payment for their tickets.

"Will you be checking any baggage on this trip?" the airline agent asked.

"No," one of the survey party members succinctly responded.

It was obvious from the airline agent's body language that she felt something was wrong. Not having to probe the agent's thoughts, Gralp erased this occurrence from the agent's memory and directed her to process their transactions without issue. The agent complied.

Gralp and his survey party waited at the gate for hours among unsuspecting humans.

"It will be all too simple to eradicate these humans before our permanent arrival, regardless how abundant their population," one of Gralp's survey party members relayed to the others.

Shielding his thoughts from the others, Gralp was concerned about the future of the humans should Jarga designate Earth to become their new host planet. Unfortunately, he realized that if it were not to be Earth, it would be another planet with its population of beings that would likely be mercilessly murdered under Jarga's rule. Despite recognizing his future and the future of his people were at stake, he hoped there would be a better way that would not involve yet another eradication of an entire race of beings.

Travel back to Mborokua was uneventful, and they arrived there in two days. Upon their return, many members of the initial survey party were missing. The surviving members shared their experiences and other memories, including the cause of each survey party member's death, with each other. The apparent cause of death for all of the lost survey party members was exhaustion.

Given they were aware of the effect that prolonged, extensive brain usage had on their bodies, it was unprecedented that so many of them would reach their demise in this fashion given the granular and precise control they had over their faculties. Gralp determined his peers that perished during the survey must have been distracted and did not effectively manage their energy levels. This was easily understandable to Gralp considering the promise Earth yielded as their next host planet, as well as everything else the planet had to offer.

Although Gralp was comfortable assuming other absent and unaccounted for survey party members had died from exhaustion, he was slightly uneasy regarding the fact that, similar to Langi, the remains of approximately forty of them were not recovered or accounted for. He was unaware that Mairia and Vingu, both of whom were Flares, had died in a plane crash. Gralp's uneasiness dissipated when he reflected upon the wealth of information that had been compiled by each of the survey members. Everything consistently reinforced the viability of Earth being their next host planet.

"We have a two-month journey ahead of us. Hamla, return the ship to the Earth's surface. We leave first thing in Earth's morning," Gralp directed.

Gralp spent the remainder of the night reflecting upon the imminent demise humans would experience should Earth be selected by Jarga to become their next host planet.

As Gralp and his survey party entered the ship, he had not been able to formulate a way in which the humans' lives could be spared.

It was not long ago when I mindlessly and cowardly did Jarga's bidding during the civil war. How could I have done that and allowed what transpired to occur? Not again. Life is precious, and everyone should be entitled to live their lives as they choose. Who are we to strip them of it? The killing must stop.

The vessel was powered up and prepared to return to Shangten. As the ship left the ground and instantaneously disappeared into the Earth's sky, Gralp thought, *I vow not to allow Jarga to murder these people. I will find a way to save them, or I will die trying.*

Chapter 18
Worldwide Conflict

April – June 2146

"A protest in Boothbay Harbor, Maine turned violent as twenty-one people are currently reported dead, and forty-six more wounded, the aftermath of a bomb that detonated in the police department located at 11 Howard Street," a news anchor stated on a television in a break room.

"How could this happen at Boothbay Harbor, Maine, of all places?" Luallen questioned. "I used my Ocuporter to see first-hand what has been occurring through fellow FBI field agents at these crime scenes. Racial tensions are mounting, and taking into account what we learned yesterday, Middle Eastern terrorist cells are becoming more aggressive than they have been in years as they execute their global agendas. The Middle East is a catastrophe, with hundreds of innocent people being killed in the crossfire every day. Nearly all of Europe's, Africa's, and South America's economies are collapsing, causing unavoidable increases in crime. The entire world is going to hell, and now we need to worry about aliens taking over our planet?" Luallen commiserated with Kent as he watched the news.

"I've used my Ocuporter in some instances as well, sir, so I, too, could gain a full appreciation for what's been occurring globally. While all this crime and tension is extremely disconcerting, we must treat it separately from the potential alien threat we are investigating. We don't know what the aliens' agenda is," Kent replied, even though in the back of his mind he concurred with Luallen's concerns. "What I can say is we're making good progress. If we continue at our current pace, we'll learn of their intentions very soon." Kent attempted to instill some optimism in his superior's mind.

"This is a terrible distraction. The world needs us. No one has peace of mind once they leave their homes, and may not even while they are in the 'comfort' of their own homes. We need to instill a sense of peace and safety in their lives again. Accounting for all I know, my combat training, and all that I have seen throughout all of my tours, I do not feel safe, myself, anymore. A bomb, armed terrorist, compromised civilian—something that would threaten my life and the lives of those I love—could be waiting at every corner," Luallen continued, failing to react to Kent's attempt at optimism positively.

"This isn't the time to panic." Kent did not understand the gravity of his words until after he had already uttered them.

He knew in an instant that he would live to regret what he said. He had gotten too caught up in the moment. Regardless, he was correct: Luallen was panicking.

Luallen received Kent's words like a slap in the face. He appeared visibly enraged as his face changed to a reddish-purple color. Even his bald, scarred, and calloused head was turning red. The silence that followed Kent's words seemed like an eternity, although in reality, it was only a few seconds. Everything that followed seemed to progress in slow motion.

Kent began to see Luallen's lips move. The words were indistinguishable although he could hear Luallen speaking. It sounded like many baritone wind instruments chaotically competing with each other for attention via long duration monotone notes in an orchestra. Kent was feeling queasy.

"Excuse me, sir?" Kent responded, desperately trying to recover from his compromised state.

"You're right, Kent. I don't know what's come over me. I am not myself," Luallen softly replied. "We need to rethink our approach. There is a lot occurring at once, and we are too reactionary. We need to integrate with other agencies to orchestrate and execute a proactive global remediation, containment, and eradication strategy."

"I concur, sir. We need to make this country, our world, safe again."

"This is becoming a habit these days, but I'm going to speak with the President. Assemble your Special Task Force; we're going to have a closed urgent-action meeting at 1330 today," Luallen said, and then he left the break room.

Wow, now he's speaking for the President? What makes him think the President is going to accommodate his schedule? Kent thought. *However, we are facing very desperate times these days.*

As Kent stood up to begin coordination of his Special Task Force in preparation for the impending closed urgent-action meeting, Hendrix appeared from just outside the doorway.

"What is it, Hendrix? You look like you've seen a ghost."

"It's worse than I thought. Stacey Smith and Jennifer Cole are clearly up to something, and they are shadows in the wind."

Chapter 19
Revenge

July 2146

Nearly six hours elapsed before Jake regained consciousness, finding himself once again engulfed by ice and completely refreshed. After disposing of the ice by melting and then forcing it into the ground without issue, Jake went to his car and drove home. Sensing his parents in the living room, anxiously awaiting his arrival, Jake parked his car in the driveway and entered his house via the front door. *Thank God I'm getting better at all of this.*

Before either Debbie or Glenn could speak, Jake said, "I'm fine. I'm fine. Everything is OK. I'm starving, can we go out for dinner?"

"Sure, going out for dinner would be just fine if it wasn't 1:00 am in the morning," Glenn said in an agitated tone.

I thought I was getting better at this.

"You can't continue to leave us here waiting up for you, wondering when, or if, you're coming home. Wondering whether something horrible has happened to you, whether you're alive or dead," Debbie said frantically.

"Debbie. *Mom*, I'm sorry. A lot is going on in my life right now with school, Julie, and some other stuff. Please be patient with me."

INTROSPECTION: TRANSFORMATION

Debbie did not hear anything Jake said after addressing her as 'mom.' This was the first time Jake had called her that.

"Mom?" Debbie said faintly.

"Yeah, of course," Jake promptly responded. "You're taking care of Allie and me just as *she* would have. You're my mom now."

Debbie began crying. She was very grateful, not only for Jake feeling this way toward her but also for him sharing his feelings with her. Observing her reaction, Jake realized for the first time how difficult it must be for Debbie to be his and Allie's stepmother, to insert herself into a pre-existing family once led by their biological mother.

"I love you, Mom, and I appreciate everything you do."

"Thank you so much, Jake," Debbie responded just as she lunged herself toward Jake to give him possibly the tightest hug he had ever experienced.

"OK, so, forget dinner now. Can I go to bed?"

"Of course you can, Jake. Sorry, all of a sudden, I'm so emotional," Debbie said.

Jake gave her another hug and then hugged his father. Glenn rubbed Jake's recently buzz-cut head as an additional sign of affection and support. Jake then went upstairs to his bedroom, entered, and locked the door behind him.

OK, all I need to do is what I did to find Dylan Pickel.

Jake telepathically began searching for his person of interest by probing people's thoughts, just as he had done before.

Oh man, this is going to be hard. I must probe people's thoughts much more deeply than before, he thought, since the specific thoughts he was searching for applied to an event that occurred five years ago.

Jake decided to lie down on his bed since he knew it would require the exertion of an extreme amount of energy to find who he was seeking. Recalling that he had neither eaten lunch nor dinner, he went downstairs and inhaled a half-gallon of cookie dough ice cream and half a bag of sour cream and onion potato chips.

He jogged back upstairs, laid down in his bed, and began probing people's thoughts. Jake started focusing on people near his house and then continued radially from there. Since most of the people Jake was scanning were sleeping, he had to delve into their subconscious minds. While it was challenging for him to probe into people's innermost thoughts, it was much more straightforward than investigating an active mind engaged in many random, and sometimes extremely awkward, thoughts. Jake was fascinated by the themes he encountered among people's subconscious minds.

Many people suffered from a severe lack of self-confidence, and sexual fantasies monopolized many of the adults' subconscious.

Then, abruptly, in an instant, Jake found her.

I feel you. I see you. I'm coming to kill you, you heartless bitch.

Jake discerned from her subconscious that she lived in Indianapolis, Indiana. Jake ceased the probing process and prepared for his trip to Indianapolis, which required only a two-hour drive. Lucky for Jake, it was a Sunday, which was an easy day for him to be away from his parents without having to go to school.

Rather than causing his parents alarm by leaving without notice, he waited until they woke up and had breakfast with them. Debbie made Jake and Allie's favorite breakfast, which was cinnamon roll pancakes. However, just as she had done many times before, Allie dipped her entire hand into the frosting Debbie had made and then picked up Jake's glass of milk without him noticing. Like clockwork, Jake picked up his cup, only to once again have his hand covered with the sticky and gooey icing.

"Allie. Why do I always fall for this?"

Allie was laughing too hard to respond. In an attempt to stop the laughter, Jake wiped the icing from his hand onto her nose and cheeks. Jake's plan backfired since the act caused Allie to laugh even harder. The family continued the meal in light-hearted conversation, complemented with frequent laughter.

As Jake was clearing the table, he told Debbie that he was going to hang out at Cherokee Park for the day and do his homework.

INTROSPECTION: TRANSFORMATION

Since this was somewhat routine for Jake, neither Debbie nor Glenn suspected anything unusual was occurring. Jake packed his backpack, dropped it into the trunk of his car, and then backed his car out of the driveway.

As he began his drive to Indianapolis, his positive demeanor deteriorated, and he transitioned from happiness to a state of fury.

How could you do this to me? Why did you do this to me? he thought. *You're going to tell me, and then you're going to die.*

Before he knew it, he'd arrived. He parked his car across the street from the front of her house. It was 1:30 in the afternoon. He sensed that she was playing with her one-year-old daughter in their backyard.

Maybe I'll kill her daughter, too.

Jake walked into her backyard via the gate in the fence that established a perimeter around her house.

"May I help you?" she asked, in more of a confused than an alarmed tone, since Jake was just an adolescent versus an adult stranger.

"Whee. Go play in the sandpit, Lexi, while I help this young man," she said to her daughter.

Given that Lexi was only one, she did not understand what her mother had said. However, she resonated with the calm and playful tone of voice and welcomed her mother placing her in the sand pit.

"May I help you?" she repeated to Jake since her first inquiry had elicited no response.

Jake's face was bright red at this point from the rage and fury that were boiling within him. Tears were forming in both of his increasingly bloodshot eyes.

"Are you OK? Is there anything I can do?"

"You killed my mother and brother, you fucking bitch."

"What?" she responded, completely mystified. "I certainly didn't kill anyone. You must have me confused with someone else."

"Do you recall doing anything out of the ordinary five years ago?"

"What do you mean? I don't understand."

Even though she did not feel threatened by Jake, she was becoming increasingly concerned that he was not in his right mind. She did not know how to handle this situation. She reached for her cell phone in the pocket of her sundress.

"No."

Immediately after Jake expressed his opposition to her reaching for her cell phone, she recognized that she was unable to move her arm any further toward it.

"You killed my mother and brother, Kathy Fretzin," Jake shouted. Tears had just accumulated enough in his eyes to fall down each of his cheeks.

"How do you know my name? I don't understand what's happening. You must have me confused with someone else." Kathy did not realize Jake was responsible for her inability to move her right arm. "I think I'm having a heart attack."

Lexi sensed her mother's concern and began screaming and crying. Jake promptly silenced and immobilized Lexi without inflicting any harm upon her. Simultaneously, he probed Kathy's mind to learn more about the day his mother and brother had died in the car accident.

"Do you remember hacking a level-crossing protection system?"

"A what?"

"You hacked a railroad crossing?"

Noticing that Kathy did not understand anything, Jake extracted more experiences from Kathy on that day. After he'd extracted all required context, he resurfaced the memories into Kathy's consciousness.

"Do you remember now?"

"Yes, yes I do," she responded, thinking that she had independently recalled what she had been doing five years ago as it pertained to a railroad crossing, completely unaware that Jake had resurfaced the memories for her. "I was studying various hacking tools as part of my computer science curriculum at college. I downloaded a penetration testing framework and used it to open and close railway gates." Kathy broke down in tears, genuinely remorseful for what she assumed must have transpired.

"We were on our way to the zoo. Gabriel was only nine years old. My mom was everything to me. The Federal Railroad Administration said that some of their infrastructure was compromised. The railroad gate arms didn't go down, the crossing sign lights didn't flash, and the crossing bell didn't sound. They said the systems were hacked by an unknown person who was experimenting with a highly dated and freely available suite of tools called Metasploit. Their systems should have been protected from this sort of thing since the tools dated back to the early 2000s.

"'You and Allie are fortunate to be alive,' and, 'You two should be dead,' my father said to me over and over again with tears pouring out of his eyes. This was the first and only time I've seen him cry. Glass shards damaged my diaphragm, aorta, and nicked the base of my heart. It's funny that the doctor who helped me after the accident considers the fact I was able to get my sister and myself out of the car to be nothing short of heroic and miraculous. And the police at the scene said my brother and mom were likely dead before the car stopped flipping."

Jake paused to regain his composure and very quietly said, "I'm no damn hero. I couldn't save them."

Kathy fell to the ground, grimacing as she applied pressure to her left temple with the palm of her left hand in hopes of relieving some of the pain she was experiencing. She was still unable to move her right arm. "Help me. I'm having a heart attack."

Jake walked closer to Kathy as he psychokinetically applied more pressure to her brain. He looked down at her with a sinister expression on his face as he stood only inches away from her. Kathy's daughter was still silent and motionless in the sandpit.

"You must not do this, Jake. This is not in your nature, your consciousness," a voice uttered in Jake's head. Initially mystified about from where the voice was originating, he ultimately deduced who it was.

"Langi. How is this possible?" he asked. "Leave me the hell alone."

"I am now and forever tied to your consciousness and subconscious. This is not in your nature. She knew not the consequences of her actions. You must not harm her or her child." Langi insisted.

Ignoring Langi's wishes, Jake continued to inflict pressure on Kathy's brain while immobilizing all of her extremities. Kathy began screaming from agonizing pain. In an instant, and not at his discretion, Jake relinquished his telepathic hold over Kathy.

"Leave me alone. She doesn't deserve to live," Jake relayed to Langi.

"Let her be. This is not the way," she said. "Do not succumb to anger. Do not do what you will later regret for the rest of your life. There is another way."

Langi then implanted an image of Jake's mother along with the sensation of her hugging him into his mind to decrease his rage. His resistance to Langi's will was nearly completely eliminated. Langi assumed full control over Jake. Jake turned around and began walking to his car.

Regaining her composure, still on the ground, Kathy said to Jake in tears, "I'm so sorry. I'm so sorry. Please forgive me. I had no idea. I never thought about the consequences of my actions. Please, please forgive me."

Jake continued silently toward his car. He opened his car door, and sat in the driver's seat, as Kathy exclaimed, "I promise. I'm going to turn myself in. I'm so sorry."

You're damn right you will, Jake thought.

Completely numb, Jake closed the door, started the car, and left for Cherokee Park to gather his thoughts and regain composure before returning home.

Chapter 20
Earth, the New Home

August 2146

Gralp's ship landed in the main military hangar, marking the conclusion of the just more than two-month journey back to Shangten. The nearly-empty hangar suggested that many of the other survey parties had not yet returned. This was curious to Gralp since he'd relayed specific orders from Jarga that all survey parties were to return to Shangten within fifteen months. However, he expected the missing survey parties to return by the end of the following day since that would mark precisely fifteen months since the survey parties had left.

Gralp decided to take advantage of his returning to Shangten a day early by trying to formulate a means to downplay Earth's potential as a host planet due to his fears that Jarga would execute the humans. He hoped more survey parties would return with reports of other viable host planets that would not inhabited by beings Jarga would be motivated to eliminate. Gralp was at a loss as to what to do since he knew he likely could not suppress his real thoughts and intentions from Jarga. He was also demoralized by the fact that all survey party leaders were scheduled to congregate with Jarga, Leese, and other key Ungdens in two days.

Each survey leader was required to share all thoughts and experiences they and their respective survey party members had compiled during their surveys with each other and with the Ungden leaders, including Jarga, during the scheduled mind integration. Gralp reluctantly accepted the fact that suppressing thoughts regarding the viability of Earth becoming their next host planet was futile. It was just too big a subject with too many details to conceal from Jarga at a minimum. The best contingency plan he could formulate was to convene all survey party members, and not just each survey party leader, to conduct a preliminary sharing of thoughts and experiences before the official mind integration that would subsequently occur with Jarga.

In doing so, Gralp hoped that another, at least equally viable, host planet would emerge, where, at a minimum, he would not have near the compassion towards whatever inhabitants there may be as compared to his compassion for earthlings. That evening, Gralp instructed all survey party members that had already returned to Shangten to collaboratively share all thoughts and experiences associated with their respective expeditions. In addition to wanting to learn whether other viable host planets existed, he merely wanted to learn everything before Jarga would.

It seemed like an eternity to Gralp before the following morning arrived. Once morning came, all survey party members participated in the mind integration. Gralp was extremely deliberate regarding the manner in which he selected each survey party member of each survey group. With very few exceptions that only applied to those he trusted, the primary objective of his survey party member selection process had been to ensure each member's intellectual abilities were inferior to his own. This was to serve as a contingency plan should he determine one became required for an unforeseen purpose.

Because of Gralp's superior telepathic abilities, he was able to direct each survey party member's thoughts to himself first and then relay thoughts he felt would be of little consequence to all of the other present and participating survey members. Gralp executed this filtering process in such a way where he effectively concealed his presence as intercepting and filtering all survey party members' thoughts.

Many of the thoughts relayed by the survey members involved suffering and death. Gralp was extremely disheartened not only because of the loss of life experienced among the deployed survey parties, but also because it became increasingly apparent that Earth was going to emerge as the most viable host planet for all inhabitants of Shangten. He was hugely disappointed to learn through Umal's thoughts that Carpul consisted of a toxic environment incapable of sustaining life.

Gralp had high hopes for Carpul since life forms on that planet were minimal compared to the number of humans on Earth, and because its atmosphere and environment were very similar to Shangten's. He concluded that life on Carpul would not be viable considering how violent the environment proved to be for Umal's survey party members and how toxic it was to the materials comprising their ships.

Gralp was also deeply saddened to learn from Umal that he'd had no choice but to leave potentially living members of his survey group behind at Carpul, since he knew he would otherwise soon meet his demise, and since the ship would be destroyed. Gralp sympathized with Umal and appreciated Umal's commitment to surviving so he could report the outcome of his survey group's expedition. Gralp was very troubled to learn that Umal had returned to Shangten only two months after leaving for his expedition.

Two months hardly afforded Umal an opportunity, with appropriate preparations and adjustments, to determine whether Carpul could indeed serve as a host planet for our people.

Accounting for what Gralp had gleaned from the others, he found no reason to attempt to suppress any of his thoughts and experiences when on Earth from Jarga. There was no reason to mask the fact that each of them would perceive Earth as the most viable host planet since Gralp knew that Jarga would reach the same conclusion himself the following day. The mind integration lasted nearly four hours, and everyone was exhausted. Of the 132 survey parties represented in this group of survey party members, 115 of them met similar outcomes to those experienced by Umal and his survey group. A majority of the survey party members did not survive, leaving Gralp to question himself.

Despite my research, I sent so many of my people to die. Which is worse, intentionally murdering people or causing so many deaths because of one's ineptitude and mistakes? Am I any better than Jarga? Am I equipped and capable of fulfilling my purpose?

Gralp was extremely fatigued. He completed his thoughts as he retired to his living quarters to enter mental stasis for rest in preparation for his meeting with Jarga the following day.

Chapter 21
Insanely Fearful

March 2146

Recognizing that he had not eaten in nearly two days, Dr. Agon broke away from his unrelenting research and analysis of the alien remains and went to eat at a nearby fast food Mexican restaurant. During his walk of six blocks, the surroundings were uncharacteristically quiet for 4:00 pm. There was hardly any pedestrian traffic, and there were many abandoned cars throughout the streets.

Dr. Agon encountered a horrible odor as he opened the door to peer into one of the abandoned cars. Quickly identifying the direction from which the scent had originated, he looked down at the driver seat to find what appeared to be entirely liquefied human remains. Noticing a swarm of flies hovering around the back seat in addition to those hovering over the driver seat, Dr. Agon transitioned his focus to two car seats in the back seat of the car.

Completely liquefied smaller masses of human remains filled the car seats. The remains were not bloody and contained no solid substances, such as bones and teeth. The color of the liquid was pale peach with randomly dispersed intermittent red, yellow, and white spots. Although Dr. Agon commonly encountered varying states of deceased humans, the appearance and odor of these remains made him violently nauseous. He left the car and mustered all of his strength to prevent himself from vomiting.

He continued toward the restaurant, noticing human remains along the street and sidewalks similar to those that he'd encountered in the car. Dr. Agon was completely mystified about what caused all of this death and what could have transformed these people into puddles of remains. He finally reached his destination and heard stirring noises in the kitchen area, which was concealed from the entrance. After noticing tables and chairs ridden with liquefied human remains, he turned around for the door.

As he put his hand on the door handle, tentacle-like arms wrapped around both of his ankles, pulling his feet out from under him. He fell, and his face was the first part of his body to hit the ground. His nose shattered instantly upon impact, and his eyesight was severely impaired due to the abundance of accumulating tears in his eyes. The appendages rapidly dragged him all the way back to the kitchen, his limp body violently colliding with chairs, the table mountings fastened to the floor, and the food assembly counter.

Dr. Agon was nearly unconscious when he stopped moving, still face-down, with a viscous stream of blood originating from his nose. Hysterically crying out of fear at this point, he mustered his remaining strength to turn himself over, only to learn from where the appendages originated. The blue alien stood approximately nine feet tall with too many appendages from its torso to count. Some were hanging limply at its side while others were erect and either waving randomly or grasping other objects.

A liquid similar to the human remains he observed in the car surrounded Dr. Agon and was dripping from the alien's two mouths, one on each side of its massive head. Horrified by the sight of the alien, he felt a burning sensation on his ankles. As he looked down at his feet, they were detached from his legs at his ankles and were instantly picked up and consumed by the alien. He screamed, out of agonizing pain and terror.

INTROSPECTION: TRANSFORMATION

Blood was spewing out of his legs as a flat beach-towel-like object extended from the alien's torso and nearly covered Dr. Agon's entire body from just below his neck to beyond the base of his severed legs. Soon after that, he felt a burning sensation throughout his body similar to what he felt at his ankles, and then the object was removed. Unable to lift his head, he directed his eyes downward. His entire body was dissolving from its natural state to the same liquid that was surrounding him and occupying the restaurant.

Recognizing the only remaining intact part of his anatomy was his entire head, he screamed hysterically. The screaming subsided, and he began losing consciousness.

"Ah," Dr. Agon screamed, awakening from his sleep, striking beakers and other glass objects with his flailing hands and arms.

Recognizing that he had just awoken from yet another of his frequently occurring nightmares, he calmed down and noticed that shards of glass had cut his hands and arms. Before addressing the bleeding, he got some forceps and began removing the shards of glass.

After removing the last of the glass shards, he removed his lab coat and rinsed off the blood from one affected area to the next. He then applied gauze to constrain the bleeding. Once everything was back in order, he returned to his analysis of the alien remains. Recalling a sample he was closely observing, Dr. Agon turned his attention to one of his microscopes.

"This can't be," he said, looking at the sample through the eyepiece lens of the microscope.

Chapter 22
Newfound Purpose

February 2016

"Come, walk with me," Qarta requested of Jarga.

*"Look at our people. They are weak and require guidance from those, that is, **the one** that is capable of being a leader."*

"And why is it that you are our leader?" Jarga asked Qarta.

"It is because our society cannot afford to possess a conscience. Given that most despise me and consider me a ruthless ruler, it is because of their inferior and incomplete perspectives that they deem me so."

"I do not understand."

"Having a conscience is a vulnerability that can easily be exploited. All it takes is one nefarious act to inflict great harm upon us. It is my responsibility to protect us all."

"But if you are protecting us, why do you kill some of us?"

"You are too innocent and naïve, Jarga. You are so very young. You still have many centuries before you, however, and in time, that vast intellect of yours will serve us well..."

"Why is it that you kill some of our people?" Jarga again inquired, not acknowledging the rare compliment Qarta afforded him.

"Because instilling fear is required to maintain obedience. All must understand and be frequently reminded that there are consequences to disobedience. There must be no tolerance for disobedience."

"I understand," Jarga affirmed to Qarta.

"Very good then. This brings me to your next task, Jarga, a critical task."

"What is it, Qarta?" A few moments elapsed in silence until Jarga noticed that an Argas was telepathically constrained by Qarta.

"What are you doing to this Argas?"

"This Argas is in the process of creating a coup against me, which cannot and will not be tolerated."

"Why am I here?"

"This is the moment when you will demonstrate your allegiance and commitment to the wellbeing and future of our society."

"You want me to kill him? He did nothing to me."

"He has not yet done anything to you, but in time, if unattended, he will. We must take his life to demonstrate the fate that awaits the others if they do not cease their crusading against me."

Before Jarga could express further opposition and reluctance, Qarta facilitated a mind integration between Jarga and the Argas. Within an hour, the Argas's consciousness, an entire history of life experiences and those he'd previously inherited from others, were transferred to Jarga. Argas then fell lifeless to the ground.

"Why? Why? Why did you do this, Qarta? Wh—"

Qarta interjected, *"No. I did nothing. Your subconscious, the purest element of your mind, performed thy bidding. This is very encouraging, Jarga, as I am now convinced that you understand your purpose and accept your destiny."*

"I do not understand."

"Worry not, young child. You will in due time. Now absorb the Argas's remains and complete the life-transfer process."

June 2145

"You summoned me?" Langi inquired of Jarga as she entered his living quarters.

"Gralp assigned you to accompany him on his survey party in support of his expedition to Earth?" asked Jarga.

"That is correct," Langi answered somewhat impatiently in light of her being aware that Jarga already knew this to be true.

"I am asking you to do this of your free will, even though I could manipulate you to execute my wishes," Jarga continued.

"What is it you would like me to do?" Langi was offended by Jarga's vanity and demeanor toward her. However, she knew she was afforded no discretion related to Jarga's wishes. She must do whatever he asked of her, or he would likely kill her.

"Gralp informed me that planet Carpul in the Farna region and planet Earth in the Galma region are the two most viable candidate host planets for our people. I want you to evaluate earthlings' intellectual abilities and how resilient they may be should we decide to inhabit their planet. I encourage you to engage in whatever activities you deem appropriate so you may independently formulate your own conclusions. Causing loss of life is to be of no consequence in achieving this objective. I already asked the same of Umal in regards to his expedition to Carpul.

"Very well, Jarga," Langi responded, and without question, she turned to leave his living quarters.

"One more thing, Langi. You are not to inform Gralp that this conversation occurred." As Jarga relayed this demand, Langi could sense him invading her mind.

Langi exerted every possible effort to conceal her true Lumar identity from him. She felt it was imminent that Jarga would become aware of her deceit. The sensation she felt was utterly foreign to her. It was because this was the first time she had experienced this type of manipulation, which only the most superior intellects among the Ungdens were capable of performing.

Jarga had implanted this demand into Langi's mind with his unique signature that only he possessed and, therefore, only he could extract. Unbeknownst to Gralp and Langi, Jarga had implanted the same demand into a select few other members of each of Gralp's and Umal's survey parties. He implanted this demand into the minds of members that were most prone to violence to obtain firsthand practical information regarding how susceptible the native alien species were to their intellects.

July 2146

"Click ...click ...click" were the sounds made by a boy's stick as he banged it on a pile of ice he found as he was walking through a wooded area in Cherokee Park with his father.

Jake frantically regained consciousness and emerged from a large mound of ice that engulfed his entire body. He was disoriented because initially, he thought the flashback regarding the aliens reenacted his own experience. For a moment Jake thought it was him and not Langi that interacted with Jarga. Quickly regaining his composure, the recurring presence of ice was no longer a mystery to him. Contrary to what humanity derived from science, Shangten consistently sustained temperatures extremely close to absolute zero. In consideration of his encounter with Langi, Jake presumed that somehow his chemistry had been altered so his body, especially when resting, engaged in some form of an exothermic reaction. He was sure his body temperature dropped to well below freezing.

Concurrent with his realization, Jake noticed the boy and his father were shocked and startled not only to learn of his presence, but also to find him emerge from a large mound of ice since it was the middle of summer and nearly 90 degrees outside. Before the father verbalized concern, Jake sensed his thoughts and purged this entire incident from both the father's and his son's memories and directed them to continue with their walk as if they had never encountered him.

As Jake continued to regain consciousness and become further acclimated to his surroundings, he was overwhelmed with sorrow regarding Langi's death. He was mourning her loss as if she were a close family member, or even his mother, although his only exposure to her was during their encounter. Further contributing to his sorrow was recognition of Langi's resilience against Jarga's bidding. It was evident to Jake that, despite the relentlessly insensitive demands Jarga had injected into Langi's subconscious, her non-violent nature and unconditional respect for life prevented her from exercising his bidding as it pertained, in this instance, to killing humans.

Offsetting his sorrow was his ever-growing fear of Jarga and his desire to eradicate the entire human race should Earth become his host planet. Considering his reign over all that lived on his native planet of Shangten, Jake was convinced he would be no match for Jarga and could do little, if anything at all, to prevent his invasion of Earth. Amidst the opposed feelings that were presently consuming his thoughts, Jake was able to keep himself calm and composed.

Additionally, following this 'sleep' as Jake characterized it, he realized all remaining thoughts and experiences possessed by Langi had been absorbed and processed by his brain. Jake recognized all of Langi's prior thoughts and experiences could be retrieved with incredible clarity seemingly in an instant. The same was true regarding all of his own experiences throughout his entire life.

Through the thoughts and experiences he inherited from Langi, Jake gained a profound understanding of Jarga, his stature, intentions, behaviors, and everything else associated with him. Jake gained comfort knowing he now knew everything about Jarga while the ruthless ruler did not even know that he existed. *In battle, outcomes tend to favor those who know the most about their enemies.*

Jake also acquired a complete account of the history of the various races that had lived on Shangten, as well as the history of the planet itself, which he realized was why Langi transferred her consciousness to him; she didn't want the history she possessed to die with her. Jake remained mystified regarding how Langi was able to insulate her true Lumar race and identity from Jarga, given that he believed all Lumars had been exterminated.

The memories Langi had obtained from her ancestors dated back thousands of years and dozens of host planets. Jake learned of the aliens' propensity to deplete their host planets' resources, rendering entire planets incapable of sustaining life. Jake never imagined a single being could retain and retrieve so many memories and possess what appeared to be infinite intelligence gleaned from thousands of years of history of one's people.

However, it was evident to Jake that the aliens were not effectively benefiting from the knowledge of their history. To the contrary, they were using it to acquire power and fulfill self-serving desires. This realization was tied to the fact that while Jake gleaned that Jarga manipulated his society into believing detrimental changes in environmental conditions were necessitating relocations to each new host planet, it was evident to Jake that the ruler and his subordinates were at fault.

In contrast, Jake also learned how much many races of aliens valued and respected each other and their history. This was very prevalent in the context of Langi's history and the history of her lineage, and was more profound than anything that Jake had ever experienced within himself or had observed among others.

Aside from his growing fear of Jarga and his intentions, Jake's remaining anxiousness revolved around his not understanding the extent of his abilities. He knew he would not gain sufficient comprehension of them until after encountering and interacting with at least one alien. Jake determined that he needed to locate and communicate with an alien with the sole purpose of understanding the extent of his abilities and how they compared with an alien from Shangten, preferably an Ungden.

This decided, Jake was completely at peace with himself and his surroundings for the first time in his life. Previously reconciling that his greater-than-average intellect was a burden, he now understood his inherited enhanced intellect and accompanying abilities were indeed a gift. This was a gift Jake knew he must apply so he could save his planet and all humanity. Jake was no longer anguishing over what his purpose could or should be.

I know my purpose. The gifts of knowledge, telekinesis, and telepathy transferred to me by Langi to serve a higher purpose will not be wasted.

Chapter 23
Discovery

April 2146

"We found our initial intelligence was inaccurate; the names of the two people of interest are Cindy Thompson and Cheryl Jennings. Regrettably, they were kidnapped when visiting Israel with their families and sold to a child trafficking circuit in the Middle East. During the time they were subjected to child trafficking, Ms. Thompson and Ms. Jennings were forced into prostitution and subjected to physical labor amidst unimaginable environmental conditions.

"We have learned that subjecting children to this form of trafficking enables terrorist cells to desensitize them to the point where death becomes a welcomed alternative to living amidst their conditions. As these children grow up, these terrorist cells assign them multiple aliases, making it virtually impossible for anyone to track them. Ms. Thompson was concurrently masquerading under four distinct aliases, and Ms. Jennings was perpetrating seven identities," Hendrix explained as the closed urgent-action session continued.

INTROSPECTION: TRANSFORMATION

"Are any of their aliases of particular notoriety?" Luallen inquired.

"Yes," Kent interjected. "You'll be interested to know that one of Thompson's aliases is Aakifa Shehadeh. Aakifa is currently a leader of a terrorist cell that is executing its agenda in Eastern Europe."

"Isn't she of American descent? How can she possibly pass as Iranian?" Luallen asked.

"Photographs of Aakifa are very limited, and as we have learned, not authentic. Since she was kidnapped at such a young age, Middle Eastern terrorist cells used this to their advantage; they overlaid and applied the appearance they wanted her to assume. This has proven to be extremely effective, as only her closest direct-reports and only very few superior ranking extremists are familiar with her true appearance," Hendrix presented, conveying continued self-fulfillment from the fruits of her relentless research and investigative efforts.

"Are there any other notable aliases assumed by these two terrorists?" Luallen requested, not yet completely satisfied with the amount, or lack thereof, of intelligence presented by Kent's Special Task Force.

"Yes, one other: Nomsa Swanepoel. This development was extremely unexpected since she is a South African leader who has dedicated her life toward achieving peace and equality for all, regardless of race and religion," Emily responded.

"Now how in the hell does this fit into these terrorists' political agendas?" Luallen asked.

He was becoming increasingly annoyed and frustrated as Kent's Special Task Force continued providing more information since it was accompanied by an increasing number of additional questions and unknowns.

"Our intelligence indicates that these terrorist cells have been training their soldiers in Lesotho, South Africa. Further, they have been using Port Elizabeth as a major hub for aggregating trafficked children for terrorist cell recruitment purposes. Similar to Aakifa Shehadeh, photographs of Nomsa are very limited, where only very few high-ranking terrorist cell members are familiar with her true appearance," Hendrix responded.

"This is beneficial intelligence. It is evident that these Middle Eastern terrorist cells are a key concern. However, we cannot allow these concerns to distract us from the fact that there are extraterrestrials on our planet. Have we learned anything useful regarding the alien remains recovered at the airliner crash site?" Luallen inquired, redirecting the group's focus.

"I have been able to ascertain that most of the elements comprising the remains are alien. I know you do not find this useful, but alien is alien," Dr. Agon responded in a tone that conveyed that, given he knew Luallen would not be satisfied with his response, he was just tired of his attitude toward him.

"OK, OK, OK," Luallen mumbled softly.

"Is it possible to use this substance to benefit us in some way?" Luallen asked out of desperation.

"It does not appear so. From all of the tests that I have performed, my conclusion is that this is a completely dormant substance that cannot be used in combination with our elements or materials to benefit us in any way beyond what we are already capable of achieving ourselves."

"Enough with this. We cannot squeeze water out of this rock," Luallen concluded. "Kent, meet me in my office at 1400; we need to formulate a strategy to isolate and eliminate these terrorist concerns."

"Wait," Dr. Agon shouted. "Wait."

"What is it, Agon?" Luallen inquired in an annoyed tone, having convinced himself that Dr. Agon had nothing impactful to share with the team.

"Uh...I...uh...I had somewhat of an unexpected breakthrough this morning. I—"

"Well, is it, or is it not a breakthrough, Agon? Get to the damn point. Now." Luallen growled, confused as to why Dr. Agon did not just open with this 'breakthrough' when he first began speaking during the meeting.

"In the act of awakening from a silly nightmare, I was startled and cut my wrist on broken glass. I then inadvertently splashed some of my blood on a sample of the alien remains sitting on a slide mounted in my microscope whose coverslip had fortunately not entirely covered the sample—"

"And...? What is it? I'm not tracking what you're saying," Luallen insisted.

"Either fire me or show me some respect, dammit. Enough of you treating me as if I am a useless and incompetent idiot. It stops now, or I quit."

Everyone, including Luallen, was speechless.

"Inconceivably, a chemical reaction occurred. After days of research and subjecting the alien remains to numerous chemicals and diverse environmental conditions, finally a chemical reaction occurred in response to exposure to my blood," Dr. Agon resumed very calmly as if his prior outburst had not occurred.

"All of its properties changed. Its odor dissipated, its color changed from blue to white, it changed phases from a liquid to a solid, and most importantly, all of its alien components were eradicated," Dr. Agon continued.

"Holy hell," Kent said under his breath, inaudible to everyone else in the meeting room.

"Despite me being no closer to understanding the composition of the alien remains, the chemical reaction that occurred gives early indications that something in our blood could be harmful to them."

"This is incredible, Agon," Luallen said in high praise. "What's next?" Luallen continued.

"The quickest way to proceed, I mean, I would like to take blood samples from each of you. I want to understand whether human blood universally reacts with the alien remains similarly to my blood, or if solely distinct properties in my blood are required to create the detrimental conditions."

"I think I understand your thought process, Agon. Excellent work. We will all have you take blood samples before we conclude this meeting. However, it is evident that you need to get some rest. You are on edge, and you need to be at your best moving forward."

I cannot sleep. I will not rest, Agon thought. His nightmares were worsening and occurring more frequently.

"I will not sleep. I will not sleep," Dr. Agon repeated, each time escalating in volume.

"What's the matter with you, Dr. Agon?" Kent asked.

"Yash," Emily calmly interjected. "You're working very hard, and you're not taking enough time to relax, rest, reenergize, and have some fun. You're allowing yourself to become too consumed by your work. We appreciate the urgency you have assigned to your efforts, but you're only human. Let's get these blood samples, I'll take you to my favorite place for some pho, and then I'll walk you home."

"No," Dr. Agon replied.

Emily responded to Dr. Agon's outburst by putting her hand on his back in an attempt to further calm him. Emily's gesture proved useful. Dr. Agon spent a few minutes reflecting upon the current situation and eventually returned to his typically calm demeanor. He finally broke the silence by saying, "OK. That sounds good, Emily. I am sorry. I don't know what has come over me."

"It's no fault of your own. Kent, we should look into getting Yash one of our BioSense implants so he can better manage his health." Emily said sympathetically on Dr. Agon's behalf.

"We are done here," Luallen stated.

"We're not done, Luallen. I mean, sir," Hendrix blurted. She regretted her outburst, biting her bottom lip.

"What do you have to say, Hendrix?" Luallen retorted with a glare.

"I leveraged relationships we have with numerous other countries to pursue a theory."

"A theory? What the hell kind of theory do you have, and why does it matter?"

INTROSPECTION: TRANSFORMATION

Hendrix went on to explain that she had reviewed the audio and video captured from Tranquility Airlines flight 2122 nearly forty times and had yet to formulate an explanation regarding how or why a defect in the video capture mechanism within the flight recorder all of a sudden was overcome, resulting in the video feed initiating shortly before impact. In cooperation with relevant overseeing governments, Hendrix contacted thirty-seven other non-domestic airlines and learned that there had been a total of forty-eight similar instances of defective flight recorders where video was not captured only during specific flights. Of the thirty-seven airlines, six of them experienced faulty video recording mechanisms within their flight recorders. The first instance Hendrix could identify of video not being captured by a flight recorder had occurred on September 16th, approximately three and a half months earlier.

My god, aliens have been right under our noses for six months, and we didn't even know. Kent was aghast at Hendrix's new intelligence.

"Hendrix, how were you able to obtain video recordings from the other countries?" Luallen asked, hoping she had not informed any of the foreign governments of their discovery.

"I simply told them we were tracking one of our most wanted criminals, Ian Wagner, who is currently number two on the FBI's most wanted list," Hendrix replied. "I also combined it with covert hacking activities performed by the NSA."

"Good thinking, Hendrix. Good thinking," Luallen said, obviously heavily distracted by both Hendrix's and Dr. Agon's recent discoveries.

What mystified Hendrix, as she subsequently expressed to the team, was that the affected flight recorders experienced no issues during flights completed by the same aircraft both before and after each flight where video was not captured. This caused her to suspect that either particular passengers or aliens had to have tampered with the video recording mechanism to conceal their true identities. Since it was difficult for Hendrix to imagine anyone being able to render only the video recording mechanism of highly secured, and mostly inaccessible, flight recorders in distinct aircrafts globally distributed during isolated flights inoperable, Hendrix suspected the aliens performed these acts through some superior ability that is foreign to humans.

"I know this sounds like an excerpt from a science fiction novel, but I cannot conceive of a single scenario where a human could accomplish such a feat," Hendrix expressed preemptively as a feeble attempt to salvage whatever remaining credibility she may have acknowledging how ludicrous her theory must have appeared to the Special Task Force.

"But why? What do the aliens have to gain by disabling the video recording capabilities of airliner flight recorders? And why in the hell are aliens flying around in our airplanes? Are they playing with us?" Emily interjected.

"I have no idea. Another important discovery is that I found no correlation between any of the flights where video was not recorded. There were no roundtrip itineraries involving either a single airline or across multiple airlines, and I have not found any discernible relationship of dates and times at which these particular flights of interest occurred. There are simply no patterns," Hendrix continued.

"What about individual passenger manifests for each flight? Anything suspicious?" Kent inquired in a hopeful tone.

"Nothing," Hendrix said in a disheartened tone.

Silence overtook the room for nearly ten minutes until Luallen broke it.

"This alien matter is currently a dead end. Each of you are to keep your eyes open and all other senses sharp to effectively continue pursuing any other viable courses that may reveal themselves that will help us identify at least one of these aliens and understand why they are here. Additionally, the terrorist threat to our safety and ability to maintain our quality of life throughout the United States and globally continues to grow. They have murdered thousands of people around the world, and they are steadily becoming more bold and aggressive, as there have now been a total of five related terrorist incidents on our soil during the past three months alone.

"Racial tensions are soaring in our country. We need to apply sufficient resources toward mitigating these and other domestic threats. This country, actually, the entire world, is going to hell: terrorism, religious wars, hate crimes, racially-fueled violence...I could go on all day. But let me be clear, I am in no way suggesting we turn a blind eye to whatever may ensue and to what has already transpired regarding our discovery of aliens on Earth. Agon, get our blood samples and resume your work. However, focus also on returning to your everyday life. You are currently on a self-destructive path. Kent, effective immediately, your Special Task Force is to consist only of you, Emily, Agon and Hendrix. That is all. Dismissed."

The unnamed members of Kent's Special Task Force were in disbelief, mystified as to how Luallen could essentially terminate the large-scale effort of trying to identify and locate aliens while trying to understand their purpose and intentions. Since President Claring was not present at the meeting, Emily suspected that maybe it was her, and not Luallen, who'd mandated this redirection of resources.

"This is ludicrous. Luallen may as well have just relieved us of this effort, too. Four people staffed to investigate what could be a global threat?"

"Maybe this isn't such a bad thing," Emily replied to Kent. "Look, now it's up to essentially just you and me. We can continue leveraging Hendrix to crunch the data, and Agon can continue with his science experiment. This is an opportunity for us to take a fresh start, to maybe apply an out-of-the-box approach."

"I'm going to get to the bottom of this, Emily," Kent said, almost maniacally. He was struggling to tolerate the idea of the presence of aliens but mostly was engulfed by fear about what their intentions could be.

"*We're* going to get to the bottom of this together, Kent." Emily put her arms around Kent to console him while he remained motionless, expressionless, and with his arms at his side, completely numb and oblivious to the outside world.

Chapter 24
Powerlessness

September 2146

The mind integration had been completed among all survey party members, Jarga, and his subordinates. Following the mind integration, Jarga requested a closed meeting to be attended only by Gralp and Leese.

"It is obvious that Earth is the clear choice. I underestimated your assessment of the fate of our planet, as well as the viability of Earth being our next host planet, Gralp. Your conception and execution of your surveying strategy were impressive and effective. I greatly appreciate your efforts. However, do not get too comfortable. For reasons I cannot understand, I learned during our prior mind integration that both you and Langi were successful in concealing her true race from me. Perhaps my complacency is to blame, and I will accept her death as consolation. Know moving forward that I will dissect every thought in your inferior brain with increased scrutiny."

During the mind integration, Jarga became aware of Gralp's desires to kill him due to his intentions of eradicating the entire human race upon inhabiting Earth. Regardless, Jarga knew he was still dependent upon Gralp until the full migration of all remaining

Sellenians, Grunats, Flares, and Ungdens to Earth was completed, despite being resolute in his desire to kill Gralp when sensible. Jarga sensed, by penetrating Gralp's mind and scanning his thoughts while concurrently telepathically manipulating him, that Gralp's hostility towards Jarga was inexplicably decreasing.

"You are now promoted to First Lieutenant, Gralp. You will report directly to Leese regarding all matters. You have served me, your people, and our future well, and you deserve to be rewarded," Jarga relayed to both Gralp and Leese.

"This is an important time. Seventeen months remain before we must leave Shangten, never again to return. Gralp and Leese, form a survey party and conduct final observations to confirm beyond a doubt that Earth is indeed a viable host planet," Jarga continued.

"I mean no disrespect, but considering the amount of time required to complete this task, it will leave no other option for our next host planet," Gralp relayed to the others. "Further, given the growing complexity and increasing loss of life involved in our recurring searches of subsequent host planets, I urge you to begin considering how we may be more mindful of our next host planet's resources so that we may potentially live there indefinitely."

Dismissing what Gralp had suggested as if he had never spoken, Jarga continued. "You indicated during our mind integration that two and a half Earth months were required to reach Earth from Shangten, requiring a total of five months to reach Earth and return here. Is it possible to reduce the travel time in either direction?"

Leese explained that the travel time could be reduced by a total of 20%, condensing the round trip to Earth to four months instead of five. Jarga dismissed them both after informing them that he would begin designing and executing the migration plan for Shangten's entire population very soon after they left for Earth. Gralp and Leese decided to meet with each other in two hours to perform required preparations for their trip to Earth. Gralp returned to his living quarters and anguished over the increasingly grim future of humans.

INTROSPECTION: TRANSFORMATION

There must be something I can do. Creating a mutiny against Jarga was not feasible since the vicious leader would simply be able to telepathically extract Gralp's intentions from any participants in his cause. Gralp had to conceive something that would be shielded from Jarga's probing. He conceived and dismissed plan after plan—it was hopeless. Even if he executed a covert agenda that was shielded by an outer layer of actions deemed acceptable by Jarga, or even Leese for that matter, either of them would be capable of penetrating all of Gralp's thoughts and therefore become aware of his true intentions.

Gralp spent the remaining time in his living quarters entering a mourning process on behalf of the earthlings. Since nearly two hours had elapsed since his meeting with Jarga and Leese, he left his living quarters to reconvene with Leese.

"We need to obtain a complete understanding of the extent to which earthlings will be capable of resisting their eradication. This is the primary objective of our next visit. How much time do you believe will be required to perform this assessment?" Leese asked Gralp, sensing Gralp's unrelenting remorse for the fate of earthlings.

"It is complicated to know, Leese. Earth is a vast planet with a circumference of approximately 25,000 miles, and that consists of many distinct populations of humans possessing different defensive capabilities. Further, we did not have sufficient time during our previous survey to ascertain each distinct population's defensive and attack capabilities. What we do know is that humans' minds are defenseless against our intellects and our telekinetic and telepathic abilities," Gralp responded.

"Then I hope that the members of your prior survey group will have valuable intelligence to share with us regarding this matter," Leese relayed with optimism.

"I regret to inform you, Leese, that members of my survey party we left behind did not survive for several reasons. Whatever intelligence they gleaned regrettably died with them."

"I am hopeful your understanding is inaccurate, Gralp. I sense you are unaware that Jarga instructed select members of your survey party to remain behind on Earth despite whatever instructions you may have provided. Now that you have been promoted, I believe a heightened level of transparency is appropriate and warranted."

Gralp was furious. *What could be happening right now on Earth? If they are not dead, what could Flarga, Claag, Bantaq, Flannan, and the others be doing? How many humans have they murdered? How many humans are being murdered right now?* Gralp recalled Mangar's violent tendencies during their short time together on Earth.

Gralp refocused on the task at hand and continued preparations for his second and final survey of Earth, this time with Leese. Gralp and Leese agreed the survey party should consist of 300 members so they could explore as many of the dominant populations of humans as possible, within various climates and geographies to ensure such variances would not be detrimental to their wellbeing. It was imperative that this exploration be completed within the six-month duration of their final expedition on Earth.

Gralp and Leese agreed to spend the next two days assembling their survey party. As Gralp tried to condition himself to focus on necessary survey preparations, he struggled to come to terms with the imminent demise of yet another entire race of beings much larger in number than any other race previously exterminated by them.

There must be something I can do to prevent this act of mass genocide. I cannot accept that I am powerless to protect these beings.

Chapter 25
Deception

June to August 2146

Jake woke up wholly buried in another mound of ice in his bed at his usual waking time of 10:00 am on a Saturday morning. Regaining consciousness under a pile of ice was now commonplace for him. Jake decided he would formulate a way to inform the United States military of the presence of aliens on Earth and their intentions to eradicate the entire human race. Before doing so, he was adamant that he first needed to interact with an alien.

Knowing that he was capable of manipulating his parents', as well as his teachers', friends', and anyone else's thoughts and memories, he was not concerned about the extended amount of time he may need to be away from his hometown to achieve this objective. Further, as advanced as his intellect already was before his encounter with Langi, as evidenced by the straight "As" he was receiving in high school, he was also not worried about missing classes.

After routinely telekinetically removing the ice and moisture from his bed, he got dressed, sat in his chair, and began the cognitive searching process. Not knowing what unique mental qualities or thought processes to seek out initially, he started probing the minds

133

of all residents, that is, all creatures, present in his neighborhood. Since he figured thoughts possessed by the aliens would be distinctly different from humans, he scanned past-encountered, insignificant human-based thoughts. Jake was unable to interpret the thoughts of all present organisms, such as insects and animals, and his heightened awareness of their presence made him uncomfortable.

Instinctively, through his inherited abilities, Jake was able to discern the distance each person was located from himself as he scanned their minds. Jake inventoried themes of thoughts he encountered so he could further hone his mind probing process. Among common themes were how one was going to make ends meet considering all of the living expenses needing to be overcome, how one would endure specific relationship challenges, fear of first-hand or family safety in light of current racial tensions, and fear of ongoing terrorist threats. This allowed him to spend less time processing such thoughts and more time further honing his targeting ability on what he suspected would be vastly different than ideas conceived by humans.

Jake's scanning radius continued to grow until he recognized that his probing likely just crossed the Kentucky state line, at which point he became distracted by his intellectual abilities and abruptly discontinued his scanning activities. He opened his eyes and noticed ice had begun accumulating atop his entire body, with higher concentrations present on his face and head. He was neither cold nor chilled. It became evident to Jake that the more he used his abilities, the colder his body temperature became. In recent days, given the extensive processing in his brain during sleep and meditations, he was once again reminded that this cognitive exertion is what caused himself to be entirely engulfed by ice upon awakening.

Surprised to realize that 90 minutes had elapsed since he'd begun scanning minds, he decided it would be best for him to go to a remote and isolated location so he could relieve himself of having to remain aware of anyone, including his parents and sister, who may interrupt his scanning process. Additionally, relocating would reduce the likelihood of anyone becoming suspicious of, or alarmed by, his activities. Because of the previous interruption inflicted by the father and his son when they'd found him buried in a large mound of ice on the ground during one of the hottest days of the summer, Jake decided to go to a much more remote location within Cherokee Park.

Jake reached his destination. Due to his heightened sensitivity to potentially being discovered, Jake manipulated the ground so he could completely submerge himself in dirt; only his nostrils remained exposed so he could continue breathing without any obstructions. Jake buried himself under tree branches, leaves, and dirt, hoping that any accumulation of ice would be undetectable should anyone randomly pass by his location. He then reentered a meditative state and promptly focused his attention on reading thoughts from minds that were located just beyond Kentucky's state border.

Jake systematically scanned minds radially from his location. He initially studied thoughts emanating from people located in Illinois, Indiana, Ohio, West Virginia, Virginia, Tennessee, Arkansas, and Missouri. It was inconceivable to Jake how rapidly he could extract thoughts originating from so many people over such vast distances; he realized he still was not fully acclimated to his new abilities. Feeling a bit discouraged by not locating any of the aliens' thoughts in the states above, he continued his search by penetrating the thoughts of people in each state adjacent to the ones he had already telepathically traversed.

Jake's scanning activities continued until he absorbed disconcerting thoughts located in Fayetteville, North Carolina. The thoughts were from an alien that was impersonating a janitor at Fort Bragg, which was still the United States' largest Army installation and command. By probing the alien's mind, Jake was able to ascertain that it had stationed itself at Fort Bragg to gain the United States' military intelligence that could be relayed to superiors upon their imminent arrival on Earth. It instantly became apparent to Jake how dire the alien threat was to the future of humanity and the future of Earth. Distracted by his fears, Jake abruptly regained consciousness.

He was amazed to see the amount of ice that had formed around him. Possibly because of being buried under the branches, leaves, and dirt, the ice had extended horizontally from his feet and head versus the way it had accumulated in prior instances, which was vertically from atop his torso and face. As he melted the ice and returned the ground's surface to as near an uninterrupted state as possible, he realized he needed to apply more thought regarding how to conceal his planned extended absence from his family, friends, and school. Further, despite being confident in his abilities, he still did not know how they compared to those of the aliens.

Jake returned to his car and drove home. He was famished and desperately needed something to eat. He knew quite a bit of time had elapsed because it was dark outside. He parked his car in the driveway, and just as he was about to open the front door to his house, Allie was there to greet him.

"I don't know what's going on with you, but Mom and Dad are mad," Allie said, chuckling. She anticipated their parents would punish him severely.

"What did I do this time?" Jake asked Allie, genuinely mystified.

The likely reason hit him like a ton of bricks just after he completed his question. He realized he'd inappropriately trivialized the fact he was away from home and out of contact with everyone in his family for the entire day.

"The last time any of us saw you was Saturday morning. Any guesses now why they're so pissed?" Allie asked, laughing harder than before.

"What do you mean? What day is it?" Jake asked, dismissing Allie's sarcastic tone.

"What day is it? What, did you forget the days of the week and how to tell time? What is wrong—"

Jake transitioned Allie and his parents into a state of paralysis so he could assimilate their current thoughts, as well as to discern what had transpired since he left the house on Saturday.

I N T R O S P E C T I O N: TRANSFORMATION

No way. I've been gone for nine days? How is this possible? Why am I not dead? My God, I am an alien.

He learned that his parents had contacted the police and that a search, co-sponsored by his parents and his school, had begun on Monday afternoon. He also learned that the search had been continued in shifts throughout the subsequent days and nights. He did not know what to do; his absence had created extensive commotion. He had done the one thing he did not want to do—directed excessive attention to himself.

Jake fell into a state of panic. *What am I? Who am I? What am I going to tell my parents? What am I going to do?* Jake became overwhelmed and felt a sharp pain in his head that caused him to fall to his knees. He firmly applied pressure to his temples with his hands, hoping to relieve some of the pain.

He determined he was likely processing too many thoughts and emotions concurrently. More thoughts continued to accumulate; he could not stop the introduction and processing of their ever-increasing volume. The pain in his head intensified as he became more overwhelmed. Realizing his thoughts were out of his control, he stopped attempting to constrain them and fell unconscious at Allie's feet.

"Jake? Jake. Jake." Allie screamed as she regained control over her mind and body, her laughter instantly transitioned into genuine concern. "Jake, get up."

Jake regained consciousness, finding himself in his bed with his mother, Amy, at his side.

"Mom? How...how is this possible?"

"Relax, my little daredevil. One day, I hope not too long from now, you're going to learn your limits," Amy said.

"I'm sorry, Mom. I don't know what happened."

"It's OK. You're doing what every normal child would do at your age."

"I mean it, Mom. I'm sorry."

"Listen to me. You're a child. You need to have fun. You're not grown up yet, and that's fine. I'm OK with that. One day you'll be all grown up, and your mistakes won't be my concern, assuming I'm even aware when you make them."

"Huh? What are you talking about?"

"I'm sorry, sweetheart. I'm talking over your head again."

Wait, I remember this. This has already happened. I was only seven years old. My mother is dead. I forgot how beautiful you were, and how much you loved me. I'm so sorry I couldn't save you, Mom. I miss you so much. I love you, Mom. I –

Jake opened his eyes. Unbeknownst to him, nearly three more days had passed. He was in his bed, with Debbie at his side.

"How are you feeling, Jake?" Debbie asked as she caressed his head and wiped his arm with a warm washcloth.

"I...I...I'm fine. Ouch. That cloth is hot," Jake responded.

Taking into account the cold temperatures Jake had become accustomed to when resting and meditating, he was becoming increasingly sensitive to warm objects and temperatures.

"I'm sorry," Debbie said, immediately removing the hot washcloth from his arm. "What happened to you?"

"I lost track of time. I'm sorry. I promise I didn't mean to upset you," Jake said as tears welled up in his eyes.

"You were covered in dirt when you came home, and when I came into your room to check on you, you had small pieces of ice on you."

Jake did not know how to respond, and he did not know how he was going to concoct a believable explanation for his absence. Thinking as clearly as possible, Jake came up with an interim solution. He acted a bit disoriented, started moaning, and then acted like he became unconscious.

After a few minutes, Debbie left his bedroom with tears in her eyes. It was not very long after she left that Jake figured out what to do. While he, at a minimum, could have simply implanted his thoughts into his parents' minds, he felt his new idea would settle in better if he told his parents face-to-face. Jake got dressed and joined his parents, who were downstairs in the kitchen, very concerned and lost expressions on their faces.

"I was kidnapped," Jake said, walking into the kitchen.

Debbie dropped her glass of water, while intensifying anger and concern could be seen in Glenn's eyes.

"I'm OK," Jake followed, seeing how visibly upset his parents were.

Jake went on to explain that he had been drugged, and for reasons unknown, was buried alive in the ground.

"The last thing I remember is I was walking around in the woods at Cherokee Park. I felt a prick in my shoulder. I ignored it since I thought it was a bee sting. Then everything went dark. When I woke up, I had a horrible taste in my mouth. It didn't take me long to realize it was dirt. I'm guessing the person must have thought he injected me with a lethal dose of whatever it was that he shot me up with," Jake continued with his story, growing increasingly anxious to leave for Fort Bragg.

He also felt guilty for not feeling any remorse for the pain he instilled in his parents through his fabricated story.

Jake confirmed his parents accepted his explanation by scanning their thoughts. They expressed how relieved they were that he was home and explained that they needed to take him to the police station so they could take his statement. All this meant to Jake was more distractions and more wasted time. He told his parents he wanted to address this as soon as possible while his memories were still fresh.

Jake went to the police headquarters facility in downtown Louisville and gave his statement. They asked him numerous questions, had him meet with one of the department's most senior sketch artists, performed a blood draw for testing purposes, and then sent him home. Reflecting upon his encounter with Langi, Jake was only worried about what may appear in his blood test results;

everything else regarding his visit at the police headquarters facility was uneventful.

Because of the story he'd concocted to conceal the real reason he was away from home and school for more than a week, he knew his parents would not willingly allow him to leave for whatever amount of time that would be required to locate and interact with the alien at Fort Bragg. Against his better judgment, he decided he needed to manipulate his parents' thoughts. Jake was very nervous about this because implanting thoughts that would subsequently become fabricated memories into anyone's mind was no different than telling lies. Jake knew from firsthand experience how difficult concealing the truth in lies became as time went on. Put simply, he hated deceiving and manipulating his parents. They only wanted the best for him.

Since he didn't believe he had any choice in the matter, that evening he manipulated his parents, his sister, his friends, all of his extended family members, and his teachers into believing that his parents decided to have Jake visit his step-uncle in Atlanta, Georgia. To make his story more credible, he felt he needed to pursue a change of scenery in an attempt to help him return to normalcy after his fabricated traumatic kidnapping. Jake telepathically manipulated his teachers into agreeing to email him all of the assignments that he'd already missed, as well as those they would be assigning during his absence from classes.

Jake had done all he could to mentally prepare himself for the ongoing manipulation that would need to occur involving his step-uncle, Allie, and his parents. He would need to implant memories and experiences consistent with him being at his step-uncle's house throughout his trip to Fort Bragg. He was uneasy about whether he would be able to execute the complex, covert charade successfully. Jake packed the essentials into his backpack and went to bed.

The following morning, he went to his favorite restaurant for breakfast, Hammer's Pancake Nirvana, with his family. They were all happy for Jake regarding his impending trip to visit his step-uncle;

they knew the trip would be therapeutic for him. Additionally, considering all the tragedy he had experienced, they thought this trip would be a welcomed change of pace for him.

Still, they were all sorry to see him go, bearing in mind all that had transpired and because they had not been able to spend much time with him during the previous several weeks. They also feared for his safety, since the person who had kidnapped him had not yet been apprehended. Jake applied some more manipulation via his telepathic abilities to convince his parents to allow him to drive to the airport himself, although in reality, Jake would be driving to Fort Bragg.

After hugging Glenn and Allie and taking a kiss on the forehead from Debbie, Jake took a deep breath and left his family just outside of the restaurant as he sat into his car. Waving his goodbyes, Jake was relieved, remorseful, and terrified of the fact that he could now dedicate all of his focus during his nine-hour drive towards formulating a plan for his impending confrontation with the alien at Fort Bragg.

Chapter 26
An Unexpected Sacrifice

January 2146

"Gralp has summoned us; we need to return to the ship," Mairia relayed to each of her survey party members. "We leave for Shangten in three Earth days. Claag, why have you rejected my command?"

"I have been assigned direct orders by Jarga to remain on Earth to ensure they do not discover our presence here, and if they do, to derail their investigation efforts to the fullest extent possible," Claag responded.

"What am I to tell Gralp?"

"Tell him I died from overexertion."

"This goes against Gralp's direct orders, orders he received from Jarga."

Mairia began sensing increasing pressure on her brain.

"I will not tolerate insubordination, and neither will Jarga. Do as I say, or I will kill you," Claag demanded.

"Very well. Jarga will learn of this, and you will suffer the consequences if you are deceiving me."

Claag terminated the telepathic link and resumed tending to her matters.

INTROSPECTION: TRANSFORMATION

Since Mairia and Vingu were together, they both went to the closest international airport, Dulles International, to serve as the starting point of their return trip to the ship.

"It is imperative in all we do that we make ourselves completely unnoticed. We must not attract any attention whatsoever," Mairia relayed to Vingu as they entered the airport.

"Why not simply conceal our presence from everyone—make ourselves invisible?" Vingu inquired.

"The whole point of using air transportation to return to the ship is to conserve our energy. The amount of energy that would be required to completely conceal ourselves from everyone we encounter before, during, and after the flights would be too great. It is much easier to project human images of ourselves upon humans' receptors than to conceal our presence entirely."

"Agreed. In addition to humans, we must detect and impair the operations of their video capture, audio recording, and other tracking devices that could make our presence known."

The airport was infested with video and other surveillance equipment. Impairing the surveillance devices' operations, as warranted, concurrently with projecting their human forms proved more taxing than Mairia and Vingu had anticipated. Before progressing through the security checkpoints, they observed and discerned the inner workings of all scanning equipment that was in use as well as the practices employed by all of the security personnel.

"Projecting plausible images while traversing the security checkpoint equipment will be difficult but not insurmountable. Confirm detailed visibility into the output that is provided to the security personnel so that you may project a consistent pattern for yourself upon entering through the checkpoint equipment," Mairia advised Vingu. "And study all of their operating procedures and protocols in the event either one of us encounters complications."

Learning that each passenger simply remained in their position along the conveyor, moving at a constant speed until traversing through the security checkpoint equipment, Mairia and Vingu inserted themselves and their respective human projections behind the third person from the front of each line.

The identity verification, boarding authorization, and security checking processes were all automated through biometric scanning of each prospective commercial airline passenger seeking to enter the terminals. Since Mairia and Vingu were apparently unable to produce false data that would be processed by the scanning equipment, each of them determined the root mechanisms within the equipment that interpreted and issued alerts and disabled them accordingly. They proceeded to the security checkpoint equipment at nearly the same moment.

As they were nearing completion of the scanning process, a loud buzzing noise sounded in response to each of them. The progression of the conveyors was halted.

"All that I can surmise is our chemical composition must have triggered something in the scanning equipment," Vingu said with moderate concern. "Perform whatever telepathic manipulation is required not to create a scene and to project that the matter has been resolved calmly without issue."

Just as Vingu advised, they both manipulated the security personnel that approached them to portray the execution of all required security verification protocols and their successful completion. This entire ordeal was completed in approximately three minutes, and they were able to enter the secured area within the airport terminals.

"It is surprising to me that their equipment is more sophisticated and advanced than their intellects would indicate," Vingu said.

"It is evident these humans have become heavily reliant upon their technology. Considering the extensive presence of artificial intelligence, it is difficult for me to distinguish what the humans created versus what the computers created," Mairia responded.

"A perilous proposition; in time, this artificial intelligence-driven technology will likely inflict great harm upon these humans."

INTROSPECTION: TRANSFORMATION

Given they had little time before the airport staff began boarding its passengers, they immediately made their way to the appropriate gate. The boarding process started just before they arrived.

"How do you suggest we address the fact that we do not have reserved seats, let alone authorization to board this aircraft?" Vingu inquired of Mairia.

"As simple-minded as these humans are, I will implant in their boarding tracking and verification system that two seats of my choice have been assigned and accounted for. We will enter under these pretenses and will manipulate all humans who become involved in the discrepancy to avoid attention and conflict."

Mairia proceeded just as she planned. The discrepancy surfaced while she and Vingu were hovering over their selected seats, and Mairia performed the telepathy necessary to resolve the matter without issue, stripping all recollection of what transpired from all involved humans and equipment. Preparing for take-off, Vingu assured Mairia that he had disabled the video capture capability of the surveillance equipment within the aircraft upon entry while leaving the audio recording capability intact. Vingu also prevented the issuance of alerts regarding the absence of functioning video capture so they could remain undetected while in the aircraft.

The flight was uneventful until approximately three hours after take-off. The aircraft began experiencing moderate turbulence while at its cruising altitude. However, within a matter of a few minutes, a loud metal-on-metal screeching noise could be heard throughout the plane. Shortly after that the aircraft abruptly and severely banked to the left.

Captain Eric Comer informed all passengers that the left wing of the aircraft had suffered some form of structural failure and that an emergency landing at San Antonio International Airport was required. Most of the passengers panicked as the turbulence of the aircraft steadily increased. Everyone in the aircraft could hear people's screams and crying. Several passengers vomited in sickness bags.

Moments later, a companion of a passenger who lost consciousness paged a flight attendant for assistance. As the flight attendant made his way to assist the passenger, the plane uncontrollably rotated upside down along its length, rapidly losing altitude. The abrupt change caused the flight attendant to hit his head against the inner wall of the aircraft, instantly breaking his neck and killing him. All passengers who'd failed to fasten their seatbelts became airborne from their seats and crashed against the inner walls and ceiling of the aircraft.

Those passengers who had fastened their seatbelts were hanging upside down, secured in place at their waists, except for several whose seats disconnected from the floor and crushed their bodies against the ceiling of the plane. Screaming and crying continued among those who were still conscious. They feverishly reached for the oxygen masks released by the overhead aircraft compartments that were now below them.

"We have lost a portion of our left wing, and I am attempting to stabilize the aircraft," Captain Comer said over the PA system as calmly as possible, but panic and fear could be easily detected in his voice.

Just before he terminated his PA link, crying could be heard among his co-pilots.

Despite the captain's and co-pilots' efforts, the aircraft began spiraling out of control, slowly transitioning from a horizontal to vertical orientation. Unconscious bodies of passengers, some still alive, but most dead, limply and randomly traversed the inside of the aircraft, with progressively more blood from their bodies streaking the seats, walls, ceiling, and floor.

"I'm sorry, I don't think I can recover from this," Captain Comer communicated to the passengers.

Audibly crying at this point, the captain continued, "To minimize the carnage, I'm going to land us in an unpopulated area. God have mercy upon our souls."

"We need to leave this aircraft," Vingu relayed to Mairia.

INTROSPECTION: TRANSFORMATION

"No," Mairia retorted.

"What do you mean? If we do not, we are sure to perish."

"Gralp gave us specific orders not to draw attention to ourselves. Doing what is necessary to survive this event will surely grow suspicions among humans monitoring this flight."

Vingu did not respond.

"We need to end these poor humans' suffering; death is imminent. No one deserves to die this way," Mairia continued with a compassionate tone.

Mairia then sensed a moderate change in the course of the aircraft. "What are you doing?" Mairia relayed to Vingu.

"I am saving us. What else would I be doing?"

Before Mairia could react, she sensed Vingu saying to himself, "I do not understand."

"What do you not understand? Gralp specifically ordered us not to draw attention to ourselves."

"No, that is not what I am referring to. I am unable to manipulate the plane. My abilities have been compromised."

"All the more reason to accept our destiny and have mercy upon these unfortunate humans," Mairia responded.

"Very well then, as it is hopeless for us anyway."

As the aircraft and all passengers were just moments away from outcome gruesome death, Mairia and Vingu systematically relieved all remaining living passengers of their suffering by affording them an instantaneous death through applying deadly pressure to their brains. Consequently, from the amount of effort that was required to spare the passengers of unnecessary suffering, Vingu inadvertently relinquished his hold over the video recording device.

"It is done," Mairia relayed to Vingu.

The plane was rotating about its length, completing full rotations in a matter of seconds. Not even a minute later, the plane crashed into the ground, emitting a loud and enormous explosion. The plane instantly transformed into fragments while engulfed in flames, leaving a trail of wreckage nearly three miles long. The captain, with a moderate and undetectable amount of assistance from Mairia, was successful in his attempt to crash the plane in an entirely unpopulated area, not causing additional loss of human life.

Chapter 27

More Alien Remains?

August 2146

"Man, I love this place. Their barbecued calamari and smoked turkey are second to none."

"It's no wonder you've gained a hundred pounds in an hour given all the crap you eat, Kent," Emily said while looking at all of the barbecue sauce on his face. "Of course, given that you're wearing more than you've eaten on your face, I guess all of the weight you've gained is indeed surprising."

Emily chuckled and then used her right index finger to wipe barbeque sauce off of the corner of Kent's mouth. Emily's action caught Kent off guard. She then grabbed hold of Kent's left hand with her right hand and urged him to lose some weight. "You know, I don't want anything to happen to you. I can't handle the thought of having to work with a different partner."

"Nothing is going to happen to me, Emily. And I know I need to lose weight. You don't have to keep reminding me about it. I'm constantly reminded of it when I look at myself in the mirror, and when I put my shirt and pants on. It seems like every day they're both just a bit tighter."

149

"I'm sorry, Kent. I don't mean to upset you," Emily said while still holding Kent's hand. "You know, I only say this stuff because I –" Emily stopped speaking. A few seconds elapsed before Kent responded with, "I know you care about me Emily, and it's because of that you constantly urge me to lose weight."

"Well, yes, I do care about you, but not just as my partner."

Kent had a blank look on his face, bewildered by what Emily could mean. Emily then stood from her seat and kissed Kent's lips, which were covered with barbeque sauce.

"I love you Kent."

"I love you too, Emily. I've wanted to tell you for a long time, but I've been too chicken-shit to say anything."

They quickly left the restaurant and went to Kent's apartment.

"Good morning, sleepy head," Emily said after the night became mid-morning with a smile on her face as Kent rolled over toward her in his bed.

"Uh, hi. You sure you're good with this?" Kent asked, fearing Emily may have regretted evolving their formerly solely professional relationship to both a professional and an intimate one.

"Of course, you slowpoke. I've been ready for this for quite some time. You would have noticed sooner if you weren't so consumed by work, and if you weren't such a blind dumb-ass."

Emily put on one of Kent's dress shirts, which was long enough to extend down to her thighs, and went to the kitchen to start some coffee and prepare a simple breakfast.

"I can't make any sense of why Luallen would essentially give up on further investigation of the extraterrestrial concern," Kent said as he started getting dressed.

"All that we've learned is that there *may* be aliens on our planet. However, we can't lose sight of the fact that all that was recovered was a liquefied substance of potentially extraterrestrial origin. We don't know whether it is actually remains of an alien life form or if it is simply an alien substance. And considering the FBI's concealment of what happened to Hendrix, this, too, could be part of some cover-up. Regardless, we don't know whether we're facing any alien threat."

"I just don't know where to begin, and in all of the time we've spent on this investigation, I don't feel like we've gotten closer to any answers whatsoever," Kent said in a very defeated tone.

Just then, Kent's cell phone rang. The caller was a long-time friend of his from college, Billy "BeefMo" Richmond. Billy had decided to pursue becoming a police detective rather than joining Kent to pursue a career within the FBI at Quantico. Kent accepted the call, and Billy wasted no time for greetings: "There's something you need to see. Come to Theodore Roosevelt Island, east of the Three Sisters. Now."

"What is it, BeefMo? I don't hear from you for nearly two years, and this is how you break the ice with me? Are you OK?" But Billy had already hung up.

"We need to go, Emily. Now."

Leaving the coffee brewing and the uncooked food on the stove, Emily put her clothes on and rushed out the door to catch up to Kent.

"What's going on?" Emily said to Kent as she was jogging to keep up with his quick cadence. "Slow the hell down."

"I think BeefMo is in trouble...I mean, Billy."

Given Emily had no idea who Kent was referring to, she figured it was a personal friend from his past. She was out of breath when she finally caught up with Kent at his car. Kent wished FBI agents were permitted to use tandem-driving vehicles. However, due to their margin of error, only taxi services and civilians were permitted to use that nanotechnology. He drove as fast as he could, as if he were in pursuit of one of America's most wanted convicts, to reach Billy as quickly as possible.

Fifteen minutes later, Kent knew he was in the right place since he encountered several ambulances and a plethora of police squad cars. Unable to proceed further, Kent stopped his car, and he and Emily ducked under the "police line, do not cross" barriers to reach the dense concentration of police officers, first responders, and emergency medics. Pushing his way through the tight grouping of people, displaying his credentials when necessary, Kent could finally see Billy, with a dead body at his feet.

"You OK, BeefMo?"

"Holy shit, Kent. When did you become such a fat ass? Don't you guys have those implants that make it virtually impossible to become overweight due to the constant reminders it reports in your frontal lobes or something? And BeefMo? No one has called me that for years. Like, *a lot* of years."

Billy chuckled, and Emily was visibly mystified by how someone could end up with "BeefMo" as a nickname.

"I wish I could say the same about you, BeefMo, but you look great. I guess I picked up the thirty-five pounds you lost."

"Yeah, I'm fine, Kent. I've seen a lot of dead bodies, but I've never seen anything like this," Billy continued, too consumed by the dead body to acknowledge Kent's compliment.

Kent and Emily looked at the dead body to decipher what was unusual. Starting at the deceased male's feet, Kent and Emily walked along each side of the body until they met up with each other at the head. Both Kent and Emily identified the anomalous attribute at the same time.

"The top of his head is excessively concave, yet it doesn't appear there was any blunt force applied since there's no blood or laceration of any kind."

"Exactly," Billy responded to Emily's observations.

"We need to get this body to the morgue and have an autopsy performed. And do we know who this is?" Kent interjected.

"Yeah, it's a Scott Siegel. No priors, no criminal record. Not even a parking ticket. His wallet was found with a couple of hundred bucks, credit cards, the usual. Theft doesn't come into play on this one," Billy responded.

"So why did you call me? Maybe this guy simply died of natural causes."

INTROSPECTION: TRANSFORMATION

"The emergency medics are spooked by this. They, like me, have never seen anything like it. They see all sorts of inconceivable things in their line of work. Their being spooked also spooked me, so I didn't know what else to do but to call you."

"No, it's all good BeefMo. Send this guy to the morgue and let me know what they find from his autopsy."

Emily enjoyed the relaxed language Kent used when communicating with Billy. She knew this was a sign that he'd released a great deal of tension that was consuming him only a day ago.

Billy, the emergency medics, and the police officers began clearing the scene since they had not located anything in proximity to the dead body to suspect foul play.

"Let's take a look around, Emily," Kent said with sheer curiosity as he began walking toward the water.

Emily went in the opposite direction so they both could collectively cover more ground. Approximately five minutes had elapsed when Kent heard Emily summon him. Until Kent could make his way to Emily, he used his government-issued Ocuporter, which enabled him via an ocular transmitter to see through the eyes of another, in this case, Emily, also equipped with an Ocuporter in broadcasting mode. He jogged over to her location to see with his own eyes a blue-colored viscous fluid at her feet that strongly resembled the substance that was recovered at the Tranquility Airlines crash site. The fluid along the inner bank of the river and spanned approximately fifteen feet. The water had diluted its concentration and appeared to have stretched the fluid along the direction of the river's current.

"Are you thinking what I'm thinking, Emily?"

"Yes. I think we have a problem. I don't think it's too far-fetched to assume an alien killed that poor guy. Let's get something to take as much of this fluid we can gather with us, and then I'll call in a favor to Dr. Agon. My guess is he'll confirm this is the same alien substance that was found at the crash site."

Chapter 28
Cancer Is The Cure?

April 2146

"I don't understand. None of the other blood samples are reacting to the alien remains as my blood has," Dr. Agon yelled, as if to a team of collaborators, even though no one else was present in his research facility.

He was completely consumed by his work and was delirious.

"Either my analytical processes are flawed, where others' blood samples are consistently being compromised by my practices, or…"

Silence engulfed the lab as he reflected on formulating an alternate explanation to his potentially compromising the integrity of his analytical processes. Nearly thirty minutes elapsed as he stood motionless directly in front of his microscope.

"Unless there is a unique substance in my blood," he muttered.

Dr. Agon feverishly inventoried and organized all chemicals and equipment that would enable him to conduct nearly twenty distinct analyses of his blood. He conducted a complete blood count, which included an evaluation of his red blood cells, white blood cells, platelets, hemoglobin, hematocrit, and mean corpuscular volume. He also evaluated his blood glucose and calcium levels, electrolytes, kidney function, and blood enzymes.

After conducting intermittent analyses of his blood samples over the course of several days while concurrently fulfilling other professional responsibilities, Dr. Agon encountered an abnormally high blood calcium level, lower than normal red blood cell counts, and blood properties that would indicate abnormal kidney function in his blood. He then decided to focus subsequent tests on these suboptimal outcomes, and also performed a variety of urine tests. Another week elapsed before he was able to confirm the cause of the abnormalities encountered from his blood and urine tests. He also determined the specific property of his blood that was unique from everyone else's blood samples.

My god, do I have multiple myeloma?

He then frantically rushed to the hospital wing that was attached to his research facility to visit Dr. Kevin Biles, who was among the most revered oncologists in the world.

"I need to see Dr. Biles immediately," Dr. Agon said to the nurse at the nurses' station located on the floor where Dr. Biles conducted most of his rounds.

"He's currently making his rounds, sir. May I ask what the urgency is? Are you OK?" the nurse promptly, yet calmly, responded, while establishing eye contact with a resident hospital security guard.

"I need to speak with him right now. It's an urgent matter."

"Are you in any pain or discomfort? Is there anything I can do in the meantime?"

"Page him. Now! I need him to extract and perform biopsies on fluid from my bone marrow and on bone tissue."

"As I'm sure you can understand, it could take a while before he completes his rounds. I'll page Dr. Biles now." He grabbed the PA microphone. "Dr. Biles, please return to the fourth-floor nurses' station at your earliest convenience."

After hearing the nurse page Dr. Biles, Dr. Agon began to calm down.

"In light of the invasive nature of the tests you are requesting, may I check you into a patient room and begin necessary preparations?"

"Yes, a patient room. I will wait in a patient room," Dr. Agon replied with a maniacal facial expression, sweat beading all over his face and penetrating through many areas of his shirt.

"Very well then, let's go," the nurse responded, calmly motioning the hospital security guard to monitor the nurses' station. Knowing admitting him directly into a patient room was not even remotely close to conforming to required hospital protocols, the nurse noticed Dr. Agon was an employee of the hospital system by observing the access badge containing his photograph and name held by a lanyard around his neck. The nurse knew Dr. Agon was not going to leave and that tension was only going to increase if his request was ignored.

"The tests you are requesting require a sedative to be administered," the nurse said after directing Dr. Agon into the bed in the patient room.

Understanding this also did not conform to the hospital's protocol, the nurse astutely observed Dr. Agon was malnourished and likely severely sleep-deprived. He suspected it was a combination of these two factors that were causing his distraught behavior. Satisfied with the prompt attention he was receiving, Dr. Agon complied with the nurse's suggestion and allowed a sedative to be administered. The nurse injected him with a strong enough dose of diazepam to cause him to fall asleep within a matter of minutes.

"Why did you take it upon yourself to violate numerous hospital protocols in assisting this person? And who is he, anyway?" Dr. Biles snarled to John Wagner, the nurse, after finally arriving in response to being paged.

"He was frantic, and I thought requesting the assistance of a hospital security guard would only escalate the issue. Besides, I noticed he is an employee of our hospital system. His access badge identifies him as Dr. Y. Agon."

INTROSPECTION: TRANSFORMATION

"Esteemed medical researcher Dr. Yash Agon?" Dr. Biles uttered in a barely audible fashion as he turned and walked toward the patient room where Dr. Agon was sleeping. "Yes, it is him. You said he was demonstrating frantic behavior, John?"

"Yes. If I didn't know any better, I'd say he was delusional. He showed signs of severe malnutrition and sleep deprivation, which is why I heavily sedated him. I put him on a saline drip and administered a standard parenteral nutrition cocktail."

"How odd, Dr. Agon is well-known for his very calm and reserved demeanor. I wonder what could be troubling him. Please have me paged when he regains consciousness; hopefully, he'll awaken calmer, considering he will have benefitted from much-needed sleep. I'll inform the administration you acted appropriately. Don't give your 'violations' a second thought. Thank you, John."

Dr. Agon slept for nearly 24 hours before regaining consciousness, and as Dr. Biles had hoped, he awoke much calmer.

"Where am I? What happened?" Dr. Agon inquired of the attending resident.

"Dr. Biles will explain everything. He's on his way. As I'm sure you're a bit alarmed and disoriented, would you like me to remain with you until he arrives?"

"No. Thank you. I'm fine."

"Dr. Agon, I finally have an opportunity to meet one of the most esteemed medical researchers in the country, well, in the world. Forgive me as I am a bit star-struck. However, I sincerely regret meeting you under these circumstances. What seems to be the problem?" Dr. Biles was genuinely very grateful for finally having an opportunity to meet Dr. Agon.

"I have been experiencing inexplicable and unordinary fatigue, weakness and numbness in my legs, momentary shortness of breath, and random dizziness. I thought all of these symptoms were systemic from my incessant work habits. I tested my blood and suspect I may have multiple myeloma. I was hoping you would be kind enough to extract fluid from my bone marrow and take samples of bone tissue to corroborate my diagnosis."

While the symptoms Dr. Agon shared with Dr. Biles were indeed consistent with those that would be experienced by individuals having multiple myeloma, he had not experienced any of them. However, he knew he could not disclose the real reason behind the blood tests he'd conducted, bearing in mind the classified nature of his work and the fact that Dr. Biles would think he was psychotic or someone with a very creative imagination.

"Very well then, Dr. Agon. We'll keep you here until I'm ready to perform the procedure. I sincerely hope your diagnosis is incorrect. I'll speak with you again after I've completed the procedure. And once again, I regret we had to meet under these circumstances."

"Yash, please. And think nothing of it. Thank you for your help and understanding, Dr. Biles."

Casting a smile toward Dr. Agon, the doctor responded, "Kevin, please."

Chapter 29
Foreign Intelligence

August 2146

Since time was of the essence, Leese insisted they not waste it by parking their ship in an excessively remote location. Gralp decided to park the ship approximately ten miles northwest of Ely, Nevada. It was a desolate area, one very unlikely to draw any attention. In a similar fashion as performed during the previous expedition to Earth, Gralp had survey members submerge the ship into the sand.

Having already formulated their surveying strategy during the trip to Earth, the survey party organized itself into twenty separate groups consisting of twenty members each. Before each group began their respective surveys, Leese led a mind integration. To satisfy Gralp's wishes, he instructed everyone not to harm any humans and to ensure their true identities were not discovered. He instructed each survey group to begin their efforts by reuniting with various aliens that remained on Earth while Gralp and other prior survey party members returned to Shangten following their first expedition. Upon reuniting, each survey group was to receive all intelligence gleaned, as well as to share Jarga's agenda with them.

The mind integration was completed, and the nineteen other survey groups went their separate ways. Leese performed final preparations before he, Gralp, and his eighteen other survey party members left for Washington, D.C.

"Leese, despite what you previously shared with me at Shangten, there are no Sellenians, Grunats, or Flares in addition to our current survey party members here on Earth. As I previously relayed to you and Jarga, all that did not return with us died during our surveying activities."

"That may be true for some of your previous survey party members, Gralp, but not all of them. Jarga astutely felt there was too much at stake regarding our being forced to commit to another host planet within such a short amount of time. As such, before your departure, he instructed thirty-one of your survey party members to remain on Earth."

"Why did you keep these specifics from me when we previously discussed this topic? You and Jarga had no reason not to trust me."

"Jarga suspected you would grow compassionate for humans, causing clouded judgment and the inability to engage in the activities necessary to ensure our successful migration and invasion. I can see now his suspicions proved to be correct. I have sensed your compassion for humans, as has Jarga. Once humans become aware of our presence, it will be too late. Their extinction is essential for our survival."

"No." Gralp roared and telepathically began applying extensive pressure to Leese's brain, just as he had when he killed Mangar.

Leese was in shock; never had a Grunat, or a Sellenian or Flare for that matter, been capable of gaining control over an Ungden. Leese was powerless. In an instant, Gralp's shock regarding the force he had inflicted upon Leese overtook his rage. Leese fell motionless to the ground, unconscious but not dead. The 18 other members of the survey party were also in shock. They had never before seen a Grunat overtake an Ungden.

INTROSPECTION: TRANSFORMATION

Not being aware of the extent of his enhanced abilities, logic instantly overtook Gralp. He knew he needed to erase all memory of this incident from the survey party members' and Leese's minds, mainly because, having killed Mangar, a trend in his behavior was beginning to emerge. Not sure whether he was even capable of achieving such a feat, Gralp simply willed this to occur. And to help eliminate any potential awkwardness, he willed all survey party members and Leese to sleep until the following morning. Gralp also meditated in an attempt to overcome the panic he was currently feeling.

Waking up before all other survey group members, Gralp was nervous about whether anyone would have any recollection of what had transpired the night before. As a precautionary measure, he insulated his thoughts from the survey party members and Leese to prevent them from learning about what had happened in the event he had been successful in purging the incident from their respective memories. One by one, each survey member awoke. Gralp was most concerned about Leese since, at least while at Shangten, he possessed intellect and abilities far superior to his own and those of the other survey party members. More specifically, Gralp was concerned about the consequences should Leese recall the incident.

Leese awoke and appeared to have no recollection of the incident.

"Our journey to Earth is complete, and we are now rested. We need to reunite with those who stayed behind and learn what they have learned," Leese relayed to everyone in the survey party, including Gralp. "Gralp, lead us where your prior survey party spent most of its time."

"That is Washington, D.C. It will require two Earth days to reach this destination. I have learned we are unable to endure more than twelve hours of self-travel without potentially dying of exhaustion. We do not have enough time to create false identities so that we may fly in an aircraft, which is required to minimize suspicion and eliminate the likelihood of our presence being discovered," Gralp responded.

All survey party members levitated off the sand and followed Gralp toward Washington, D.C. while performing necessary telepathic manipulations to remain undetected by humans. Once they were in sufficient proximity of Washington, D.C., Leese telepathically summoned the three Grunats who'd remained on Earth to learn as much as possible about humans' military defenses and attack capabilities. Leese instructed them to meet with him and the survey party in an Earth hour.

Chapter 30
Covert Mission

August 2146

It was only an hour into his drive to Fort Bragg, and Jake was already mentally taxed. What he'd thought would be intermittent, yet ongoing, monitoring of various family members' and friends' thoughts actually required continuous attention. Debbie dominated everyone else's inclinations to contact Jake's uncle, and the volume of her distinct thoughts and the frequency at which they were conceived were impossible for him to expect. Further, some of the subject matter associated with her thoughts was very personal, causing Jake to feel consumed with guilt for surveilling Debbie's thoughts.

Due primarily to the possibility of Debbie contacting her brother, Jake realized he needed to continually scan her thoughts and deter her from contacting his step-uncle while implanting false experiences of her speaking with him. Allie, his friends, and Glenn were a harsh contrast to Debbie. Jake was a bit disappointed that they had not afforded him much of a second thought since he'd left them at the restaurant. However, to his surprise, he was profoundly flattered to learn of the despair Julie was feeling about Jake distancing himself from her. He was also surprised that she was constantly fighting urges to call him. As was true regarding him probing Debbie's thoughts, he felt incredibly guilty for surveilling Julie's thoughts. Regardless, he could not afford to take any chances and have anyone learn that he was not going to be visiting his step-uncle.

Given how consumed Jake was in monitoring everyone's thoughts and implanting experiences to conceal his excursion, the nine-hour drive elapsed much quicker than he'd anticipated. Still, he was very relieved to have finally completed conceiving a plan regarding his impending alien encounter once he was within twenty miles of reaching Fort Bragg. Jake decided to leave his car in Spring Lake, NC, a town adjacent to Fort Bragg.

Using the Internet, Jake decided to eat dinner at a Thai restaurant with a commendable number of positive ratings that was celebrating its 54th year in business. Jake ordered his favorite Thai dish, panang curry with chicken. He ate in record time—he had not eaten anything since breakfast. Since he was still hungry, Jake ordered and devoured four more Thai spring rolls.

Feeling fulfilled, Jake began executing his plan. He left the table where he'd eaten his dinner and went into the single occupancy bathroom in the restaurant, locked the door, and began scanning for the alien he'd previously located that was masquerading as a janitor. Because of his proximity to Fort Bragg, Jake was able to locate the alien, Malau, a Grunat, within seconds.

"Malau, I am Jarga. I am on Earth with Leese and others, performing final preparations for our migration to Earth. You have served Ungden well by gaining intelligence regarding humans and their military's capabilities. We will be conducting a mind integration the day after tomorrow at 2:00 am local Earth time at Cape Fear Botanical Garden. I will provide you the specific location within the garden once we are there," Jake relayed.

Jake astutely chose two o'clock in the morning as the time to meet with Malau since he was highly confident everyone whose minds he was surveilling would be sleeping. Jake exited the restaurant and went to a nearby hotel. Since he was short on cash, he telepathically manipulated the attendant at the front desk to provide him with a room in such a way that the attendant's peers did not suspect any foul play was occurring. Jake received the room key and went to his hotel room. He stayed there for the remainder of the evening and got some much-needed rest after he confirmed Debbie, Glenn, Allie, and his step-uncle were sleeping.

Jake awoke early enough the following morning to ensure he was awake before any of his family members. Recalling how especially active Debbie's thoughts were, Jake decided to remain in his hotel room until he felt he had everything under control. Unfortunately for Jake, it was not until late afternoon when he felt comfortable going about his day. Once again famished and wanting to keep things simple, Jake decided to visit the same Thai restaurant he'd eaten at the prior night, this time for a late lunch. *If it isn't broken, why fix it?*

Jake ate exactly what he'd had for dinner the night before, except this time he ordered and ate three instead of two orders of the Thai spring rolls. Just as he finished the last one, and during him licking the sweet dipping sauce from his fingertips, he decided he deserved to have a little fun with his recently inherited abilities and go shopping for *free* electronics.

Jake headed to Barnett's Electronics, a store that carried very cutting-edge and expensive consumer electronics goods, located at the nearest shopping mall. Considering all of the stress he had endured during the past week, and because money was no object, Jake decided to acquire some tandem-driven neurotechnology-powered drones equipped with infrared, night vision, and x-ray cameras, that are operated similarly to tandem-driven taxis. Jake also dreamed of getting full-body virtual reality video game uniforms and a 5D X-Box virtual reality game console. *Hell, I'll take all the X-Box Live cards the store has so I can play as much as I'd like.*

After essentially making himself invisible to all of the personnel in the store, Jake walked over to a cashier station and took four large vinyl bags bearing the 'Barnett's' name. Jake telekinetically transported six drones, two uniforms, and two X-Box consoles into the shopping bags that were levitating in the air in front of his chest. And for good measure, Jake took a couple of microchips that would enable him to link his cell phone and watch to satellites so he could view Earth from their vantage points. After completing his shopping, Jake returned to the hotel, dropped off his new items, and took a shower.

Jake checked in with his parents and then went to see a movie since it was approaching 9:30 pm. After speaking with Debbie and describing the great time he was having with his step-uncle, Jake went to see the new Eli Spielberg movie, a science fiction thriller about mankind's colonization of Mars, at the Youkhanna Cinemas movie theater. Eli Spielberg was Steven Spielberg's great grandson, the late and extremely famous movie director. It was widely understood he would not have gained his current stature if he were unable to capitalize upon his grandfather's reputation even though Eli possessed incredible directing skills.

Leaving the theater quite satisfied, Jake knew the movie would have been even better if he'd had the luxury of affording it his full attention. However, he'd needed to continue surveilling his family's and friends' thoughts throughout the production. He decided to get some more food at a local seafood restaurant, mentally prepare for his meeting with Malau in his hotel room, and then go to Cape Fear Botanical Garden.

Jake reached the garden shortly before 2:00 am and instantly detected Malau's presence. Jake instructed her to meet him along Cross Creek, just beyond a clearing located in the garden. Jake made himself a beacon that she could telepathically follow so she could reach him while insulating his thoughts from the alien. To not cause alarm and create any complications, Jake mentally projected Jarga's physical appearance and mannerisms in preparation of Malau's arrival.

Shortly after that, Malau emerged from the trees and stopped just short of Jake's location, hovering a couple of feet in front of him. "It is good to see you, Jarga. I have not seen another of our kind in nearly 14 Earth months. It seems like an eternity because I have had to coexist with these pathetic earthlings," she relayed in complete disgust.

"I recognize and acknowledge your efforts and sacrifices, Malau. I assure you that you will be rewarded for your dedication and selflessness. Share what you have learned with me; time is of the essence."

Jake then attempted to begin a mind integration with Malau while continuing to insulate his thoughts from her. Just at the onset of the process, Malau relayed, "Do you think I am unaware that you are not Jarga?"

Jake was unaware that Malau had telepathically infiltrated his subconscious as he approached her and was able to discern that his mental signature was human. Jake was shocked by this development and instinctively inflicted harm upon Malau by applying pressure on her brain. The intensity of her chartreuse color was decreasing, and her color was flickering.

No, no, I can't kill her. I need her. I need to know what she knows.

Just as Malau was on the brink of death, Jake forced her to relay all information she had learned during her covert mission on Earth. Jake began by extracting all information regarding what Malau learned about Fort Bragg itself. It was the home of the United States Army airborne forces and Special Forces, as well as United States Army Forces Command, United States Army Reserve Command, and Womack Army Medical Center. Jake recognized Malau's perception of the strategic importance of Fort Bragg and the vital role it fulfilled in support of the United States military. Succumbing by this time to Jake's will and understanding the purpose of his psychical interrogation, Malau relayed the intelligence she gleaned about various agencies and military defense and attack initiatives Fort Bragg interacted with and supported, respectively.

Next, Malau relayed global military intelligence she had been able to glean from various Fort Bragg personnel she had been scanning on a recurring basis during her infiltration at the military base. Jake was extremely alarmed regarding the intelligence she was able to acquire in such a short amount of time. In addition to the United States, Russia, China, India, Japan, and the United Kingdom had emerged as countries possessing the most significant military forces. Malau then relayed, in detail, military personnel capabilities, infrastructure, firepower, nuclear capabilities, and other relevant intelligence specific to each of the previously identified military powers.

Next, she relayed names of specific high-ranking military personnel who were based in the world's most robust defense installations. Malau also relayed energy sources, key cross-border relationships, economic intelligence, and other information. Jake could sense she had deduced from all of the military intelligence she had gleaned that humans would be no match for them during their occupation and colonization of Earth.

However, the only concern Malau had was whether the aliens would be strong enough in numbers because their invasion would be orchestrated solely by their minds. Jake could sense Malau questioning Jarga's judgment about consciously deciding not to dedicate resources toward designing, developing, and manufacturing weapons. She was concerned that Jarga's ego could unnecessarily cost many lives since the aliens would be capable of manipulating only a specific number of humans' minds, a quantity likely less than the entire human race.

Jake was shocked to encounter Malau's insightful thought process since she was a Sellinian, whose intellects were far inferior to those of the Ungdens. However, similar to what he'd learned regarding his superior intellectual abilities, he postulated that her intellect may have been enhanced due to environmental factors on Earth.

Although Jake was relieved to learn that Malau had no intelligence regarding the inter-workings of the FBI, NSA, CIA, and other intelligence agencies, he was very concerned about the data she had gleaned regarding the United States' and other powerful countries' military structures and efforts. The extent of his concern caused him to lose his composure and prematurely terminate his extraction of Malau's research. Taking into account the extent to which Jake's mind was linked to Malau's, she lost consciousness and fell to the ground. It was approximately 4:30 am, and Jake had no idea how long it would take for her to regain consciousness. And once she did, he was concerned about unintentionally revealing his true identity to her.

Jake waited near Malau until 5:30 am. Fearing they would be discovered, he went to the most remote location he could find along the creek and began scanning for any nearby people. Things were rather quiet until 6:30 am, which is when joggers and other passersby started filtering into the garden. Malau was still motionless on the ground, and Jake was becoming increasingly concerned. The best idea he could formulate was to scan her mind in hopes of being able to discern her condition.

Jake attempted to scan the alien's mind, but no thoughts were being retrieved. Jake realized she was dead. This made sense to him after noticing her physical form had changed phases. What was originally a living, hovering gas had become a lifeless puddle of blue liquid on the ground. Jake had killed her, a living being. He was severely distraught and entered into a frenzy.

What have I done? What am I going to do? What have I done? What have I done? I am a murderer. Where were you when I needed you? Langi? How could you allow this to happen? What am I going to do?

He did not know what to do, and most importantly, he felt horrible for taking her life. He then began wondering what the aliens would think and what they may do to him if they learned he was the one who'd killed her. Having a limited amount of sound mind left, and solely out of respect, Jake buried Malau's remains along the creek's bank.

Jarga will find me and then kill me. I am screwed. Oh man, he's going to kill me.

Jake unexpectedly transitioned from raw fear to remorse. Crying in remorse, Jake returned to his hotel room, gathered his belongings, went to his car, and began heading home. During his drive, he recognized he had achieved the primary objective of his trip; he'd learned of his dominance over an alien. But it came with an ultimate price, the life of another. He realized he was powerful enough to kill another alien with his mind alone unintentionally. Not forgetting the fact that there are four living races of aliens on Shangten, and that Malau, who was a Sellinian, possessed the lowest level of abilities of the races, Jake was cognizant of the fact that Grunats, Flares, and Ungdens may possess abilities equal to or stronger than his abilities.

Continuing his drive home, he reflected upon the intelligence that Malau was able to obtain in approximately a year's time. What concerned him most was what the aliens might do with that valuable intelligence in the context of the invasion they were orchestrating. He was slightly relieved, knowing that Malau's knowledge had died with her, but what little relief he experienced disintegrated once he resolved there were likely aliens stationed in other military bases mining similar intelligence.

Jake's first instinct was to share what he had learned with an appropriate United States government agency, but he did not know how he would do so. He was nervous that any attempt to share what he knew would cause others to perceive him as insane, thereby furthering his current advancements toward a life of isolation. But the United States and, more broadly, humanity, was in jeopardy.

The aliens intended to eradicate all humans on Earth. It was a stalemate, and Jake did not know what to do. Even if he were willing to risk his safety, future, or even his life, he was not convinced anyone would take him seriously. He was not going to spend the rest of his life, albeit likely short if the aliens' invasion was successful, in a psychiatric ward. However, with his abilities, he knew no one would be able to capture and imprison him anywhere. Regardless, he knew he would be on the run for the rest of his life and that his relationship and future interaction with his family and friends would be severely strained at best.

His concerns regarding the imminent extinction of the entire human race began to waiver as mental activity from Debbie, and some friends started and continued to increase because it was currently the start of a new day for them. He was consumed by scanning and influencing various family members' and friends' thoughts, including implanting permanent memories that would corroborate his fictitious visit with his step-uncle. Hoping this activity would be a good distraction for him, Jake could not help but to remain cognizant of mankind's imminent threat and the fact that he killed Malau.

Since he did not want to deal with his family upon his return home, Jake stalled long enough so that he would arrive late in the evening. His parents and Allie were already sleeping when he got there. Jake was exhausted and went straight to bed.

Early the following morning, Debbie unintentionally woke Jake up while she was putting some clean clothes from the laundry away in his dresser drawers. Once again, Jake awoke submerged in a mound of ice, and he could sense Debbie's alarm. He telepathically purged the incident from her memory while telekinetically evaporating the ice.

"I didn't hear you come in last night, and you're home sooner than I expected," Debbie said, with mixed emotions and intense curiosity.

Even though she was delighted to see Jake, she feared something had gone wrong during his visit with her brother, Cliff.

"We need to talk." Not thinking of the magnitude of the situation entirely through, Jake decided it was time to tell his parents everything that had happened to him.

"Your visit with Cliff was that bad? I'll call Glenn now to tell him to come home from work," Debbie said, fearing the worst.

She wanted to respect Jake's wishes, still believing he had been kidnapped. Glenn came home from work, and the three of them sat down together in the living room.

"I can't explain what has happened to me in words. I need to show you something. This is going to freak you guys out completely, so I need you to do everything possible to remain calm."

Right after completing his sentence, Jake levitated himself, the end table to the right of where he was sitting, and Glenn approximately two feet above the floor.

In shock, Debbie fainted on the couch. Glenn was speechless. After approximately fifteen seconds, Jake slowly returned everything to its original resting place. Jake then manipulated Glenn's thoughts to perceive changes in Jake's appearance. He projected Allie's appearance, then a monkey's, and finally Glenn's. From Glenn's perspective, it appeared Jake had rapidly changed forms into each of them. Glenn was still speechless.

Nearly five minutes elapsed before Glenn recovered from his trance of shock and broke the silence by asking, "What are you? What in the hell has happened to you. Have you always been this way, Jake?"

Knowing that Glenn could process what had happened to him more effectively than Debbie, Jake told his father everything. Demonstrating his recently inherited abilities versus trying to explain them verbally worked well. Jake was pleased and relieved that Glenn expressed this to him rather than Jake having to resort to extracting such thoughts from Glenn.

"How do you feel? Have you always had these abilities and just learned of them now? Are you sure you inherited them from an alien? An alien? How is this possible?"

"I'm fine, Dad, and yes, I'm sure I inherited these abilities from the alien, Langi, who touched me." A long pause followed before Jake broke down in tears. "I killed one of them, Dad. I didn't mean to. It just happened suddenly, with no warning at all." Jake unintentionally scanned Glenn's thoughts just as he began crying. "No, I'm not going to hurt you. I'd never hurt any of you, Dad!"

Glenn was horrified to discover firsthand that Jake was capable of reading his mind. "Yeah, but how do you know? Can you control your abilities? You just accidentally killed an alien, Jake."

"I should have thought this through. This was a mistake. You and Mom will never be able to look at me the same way again. You're always going to fear me. I'll go upstairs and get my things, and then I'll leave you all alone."

Still in tears, Jake scrambled upstairs to gather his things, and Glenn immediately ran after him.

"Jake, you need to understand that this is a lot to process," Glenn said as he used his forearm to prevent Jake's bedroom door from slamming shut in his face. "I'm with you, Jake. You're my son. This is your home. We are your family. You need to give Debbie and me some more time to process all of this. Well, your mom doesn't even know the whole story yet. This is a lot process. Please don't leave us."

"What about Allie?"

"I don't think we should tell her about this now, Jake. She's just a kid. This is too much for her to handle. She's wouldn't be able to withhold this information from everyone else. I'm worried about Debbie; let me try to comfort her a bit. Once she's calm, let's all grab some lunch. Of course, she first needs to regain consciousness," Glenn concluded, chuckling. "What do you say?"

"Sounds good, Dad. I love you. Thanks."

"I love you too, Jake. It's all going to be OK, I promise."

As Glenn went downstairs to care for Debbie, Jake began experiencing some relief, realizing he no longer had to keep this secret from everyone, at least not from his parents. His relief did not last long as he abruptly transitioned his thoughts to the threat humanity would soon be facing from the aliens.

This is just too much. I can't handle this. Jake wiped the tears from his face and then blew his nose. *How in the hell am I going to save the world? Me, save the world? I can hardly ever get to school on time. This is insane.*

Chapter 31
Harmful Intentions

August 2146

"I just got a call from the morgue. Christine, the lead forensic pathologist, has something she needs to show us," Emily said to Kent as she grabbed her jacket from the hook along the wall in front of her desk at the Bureau and then kicked the back of his chair.

Kent and Emily left the facility and got into her car. Kent asked whether she'd heard anything from Dr. Agon while they were driving to the morgue. Emily explained that he'd recently returned to his research in Washington, D.C., from Italy, where he was a guest lecturer, and that he was planning on analyzing what they had found at the murder scene once he got settled in. Given how anxious Kent was to get to the morgue as quickly as possible, he insisted Emily activate her lights and sirens.

They reached the morgue in twenty minutes, and they both exited the car and jogged their way to Christine.

"What do you have for us, Christine?" Emily inquired, slightly out of breath from running.

"Come with me," Christine replied with an expression of mystery on her face that could neither be missed nor ignored.

Emily and Kent followed Christine into the exam room where the subject of interest was lying on a cart, covered by a sterile white sheet. Christine lifted the sheet and pulled it down toward the waist of the cadaver.

"What's the matter, Kent? In the seventeen years you've been in the FBI, you've never seen human brains before?" Emily asked while chuckling and slapping Kent on the back of his head at the same time he was gagging.

The corpse's skin was cut along the centerline of his skull, with the skin flapped over and lain on each side of the incision. The head had been opened and removed through the use of a bone saw, leaving the brain entirely exposed.

"I honestly don't know what to make of this," Christine said. "When I saw this subject for the first time, I suspected the cause of death was subdural hematoma, which is an excessive accumulation of blood in a localized part of the brain. Subdural hematomas are typically caused by, or associated with, a traumatic brain injury. I realized this was not relevant to this poor soul.

"First, if you look at the skull, acknowledging it is slightly concave and suggests some form of blunt force trauma occurred, there are no contusions. There were no scratches or penetrations in the skin. Now, look at the brain. The average volume of a male human's brain is approximately 1,300 cubic centimeters. The volume of this subject's brain is approximately 700 cubic centimeters, and—"

"It looks like someone or something grabbed hold of his brain from within his skull and squeezed it until he died," Kent interjected, recovering from his nausea.

"Exactly," Christine replied. "But that is impossible. No one can penetrate someone's skull and squeeze brains without inflicting any damage to the skin and skull. I've never seen anything like this."

In reaction, Emily and Kent looked at each other. Acknowledging the confidential nature of what they were working on, they knew they could not vocalize what they were thinking in

Christine's presence, that somehow the aliens were responsible for this person's death.

"Did this man sustain any other injuries?" Kent inquired.

"No, none. The damage inflicted to this subject's brain is undeniably his cause of death."

After profusely thanking Christine for her expeditious assistance, Emily and Kent returned to their car.

"Do you know what this means? It confirms that the aliens are hostile," Kent proclaimed as he closed the car door.

"Not necessarily. Don't allow your imagination to get the best of you, Kent. Don't lose sight of the fact that Hendrix indicated aliens have likely been on Earth for approximately ten months. This is the only death we have learned of that was potentially caused by them. Just because we found alien remains in proximity of that man's body does not definitively confirm that he was killed by an alien. Also, what if he was killed for murdering the alien whose remains we found? There is too much uncertainty here to go jumping to conclusions," Emily said with a raised voice.

"Come on, Emily, there is no other explanation here. Since when are humans able to reach into peoples' heads without any physical signs of penetration and squeeze their brains like grapes? And who, or what would do such a thing without ill intent? We need to update Luallen on this and discuss next steps. We need to address and manage this alien threat."

"Yeah, but considering aliens have been on Earth for at least ten months, if they had intentions of harming us, why only kill one person over such a long period? It just doesn't add up."

"I'm done debating this. Luallen will know how to proceed."

Kent and Emily went straight to Luallen from the morgue. Emily was horrified to see Kent's maniacal body language and behaviors again. It was as if the aliens had wronged him personally countless times over a long time frame and he was out for revenge. For justice. Emily was very uncomfortable about how to handle this situation with Luallen since they had not confirmed beyond reasonable doubt that the aliens presented any real or direct threat to humans.

Unfortunately for Emily, she did not have much time to reflect on the situation and formulate a game plan because, before she knew it, they arrived at the Pentagon. She was also very distracted by the feelings she had for Kent. The presence of the aliens was consuming him and distancing him from her emotionally.

"Jacobsen, wait a minute," Emily said to Kent in an extremely concerned tone.

"Oh man, this must be bad since you addressed me by my last name," Kent said, chuckling.

"This isn't funny, Kent. You're allowing this to consume you. You are transforming into someone… something I don't know or recognize. This is turning you into a monster. You have—"

"What do you expect from me? We don't know what the aliens' objectives are. I don't want to let up on my intensity and what I have been assigned to do, only to find out I was right all along and it be too late to defend ourselves."

"I understand, Kent. I really do. But let's slow down a bit and take emotions out of the equation. I, like you, am terrified. And I don't deny that it's beginning to appear that these aliens mean to inflict harm upon us. If this is true, we need to be sharp. On our A-game. Can you honestly tell me you're on your A-game?"

This silenced Kent, and he sat there in the driver's seat of the car for a few minutes without making a sound. Emily knew she'd got through to him as she saw a transformation occur in his expression and demeanor. His face transitioned from full fury and chaos to calmness and reflection.

"I don't know what I'd do without you, Emily. I love you so much. Thank you," Kent said with tears forming in his eyes as he laid his head on Emily's chest.

"I love you too, Kent. We're going to get through this together. I promise. You need to focus on keeping yourself grounded, especially now having been confronted with these new and alarming developments."

The ringing of Kent's phone interrupted this intimate moment.

"I'm sorry, I have to take this. I'm OK...I'm grounded. I promise." He kissed Emily on the lips and then answered his phone. It was FBI agent Bekka Rodriguez.

Before he could say hello, Rodriguez began talking. "We have a huge break in our investigation, Kent. This is huge."

"What in the hell are you doing, Rodriguez?" Kent responded. "You're no longer on the Special Task Force. *There is no Special Task Force.* And if there was, you'd need to run whatever you discovered through Hendrix, our lead analyst."

"I tried to, but Hendrix hasn't been answering her phone. You've got to get over here. I have something unbelievable to show you."

"This doesn't make any sense, Rodriguez."

"Pardon me sir, but get your fat ass over here right now. If I'm wrong, fire me."

"Fat ass? Really?" *This must be something important.* "OK, OK. Emily and I will be right over."

Chapter 32
Relationship Rekindled

August 2146

"Welcome back, Jake. It's been a long time since we have all been blessed with your presence. I've missed not having you as my go-to guy when your classmates get stuck trying to answer my questions," Mr. Plonsker said, chuckling. "In all seriousness, though, I hope you enjoyed your trip."

Jake was glad to be back in school, although he wished school was not year-round as it used to be when his great-grandfather went to school. In light of how much was on his mind, it was a good distraction for him. Recognizing the magnitude of what he was facing, he was no longer uncomfortable being in the presence of Julie. This was a good thing since she was sitting right next to him.

"You doing OK?" Julie asked Jake with an expression of genuine concern.

"Yeah, I'm hanging in there," A short yet awkward silence followed, soon broken by Jake. "Thanks for asking, Julie."

She smiled. This was the first exchange, let alone acknowledgment, she had received from Jake since they'd broken up several weeks ago. After confiding much of what he had learned and the new abilities he'd inherited from Langi to his parents, Jake decided he was going to take a break from all of that and try to return to a life of normalcy. Further, after all that had happened to Jake, he'd gained an entirely new perspective on everything. All of a sudden, the falling out he'd had with Julie, his feelings of isolation at school, and his scrawny physique no longer caused him any distress.

"What do you say we get some ice cream after school, Julie?" Jake blurted out without giving it much thought. "I mean, this isn't a date or anything, I just thought it would be nice to catch up on things over some ice cream."

"That sounds great, Jake. I'll meet you at the flags after school."

Jake felt like a new person. It seemed to him like years had elapsed even though it had only been a matter of weeks since his world was turned upside down. For the remainder of the school day, he focused on reconnecting with some friends and classmates. Taking into account the history of the aliens he'd learned from Langi, his new abilities, and further enhanced intellect, he had been afforded the gift of a new and uncharacteristic mature perspective for a teenager.

His day of reflection was interrupted by the sounding of the tone which signified the conclusion of the last period of the day. Jake broke from his trance and made his way to the school flags to meet up with Julie. As he walked through the door to leave the school building, he noticed that she was already waiting for him at the flags.

"Wow, you got here quickly," Jake said with a smile.

"Yeah, well, I'm glad we're finally talking again. Things between us ended so...abruptly."

"I'm sorry, Julie. After being friends for so long, we became something more, and I wasn't handling it very well. I don't think I was ready to take our relationship to the next level."

"I understand; it's OK, Jake," Julie said softly, with a look of disappointment.

"But I'm ready now, Julie," he promptly added, bending toward her and giving her a quick kiss on her lips. "We're meant to be together. We have a long history. We're best friends."

"Is that so?" Julie asked with pure happiness. And she was shocked since Jake had never been that forward with her physically. They had never kissed before.

"Yeah." Jake smiled.

They gave each other a quick yet passionate kiss. Julie suddenly pulled away, blushing. She was not one to publicly display affection. Instantaneously feeling some concern regarding her actions, Jake inadvertently scanned her thoughts. He was relieved when he learned why Julie had pulled away and more so once he learned that her feelings for him were genuine, sincere, and real. He was on top of the world.

"Let's go get some ice cream," Jake said as he interlocked his right hand into Julie's hand and guided her toward his car.

At the ice cream shop, Jake ordered his favorite ice cream flavor, pralines, and cream, and Julie got a Reese's peanut butter cup milkshake.

"So, what have you been up to?" Julie asked Jake as she ate a spoonful of her thick milkshake. She was not comfortable talking to him about his recent kidnapping because she figured that was a conversation Jake should initiate himself.

"Honestly, not that much. Ever since I broke things off with you like a knucklehead, I was lost. I was in a sort of haze. The only good thing that happened is I was able to spend some time with my step-uncle and his family."

He was uncomfortable sharing what had happened to him and everything he had covertly learned of Julie's thoughts while he was away even though he had confided everything in his parents. He did not want to scare her, and he did not want her to think of him any differently than she did at this moment. He sensed intense respect and affection from her, and he did not want that to change in any way.

Fearing that Julie may dig deeper, Jake preemptively told her that he thought about her a lot, which was true. Julie smiled as she looked into his eyes.

INTROSPECTION: TRANSFORMATION

"Woah," Jake said, pressing his back into the bench where he and Julie were sitting.

"What's wrong?" Julie asked with an expression of complete mystery on her face.

Once again, Jake had unintentionally scanned Julie's thoughts and sensed her strong affection and physical attraction for him, along with a desire to get physical.

"Oh, nothing's wrong...just looking at you looking at me...you're just so beautiful. I don't know what I was thinking when I pushed you away. I'm so sorry about that."

While it had only been six weeks since they'd decided to transition their friendship into a romantic one, Julie experienced great pleasure from how nervous he behaved when they were alone with each other.

Observing Julie's reaction, Jake realized that was the save of the century. However, he became increasingly concerned over his inability to control his mind scanning tendencies, especially since he was scanning Julie's thoughts without consciously wishing to do so, and, more importantly, without her permission. He knew scanning her thoughts was an invasion of something sacred. He felt terrible.

"So where do we go from here, Jake?"

"This is all so new to me. I've never had feelings for someone like the ones I have for you. I can't believe I'm saying this, but please be patient. I don't want to move too fast. I want our relationship to last forever."

Jake blushed and was visibly embarrassed.

"I haven't either. This is new to me, too, Jake. It's OK; don't be embarrassed. We have all the time we need."

We have all the time we need, Jake repeated. *Time is a luxury we actually don't have.*

"Jake? Your ice cream is melting."

"Sorry, I spaced out there for a moment," Jake said, chuckling.

Jake and Julie finished the rest of their dessert and then Jake drove to Seneca Park. He parked the car, and he and Julie crossed the street and began walking on the path together, something they'd enjoyed doing together for many years. They walked hand-in-hand for about forty-five minutes. During this time together, they talked about school and current events and then returned to the car so Jake could take Julie home. He pulled the car to the curb in front of her house and thanked her for her understanding and willingness to give him another chance. Julie gave him a big hug, kissed him, picked up the backpack sitting on the car floor between her feet, and ran into her house.

What a day, Jake thought, pulling away from Julie's house.

Driving away, he was reminded of everything that had weighed him down regarding Jarga's agenda and the aliens' presence on Earth. He decided he was going to try to locate as many aliens as he could, scan their thoughts to understand their current objectives and, to the fullest extent possible, their end game.

Jake saw it was about to rain, so he drove back home. His parents were awaiting his return as he walked through the front door of his house.

"Take it easy, guys, everything is OK," Jake said to his parents in response to their obvious concern for him.

It was then that he realized how heavily his current situation was weighing upon them. And to his surprise, they were not too concerned about the presence of aliens and the uncertainty of the human race; they were concerned about him, and more specifically, his future.

"What's going on?" Allie asked as she walked downstairs toward the foyer.

"Great day at school. Julie and I are back together," Jake responded.

"That stinks. I enjoyed you being miserable." Allie laughed.

"Thanks a lot, sis. I'm hungry, what's for dinner?"

"Chicken and crunchies packed with broccoli, baby corn, and bamboo shoots," Debbie said.

INTROSPECTION: TRANSFORMATION

Crunchies was how Jake's family referred to water chestnuts. This was one of the family's favorite meals. Jake ate dinner with his family and then asked Debbie and Glenn to follow him into his bedroom. They were both visibly concerned, yet hopeful that Jake did not have any more disconcerting news to share. They cleaned up from dinner and then went to Jake's bedroom.

"There is something I need to do, and it could require two to three days for me to do it. I'll be in my room the whole time. Using my new abilities in this way is going to cause a lot of ice to form all over me. I don't want you to be alarmed if you see it. And because of what I'm doing, I need you to make sure that Allie doesn't come into my room. I can't handle any distractions or interruptions."

After learning of Malau's agenda, Jake wanted to determine how many more aliens were currently on Earth. His parents complied with his wishes despite being extremely concerned about Jake's welfare. They locked the door as they left his bedroom. Jake had already begun the scanning process before they went. Being able to count the number of times Jake had performed this scanning process on one hand, he was uncertain of the most efficient and methodical manner to locate the aliens. He decided to scan in similar fashion to the one he'd conducted to locate Malau at Fort Bragg.

Beginning at his current location, Jake scanned radially outward as far as he could, making mental notes regarding where and how many aliens were located along the way. Unlike the millions of miles that separated most planets from Shangten, the circumference of the earth was only 25,000 miles, which was within the range of telepathic activity. Jake was capable of telepathically communicating with anyone else on Earth.

Thirty in Kentucky / Tennessee. Fifteen in Virginia. Ten in North Carolina. Twenty-five in Washington, D.C. Jesus, Jake thought, capturing his mental notes. In just a matter of minutes, he'd discerned the aliens were planting themselves in proximity to the United States' key intelligence and military infrastructures.

Fifteen in Texas. Thirty in Canada. Forty-five in China. Thirty in France. Fifty in the United Kingdom. Thirty in South Korea. Sixty in Russia. Forty in India...

Jake woke up after he figured he had scanned the entire world and scrambled to his desk to write down everything he had learned.

"Everything OK, Jake?" Debbie asked from outside his bedroom door, hearing the commotion in his bedroom.

"Everything's fine, Mom. Sorry for all of the noise."

Jake surmised there were more than 400 aliens on Earth. Although he was concerned about the extent of their capabilities, he was relieved to learn of their relatively nominal number. Knowing that the aliens needed to migrate from Shangten to Earth within approximately a year's time, he recognized the aliens' presence on Earth signified the final stages of their surveying activities. It was painfully obvious to Jake that they were researching and inventorying the world's military and intelligence superpowers—they were "sizing up" their enemy.

What are we going to do? What am I going to do? Regardless of my new abilities, I can't fight off four races and tens of thousands of aliens. This is hopeless.

Suddenly, Jake experienced a sharp and sudden sensation of fatigue and fell out of his chair and onto the floor. *What's happening to me?* Unbeknownst to him, he was dangerously exhausted. He had not learned of his limitations of exertion. Jake could not help but try to make his way to his bed and sleep regardless of understanding the urgency of the situation.

Hours later, he opened his eyes and was confronted with the presence of a transparent crystalline mass immediately above him. He was unable to move his body because he was completely encased in ice. Since he had never found himself constrained to this extent, he was curious regarding exactly how much ice was present. Jake melted the ice off of his face and part of his chest so he could raise his head up and observe his surroundings. The frozen mass, nearly three feet thick, engulfed his bed and almost covered the entire floor of his bedroom.

It was then that Jake realized the amount of ice that formed on and around him was proportionate to the extent to which he exerted himself. He melted and then vaporized what remained and then returned to his desk to complete the notes he'd started capturing before he went to sleep. Contrary to before, Jake was now very calm. He suspected this was achieved by getting some sound and much-needed rest.

Sensing that his parents were approaching his bedroom, Jake opened his door using his telekinetic abilities.

"This is going to take some getting used to, Jake," Glenn said in response. "Are you OK?"

"Yeah, sure, I feel great. I really do."

"You've been in your room for nearly three weeks. We thought you could use something to eat."

Three weeks, no wonder I'm so hungry. Three weeks? How is this possible? No one can survive without eating and drinking for three weeks. I'm a freak. I'm a freak.

Debbie put a plate containing a couple of grilled cheese sandwiches and a mound of potato chips on Jake's desk.

"Three weeks?" Jake replied.

"After Debbie checked in on you the first time, it wasn't until after nearly two weeks that we heard some commotion in your bedroom. That was the only other time we went into your room since you asked us to give you some space to do whatever it is you needed to do," Glenn said, fearing Jake's health was somehow in danger.

"Guys, we're in trouble," Jake said with a crackling voice and an alarmed expression.

"What's wrong? You just said you're feeling great," Debbie said.

"I know. I didn't want to tell you what I'm feeling. I don't want you to worry. But I remember how good I felt when I told you about all of this before, so I figured I should tell you what I'm feeling and learning. Life…" Jake paused, providing even more insight to Debbie and Glenn regarding the reservations he was feeling to share what he was thinking.

"We know this must be incredibly difficult for you, Jake, not only further adjusting with your new abilities, but also managing your feelings, learning more about the alien threat, coming—"

"That's exactly it, Dad. We're in deep shit!" Jake said as he shoved an entire grilled cheese sandwich into his mouth.

After observing Debbie's expression, he realized the profanity he'd just uttered. "I'm sorry, Mom. I'm freaking out right now."

"It's OK. Are we in danger?" Glenn asked.

"Aliens will soon be on their way, and they're looking to kill all of us. Every last one of us."

Silence engulfed the room; neither Debbie nor Glenn knew how to respond. A few minutes elapsed before the silence was broken by the sound of sirens, screeching brakes, and skidding car tires.

"What the hell?" Glenn said as he scrambled to Jake's window, fanned the drapes out of the way, and looked into their front yard.

Chapter 33
Growing Discontent

August 2146

Leese engaged in a mind integration with the three Grunats that had been assigned to remain in Washington, D.C. after Gralp's departure from Earth after his previous survey. Leese learned that the Earth is comprised of seven continents, each of which containing at least one military power of consequence. The specifics of each military power were relayed to Leese, including the particular weaponry they processed and their geographic locations. The negligible intellects of humans was also shared. It became evident to him that, other than the sheer number of humans on Earth, they posed no real threat to the inhabitants of Shangten.

"I need to learn for myself how inferior humans' intellects are to ours," Leese relayed to the others in his presence after completing the mind integration.

Assuming the appearance of a ten-year-old girl, Leese made his way to the Smithsonian National Museum of Natural History. Entering from National Mall, he transported himself to the second floor. Ignoring his promise to Gralp that no humans would be harmed, beginning upon his entrance into the Butterfly Pavilion, he decided he would kill every human he passed as he navigated through the museum.

Making himself invisible and being completely non-discriminatory, infants, children, men, and women instantly collapsed to their deaths without warning as Leese approached them. Having neither remorse nor a predetermined quantity of humans he would kill, he traversed the Butterfly Pavilion, the One Hundred Years of Technology exhibit, the Rise and Fall of Google and Amazon.com exhibit, Mummies, History of Automotive Innovations, IMAX theater, which was nearly full to capacity primarily with children, Holographic Aquarium, and then the rotunda before exiting the building. He completed his killing spree, which caused the deaths of a total of nearly fourteen hundred people, with minimal effort.

Making himself visible once again as a ten-year-old girl, Leese hovered above one of the steps leading into the same entrance he'd used into the museum and observed the escalating chaos that followed. The number and volume of screams steadily increased, as did the number of people frantically running out of the museum. Within a few minutes of Leese leaving the museum, the entire perimeter of the building started to become engulfed by first responders, police squad cars, fire trucks, ambulances, emergency vehicles, and a variety of FBI and SWAT vehicles.

Clueless and pathetic, running around like lost ants, Leese thought as he observed the reactions of the various law enforcement agencies engaged in emergency response processes.

"There is no need to waste any more time on this planet. It is time to return to Shangten and perform final preparations for our migration," Leese relayed to his survey party members.

"Why are we leaving so quickly, Leese?" Gralp relayed in response to these abrupt instructions.

"I will share my experiences with you, and my reason for leaving will become clear," Leese relayed.

INTROSPECTION: TRANSFORMATION

Leese, Gralp, and the remaining survey party members congregated at their original stopping point upon their arrival at Washington, D.C.

"We will rest here and begin our return to our ship at sunlight tomorrow morning," Leese relayed to the survey party. "Gralp, come."

Gralp followed Leese to a location isolated from the other survey party members, and then they began a mind integration. Horrified by Leese's actions at the Smithsonian and overcome by fury, Gralp, without conscious thought, instinctively killed Leese in an instant. Severing the mind integration by killing him caused Gralp to lose consciousness and fall to the ground.

What have I done? Gralp thought after he regained consciousness. *I have killed Leese. I am a murderer. I have become that which I detest and vowed to avoid. But he killed all of those defenseless humans solely for amusement. At what price should one take the life of another? Are my actions justified?*

Fortunately for Gralp, he'd regained consciousness before any remaining survey party members were motivated to find him and Leese so they could begin their return to their ship in Nevada. Gralp returned to the survey party and entered a meditative state to continue and complete his self-reflecting moral debate. He rationalized shortly before sunrise that if his actions were deemed unjustified, the other spirits that resided in his consciousness and subconscious would not have allowed him to kill Leese.

Noticing a stirring among the survey party members, Gralp alerted them that Leese decided to remain on Earth, and soon thereafter, directed them to begin their journey back to the ship. Gralp instructed each survey party leader geographically distributed throughout Earth to begin their return to the ship to depart for Shangten while he and his survey party were traveling back to the ship.

It required seven days for all of the survey parties to arrive. Once they were all present, Gralp proactively relayed a concocted reason for Leese's absence since he sensed their confusion. He explained that, recognizing his strengths in combat strategy, Leese had decided to stay on Earth to plan the eradication of humans, and that he felt the planning was necessary for consideration of the large number of humans on Earth. Gralp then removed the ship from underneath the sand and instructed some survey party members to prepare it for their trip back to Shangten.

He'd taken advantage of the six days he'd waited for the remaining survey parties to return to the ship to reflect upon his current situation, and he concluded he could not return to Shangten. Jarga would be able to glean from Gralp's memories that he'd killed Leese. As such, Gralp informed all survey party members that he would stay behind at Leese's request to assist him in required preparations for the subsequent arrival of all inhabitants of Shangten.

All of the survey party members entered the ship, and within seconds, it disappeared into the cloud-ridden sky. Gralp was all alone physically, emotionally, philosophically, and psychologically. He was overwhelmed by disgust at Leese's heartless actions as well as by Jarga's intention to kill every human on Earth. Gralp felt helpless, vacillating between deciding to end his own life and attempting to devise a means to prevent the eradication of the entire human race.

This is hopeless. I am just one Grunat among thousands. Thousands of Ungdens. Tens of thousands of Flares. Tens of thousands of Sellinians. One among more than one hundred thousand who will be against me. Jarga is going to force all of them to abide by his bidding.

But there must be a way.

Estimating that it would be approximately sixteen months before Jarga and the entire Shangten population would arrive on Earth, Gralp decided that if he was going to die, he would die while attempting to help earthlings prepare themselves for the impending invasion.

Chapter 34
Suspicion Confirmed

April 2146

Dr. Agon woke up from what seemed to be many days of sleep. He felt more refreshed than he had in weeks.

Wow, I need to take some bags of their parenteral nutrition cocktail to my lab. This stuff works wonders.

He propped himself up in his hospital bed and turned on the television. Agitated that nothing but snow and static were present on the first few stations he selected, he raced through several more.

What the hell? Can't this hospital afford satellite TV?

Just as he was about to turn the television off, droplets of blood began penetrating through the screen from inside the TV and falling to the hospital floor. In a matter of seconds, they transitioned to steady streams of blood. Within minutes, the entire floor of the room was covered in blood.

Feeling moisture accumulate at his temples and sensing perspiration forming throughout his body, Dr. Agon looked down at himself to find his entire body covered in blood. Removing the sheets lying over his legs revealed a pool of blood in the hospital bed.

Terrified, Dr. Agon rolled onto his knees, turned himself around, and pressed the emergency button located on the wall behind his bed to alert the nursing staff to come to his room. He frantically depressed the button numerous times, but no one was responding to his urgent calls for help. Recognizing an inconsistency in that he did not feel any weaker or tired from the excessive loss of blood, he jumped out of his bed, pulled the door to his room open so forcefully it made a loud smacking noise against the wall, and ran into the hospital corridor.

As he turned left toward the nurses' station, he noticed the hallway was riddled with dead bodies. The walls were covered with streaks of blood, indicating that hospital staff was clawing at them to fend off something pulling at their lower extremities. As Dr. Agon made his way further down the hall, the density of dead bodies increased.

Turning the corner, heading toward the elevators, Dr. Agon felt a sharp pain in his back. Looking downward toward his feet, he saw a pointy object that appeared to be comprised of bone emerge from within his chest, accompanied by blood spewing straight out in front of him. The object continued emerging from inside his chest, its diameter increasing the farther its point became from Dr. Agon's eyes.

Hearing a shrieking noise behind him, he turned his head to find its source. Taller than the distance spanning from the hospital floor to the ceiling, a dark form speedily approached him. As it came closer, it became evident that it was over ten feet tall. Suspecting his eyes were deceiving him, Dr. Agon attempted to rub them to clear his view. However, because of being impaled in his chest by the foreign object, he could not move his arms.

Acknowledging his current state and the excessive amount of blood he had lost, he knew his demise was near. The creature relentlessly approached closer until Dr. Agon was able to see its entire body.

INTROSPECTION: TRANSFORMATION

"No," Dr. Agon screamed, realizing it was an alien. "Let me die in peace," he continued, crying.

"Hi there, Yash." The words were spoken faintly into Dr. Agon's consciousness. "Yash?" the voice continued. "Dr. Agon?"

Dr. Agon finally opened his eyes, realizing he had suffered another horrible and graphic nightmare.

"The nurses informed me that you have been sleeping for days. You're not Rip Van Winkle, are you?" Dr. Biles chuckled.

Recognizing it was as if he was speaking in a foreign language because Dr. Agon was too young to be familiar with this short story, Dr. Biles continued, "How are you feeling?"

"I feel much better, Doctor. I mean, Kevin."

"I'm very pleased to hear that, Yash. Before I share the test results with you, I must know why you arrived famished and severely sleep-deprived," Dr. Biles inquired.

Dr. Agon explained that he had been immersed in research on behalf of the FBI and was then distracted by his health issues. He recognized and acknowledged his obsessive behavior traits and that he had ignored his own needs to understand what was wrong with him.

"Don't knock it; my obsessive-compulsive disorder got me through medical school." Dr. Agon joked.

"I was the same way, and that's what got me through all of my studies and my five years of residency. I shouldn't speak of it in the past tense. I'm still very obsessive." Dr. Biles smiled. He was relieved he had achieved his objective in consoling Dr. Agon and preparing him for the terrible news he had to share.

"Yash, I'm very sorry, but your self-diagnosis is accurate. I am afraid you indeed have multiple myeloma."

The words fell upon Dr. Agon as if an anvil had dropped on his head from far above. He had hoped he was wrong and that there was another explanation for what he'd encountered with his blood. Dr. Agon was mentally in a different place and was not processing anything Dr. Biles was saying as he was explaining the history of cancer, treatment options, and immediate next steps.

Well OK then, that's that. My life won't be in vain. I'm going to find a way to kill all of those sons of bitches, Dr. Agon thought.

"I don't know how much time I have. I need to get to work."

"Excuse me, Yash?"

"Forgive me, Kevin. I'm eager to return to my work."

Noticing that Dr. Agon was severely distracted and appeared not to have heard a word he'd said, Dr. Biles requested that he stay in the hospital for another day. Dr. Agon refused but genuinely promised to take better care of himself.

"Very well then, Yash. I sincerely wish I had better news. Sleep, a healthy diet, and a sound work-life balance will be the keys to a comfortable quality of life for you moving forward. Please contact me when you are ready to discuss treatment options. I will personally provide you with all the care you need."

"Thank you very much, Kevin. I can't tell you how much I appreciate that," Dr. Agon said as he was putting his clothes on.

He's right; if I have any chance of formulating a biologic defense against the aliens, I have to afford sufficient time. I do need to start taking better care of myself.

Chapter 35
An Alien Among Them

August 2146

Glenn peeled out of Jake's bedroom window to see what appeared to be thirty FBI squad and police cars along with two SWAT vehicles outside. FBI and SWAT team members scattered themselves around and atop their house like a fleet of ants honing in on a picnic blanket full of exposed food. Jake began scanning each FBI agent's mind just as Glenn was transitioning into a panic.

"I know why they're here, Dad," Jake said calmly with a sense of regret in his voice. "I'm sorry. I was careless."

"What do you mean? What's this all about?" Debbie inquired, fearing the worst.

"It's about my abilities; they think I'm an alien."

"How would they know about your abilities?" Glenn asked.

"I was careless. When I went to North Carolina, I had a little fun at a shopping mall. I used my abilities to steal some extremely expensive stuff. I just wanted a break from all of the stress and to have some fun. I didn't think about the surveillance cameras. They saw drones, uniforms, and Xbox consoles floating around, and they saw me walk out of the store in front of many Barnett's employees with items I didn't pay for. It was stupid, and I'm sorry. I need to get out of here."

Jake closed his eyes for a moment and then opened them again, got a duffle bag out of his closet, and began filling it with clothes and a few personal mementos. As Jake was packing, Glenn once again peered out of the bedroom window to see everyone completely motionless. All of the FBI agents, SWAT team members, and neighbors observing the commotion were still. The scenery looked like a setup of the board game Risk.

"Jake, you can't do this," Debbie said with tears in her eyes. "If you leave this way, they're not going to stop looking for you. And who knows what they'll do to Allie and us. You'll be looking over your shoulders and running for the rest of your life."

"I can't let them take me, Mom. They're not going to believe that I'm not an alien, and even if they do, I'll become a guinea pig. They'll perform tests on me until I die. I'm not going to live the rest of my life as a prisoner of the FBI and United States government."

"I'm not saying it's going to be easy, but just as Debbie said, fleeing is not the right path for you, Jake. It may take them a while to believe what you have to say, but you need to try. We are facing a threat beyond anyone's comprehension. As inconceivable as it sounds, survival of the human race rests in your hands. You need to make them understand this. I believe in you. I know you can do it. And when the time is right, we'll help you any way we can."

Jake stood motionless, not uttering a word or making a sound while deeply evaluating Glenn's and Debbie's assessments of the situation. Recognizing their logic was sound and that he was capable of escaping at any time, Jake finally responded, "OK, Mom and Dad. I trust you both. I'll do the best I can."

Before doing what he knew he must do, Jake stilled Glenn and Debbie and called Julie.

"Hey, Julie," Jake said in relief, temporarily forgetting about his troubles.

"It's so good to hear your voice."

INTROSPECTION: TRANSFORMATION

"Are you OK?" Julie inquired, sensing in Jake's tone that something was troubling him.

"Something has happened, and as crazy as it sounds, the FBI is taking me to D.C."

"What did you do? Are you OK?"

"I didn't do anything. I promise this is all just a big misunderstanding."

"I know you, Jake. I know you couldn't have done anything wrong and certainly nothing that the FBI would care about."

"I can't tell you how much it means to me to hear you say that, Julie."

"We've spent nearly our entire lives together Jake, I..."

"Julie, I'm sorry to cut you off, but I have to go. You may hear things about me in the news. I don't know what they will say. But if any of it is bad..."

"I know," Julie interjected. "I won't believe a word of it."

"It may be a long time until you hear from me again, but know that I love and care about you very much."

"I love you too, Jake. You..."

Jake hung up before Julie could finish speaking. He took his duffle bag and slowly walked downstairs to the front door while continuing to control everyone outside; they all remained completely motionless around and on top of the house. Jake turned the knob, opened the front door, and began to see the swarm of FBI agents and SWAT team members around him. Debbie and Glenn exited the front door of the house behind him and watched Jake deliberately walk up to a particular FBI agent.

As Jake stopped directly in front of Kent, he allowed him to regain control of his entire head. Kent's expression transitioned to one full of terror as his eyes and head raced around in all directions, noticing everyone else other than Jake's parents were completely motionless, powerless, and under Jake's control.

"I am not an alien, and I promise I will not hurt you or anyone else as long as you don't give me a reason to. I'll explain everything.

With my abilities, there is nothing you can do to prevent me from escaping at any time, and I won't allow you to do anything to me I don't want you to do. Do you understand?"

Kent heard and processed everything Jake said but was mystified and frightened to notice neither his lips nor mouth were moving.

"Yes, that's right. I'm communicating to you telepathically. Remember, I'm not going to hurt you unless you or anyone else give me a reason to. I will let you take me away."

Jake granted Kent complete control over his mind and body while leaving everyone else motionless.

"I need to give everyone else the impression I have you sufficiently constrained. Will you allow me to cuff you?" Kent said softly so no one else could hear, the chain of the handcuffs clanging because his hands were feverishly shaking.

"Good idea, Senior Master Sergeant Kent Jacobsen," Jake said as he turned around, put his hands behind his back, and telekinetically removed the handcuffs from Kent's hand and placed them loosely around his wrists.

"How did ..."

"I know everything about you, Kent, and I can control objects too," Jake said, sensing Kent's discomfort, though his back was still to him.

Kent very politely asked Jake to turn around and face him.

Looking into Kent's eyes and moving his arms and hands down in front of him, Jake said, "Just as a reminder..." and then moved his eyes downward toward the handcuffs secured to his wrists.

Kent looked down at Jake's wrists to see Jake slowly split a link in the chain with his mind and pull his hands apart. Jake then moved his hands closer together and reassembled the chain.

"Don't worry. I won't forget. I'll make sure you aren't harmed," Kent replied and then motioned Jake to walk toward his and Emily's car.

"Wait," Jake said, sensing his parents approaching with something they needed to say to Kent.

INTROSPECTION: TRANSFORMATION

With tears in their eyes, Debbie and Glenn insisted that Kent take care of Jake.

"Taking into account what little I've learned of your son's abilities, I want you to know that I greatly appreciate his candor and cooperation. I assure you that I'll take good care of him; he will not be harmed while under my supervision."

Debbie and Glenn were hysterical.

"Here's my card," Kent continued. "You are welcome to call me anytime. When you call, I promise I will answer. And you can see Jake whenever you'd like. Please understand that, for the foreseeable future, he will be detained at our facility in Washington, D.C. So if you want to see him, you'll need to come to D.C."

"It's going to be OK, guys. Even if they wanted to hurt me in any way, they couldn't. I won't let them. I promise I'll cooperate unless they give me a reason not to. And tell Julie I love her and miss her already...and that I'll be OK," Jake relayed to his parents.

Debbie and Glenn smiled as Kent guided Jake into the back seat of his car.

Just as Kent was about to close the car door, Jake told him that he was going to first release Emily from his mental grasp. Jake told Kent to debrief her on everything that had transpired and that he would await Kent's request to release everyone else at the scene. Jake released Emily, and Kent followed his specific instructions, updating her on everything he'd learned about Jake.

Kent then removed a megaphone from his trunk and motioned to Jake to release everyone, which he did.

"Listen up, everyone. Lower your weapons. If any of you would use your damn firearm sensors, you would have known our person of interest is not carrying. Now I know each of you is very confused. I have the person of interest in my vehicle. He surrendered himself willingly, and we will be transporting him to the Pentagon for questioning. Agents Horwitz, Brenner, and Silk, I need an escort back to our aircraft at Standiford Field."

Kent went into his car, awaited the formation of his escort, and then drove to the airport.

"No, I'm not an alien from outer space. And no, I'm not going to hurt you," Jake said in response to Emily's thoughts.

"Well, that's a relief," Emily said after taking a deep breath and exhaling loudly.

They reached the airport and entered the FBI's Critical Incident Response Group's Surveillance and Aviation Section aircraft to quickly return to the Pentagon. The aircraft began to shake and then hovered a few feet above the ground while one of the co-pilots was performing a standard visual inspection of the aircraft, and while the other co-pilot was programming the flight plan into the flight management system.

"What the hell?" Emily said as the co-pilots were looking outside the cockpit, trying to decipher what was causing the aircraft to hover above the ground.

Before anyone had time to react to the situation, the aircraft gently returned to its prior motionless state on the ground.

"I'm sorry. I just had to know whether I could do that," Jake said to Kent and Emily with an expression of guilt and remorse on his face.

"Holy shit. How did you do that?" Emily asked.

Jake started to expand upon what Kent had already shared with Emily regarding his abilities. As Jake commonly did, he performed gestures using his arms and hands when delivering his explanation.

"What the hell happened to your handcuffs?" Emily shouted.

"Oh, sorry, they were uncomfortable."

"It's OK, Emily," Kent said. "If he had any intention of harming us, he would have done so well before now."

"Wow, that's comforting," Emily responded with sarcasm.

Jake purged what had just transpired from the co-pilots' memories. They informed them they were ready to leave, and Kent motioned them to proceed. The flight was uneventful, and they arrived at Ronald Reagan Washington National Airport in approximately ninety minutes. The four of them then transferred themselves to a helicopter that took them to the Pentagon Army heliport located on the west side of the facility.

As they approached the heliport, numerous military personnel were present to greet them. The four of them left the helicopter just after landing. Kent was shocked to see Luallen there.

"No offense, sir, but what are you doing here?" Kent inquired.

"I have been buried in orchestrating a response to a currently inexplicable and horrific incident that occurred at Smithsonian National Museum of Natural History. There were nearly one thousand four hundred casualties."

"What?" Emily interjected.

"The video captured by the surveillance cameras is dark, similar to what we saw from the video feed of the black box in Tranquility Airlines flight 2122. Very few people who saw what transpired in the museum lived to tell us about it. And those who survived are consistent in their responses to our questioning. They all describe what occurred as if there was an invisible stream of death that instantly killed everyone in its path. It just does not make sense that nearly everyone in certain areas within the museum died, leaving very few but some survivors. There were no explosives, no explosions, no firearms involved, and no visible disruption other than people falling dead because of some invisible and fatal biologic agent... or aliens."

"Please don't tell us their heads were caved in with no indication of blunt force trauma," Kent said, fearing the aliens were responsible for the mass murder.

Luallen stopped walking. "How could you possibly know that?"

Neither Emily nor Kent had been aware of what had occurred at the museum, and neither responded to Luallen's question. They continued to walk. Jake had secured the handcuffs to his wrists so he could eliminate potential suspicion by those around him. Kent dropped Jake off at a secure interrogation room that was manned by guards just outside the door.

What seemed like days to Jake while alone in the interrogation room were mere minutes that had elapsed until Emily walked in.

"There are a lot of people who want to see and talk to you. Come with me," Emily said, and then she escorted Jake to a large and highly secured multi-purpose room equipped with numerous monitors, computers, and other equipment.

As Jake walked into the room, he instantly fixated on something he had not expected.

Looking at Kent sitting at the head of the far end of a huge table staring back at him, Jake asked, "How did you get an Ungden to cooperate with you?"

Seeing that neither Kent nor anyone else in the room understood what he was referring to, Jake followed by saying, "I mean, how did you get an alien to help you?"

"What in the hell are you talking about? The only alien in this room is you," Luallen responded in an enraged tone.

"Oh my god," Jake said softly after he realized they were unaware of the alien's presence.

Chapter 36
Destination Earth Confirmed

May 2018

"Ah yes, the time has come. Admittedly, it's sooner than I had anticipated," Qarta relayed to Jarga as she sensed him approaching her.

Moments later, Jarga entered Qarta's living quarters and stopped directly in front of her.

"You killed my father. You have been manipulating me ever since that day you killed him."

"I sensed curiosity and doubt had been stirring within you for the past several months. I was aware of you penetrating my thoughts and memories."

"Then why didn't you stop me; why didn't you prevent me from learning the truth?"

"Because I could not," Qarta responded, disappointed that Jarga still failed to understand the extent of his intellect, the fact that it was superior to all others on Shangten.

"What do you mean?"

"Jarga, your intellect is marginally superior to my own, making you the rightful ruler of Shangten and our people. Now get on with it, assume your role, and fulfill your destiny."

"Why did you kill my father? Why did you manipulate me into thinking I was the one who killed that defenseless Argas?"

"Because it was all part of the process. Had I not done these and other acts, you may have never assumed your rightful place and rule over Shangten. Again, get on with it," Qarta relayed to Jarga, exploiting his emotional immaturity in hopes of manipulating and taunting him into completing the final step in his transition.

In a fury, driven by raw emotion, Jarga initiated a mind integration similar to what Qarta had facilitated between Jarga and the Argas. Jarga absorbed Qarta's consciousness and all first-hand and inherited memories and life experiences. Because Qarta was nearly 500 years old, the mind integration lasted nearly eight hours before the process was completed and Qarta was dead. Qarta's remains consisted of a black pool of liquid, a life form color never before shared by any other beings on Shangten.

Upon completion of the mind integration, Jarga absorbed Qarta's remains and was infused with newfound energy and unanticipated and immeasurable malice.

I understand. I know what I must do. I will lead my people. I am ready.

September 2146

Hearing the ship approaching the military hangar, Jarga peered out of his living quarters, intently awaiting Leese's return from his visit to Earth. The ship landed, and the survey party members began leaving the ship. Jarga was surprised Leese was not the first survey party member to exit, and his impatience rapidly increased. Survey party members continued filtering out of the ship until there were no more.

Leese? Gralp? Jarga thought while telepathically directing Bly, the only Ungden other than Leese to visit Earth, to report to his living quarters.

Glaring through Bly, and with no formalities, "Where is Leese? Gralp?" Jarga insisted.

"Leese indicated those that have remained on Earth since our first survey had not advanced required preparations as quickly as planned. Therefore, he decided to remain behind and ordered Gralp to do the same, to ensure safe passage when we all arrive," Bly responded.

Bly and Jarga engaged in a mind integration, enabling Jarga to obtain the details of the current situation he was seeking. Upon completing the mind integration, Jarga sensed a splinter in a portion of Bly's memories. Although the affected memory was present, it appeared to have been slightly incomplete, giving birth to the splinter, which is typically an indication that his mind had been tampered with. This was very odd to Jarga since the only member of the survey party capable of manipulating Bly's memories was Leese. Bearing in mind that Bly was an Ungden, Jarga could not comprehend why Leese would want to alter Bly's memories. More specifically, he could not understand why Leese would want to change only one particular memory.

Because Jarga was aware that Leese split the four hundred survey party members into twenty equally manned survey groups, Jarga ordered Bly to assemble the remaining nineteen survey party leaders in the highly secured meeting room within the military hangar to perform a mind integration.

Bly assembled the various survey party members in the meeting room, and they awaited Jarga's arrival. Within minutes, each of them could sense Jarga's presence, as he appeared to be agitated. They all feared for their lives since lives tended to be lost when Jarga was upset.

Jarga arrived soon thereafter, and a brief moment later, the mind integration began. It concluded six hours later, leaving Jarga perplexed since no other splinters were encountered. In light of his superior intellect, it did not take him long to realize that he had not interacted with anyone from Leese's survey group since Leese led that group and was absent. Fatigued from the two mind integrations he'd performed that day, Jarga summoned all eighteen members of Leese's survey party to report to his living quarters the following morning.

The next morning arrived, and all eighteen of Leese's survey group members awaited Jarga's admittance into his living quarters. Once again without formalities, Jarga admitted them and immediately initiated a mind integration. The mind integration was completed in approximately three hours, and it left Jarga very troubled. He'd noticed a single splinter in the context of the very same memory, albeit a much more difficult splinter to detect than the one he'd encountered when integrating with Bly's mind. It was evident to Jarga that this particular memory had been manipulated, its integrity compromised.

The memory in question seemed to Jarga to be extremely superfluous since it pertained to a point in time very soon after they'd arrived on Earth and split into the twenty survey groups. Jarga asked the 18 survey party members whether they remembered anything unexpected that occurred during their time on Earth. The only notable occurrence they mentioned was the fact that Leese decided to remain on Earth and directed Gralp to do the same. They mentioned they were surprised since it made more sense to them for Gralp to remain behind, if necessary, and have Leese return to assist Jarga in executing their evacuation from Shangten.

Jarga concurred with the collective assessment of the group and concluded the splinter must have been caused by an environmental factor on Earth that was experienced by each of them at their specific location. He decided to redirect his focus on their impending evacuation. Approximately eleven months remained until nearly all of the resources of Shangten would be depleted, and soon thereafter, the planet would begin to disintegrate. Jarga did not have the luxury of only needing to formulate an evacuation plan, he also needed to determine how they would invade Earth while suffering as few casualties as possible.

The following day, Jarga met with Dangu and Zalm in his living quarters. Dangu was next in command of military operations after Leese, and Zalm and was the one who had orchestrated and led evacuations from their two prior host planets.

INTROSPECTION: TRANSFORMATION

"Zalm, as you have effectively executed historical migrations, you will plan and lead our evacuation from Shangten. Plan on us all leaving in ten months. I expect updates weekly until further notice. You are dismissed," Jarga relayed in his traditional demanding fashion.

Zalm left, and Dangu remained in Jarga's living quarters.

"Dangu, you will lead strategic preparations for our invasion of Earth; all of our military resources and assets are at your disposal. I expect your eradication of all earthlings to be swift with minimal casualties of our people, and especially of Ungdens. No humans are to survive or be spared. Understanding humans' intellects are far inferior to even those of the Sellenians, they are large in number, nearly twelve billion, and our military consists of only 10,000 soldiers. Given their inferior intellects, it may be viable to include non-military personnel in your efforts, as I have learned it is all too simple to kill humans. They are very fragile. Questions?"

"None," Dangu replied, relaying an emotion of excitement to Jarga in anticipation of orchestrating yet another invasion and eradicating another entire species of aliens.

Chapter 37
Convert Operation Exposed

September 2146

Hendrix was faced with a dilemma. Should she try to escape, therefore acknowledging and exposing her true identity as an alien, or should she remain in the presence of everyone and focus her efforts on convincing all who were present that she was human and Jake was the alien? She recognized Jake's ability to overcome her telepathic manipulation and discern her true alien identity, which was very disconcerting to her. She was concerned about Jake's dominance since she was an Ungden and therefore, like Jarga, was at the top of the intellect-based caste system on Shangten.

Further, she did not know what Jake was. Despite him appearing to be human, he possessed alien-like abilities she feared were superior to her own. Her great intellect enabled her to process these and other realizations and scenarios within a human instant, culminating in her determining the best way to proceed was to continue masking her true alien identity and attempting to convince at least Emily and Kent that Jake was the alien.

INTROSPECTION: TRANSFORMATION

"Your plan won't work Claag, Ungden of Shangten," Jake relayed to Hendrix. "I know who and what you are, and I will stop you by showing them who you are."

Claag was enraged. "I sense what you are trying to do to me, and surely you have come to realize that my will is much stronger than yours," she responded.

Claag became even angrier, after confirming that Jake's abilities were superior to hers.

"I can tell you're frustrated, and I know you're questioning how a petty human's intellectual abilities could surpass your own," Jake pushed, attempting to cause Claag to lose her composure and expose her alien form to everyone in the room.

Even though Claag was oblivious to Jake's ulterior motive, she remained unyielding in her strategy of not revealing her alien appearance and convincing them that Jake was the alien. However, she came to the harsh realization that Jake was preventing her from executing her plan. Each time she tried to manipulate Jake's human appearance, and each time she attempted to verbally or telepathically communicate with those in the room, Jake snubbed her.

Scanning everyone's thoughts, Jake learned that they were convinced he was the alien in light of Hendrix projecting visual expressions of her discomfort in response to harm Jake was seemingly inflicting upon her. Learning of their thoughts, Jake recognized this was going to be extremely complicated. He needed to perform the actions necessary to convince them that he was the human and she was the alien while concurrently interacting with Claag and containing her nefarious actions.

Jake was overwhelmed and needed time to think. He slowed everything down, freezing everyone in the room. He closed his eyes and focused on trying to reveal the solution to this complex situation. Nearly fifteen minutes elapsed before Jake opened his eyes and returned things as they were. He was relieved he'd fought his initial instinct to reveal Hendrix's true appearance. He decided all that were present would perceive such an action as a feeble attempt to deceive them.

"My name is Jake Moore. I was born and raised in Louisville, Kentucky. I'm a sixteen-year-old junior at Atherton High School. I know each of you are confused and scared. I promise I will explain everything. Right now, you need to understand that who you think is FBI Analyst Sherri Hendrix, a human, is actually an alien. She is an Ungden from planet Shangten, a planet very far from here. Her real name is Claag. She is critical and powerful on Shangten and is one of very few trusted associates to Jarga. Jarga is the aliens' ruler, and he is currently planning on invading Earth and killing all of us."

Jake's remarkably calm demeanor and the credible delivery of his words had everyone in the room mesmerized, though he was all the while enduring Claag bombarding his mind in an attempt to overwhelm him and create a means to communicate to everyone in the room herself directly. It was as if everyone there was in a trance, hypnotized by Jake's apparent wisdom and calming effect. A silence overtook the room but was finally broken by Kent.

"I saw you in the electronics store. Humans are incapable of doing what you did. People can't move objects with their minds. People can't make themselves invisible to others right next to them. You are trying to manipulate us into breaking in an instant the trust Hendrix has worked years to establish while selflessly serving the FBI and our country."

"When will you resign yourself to the fact that your kind's inferior intellect will be your demise? Humans cannot see beyond what is right in front of them. They will never accept the fact that I am a traitor, let alone an alien," Claag relayed to Jake.

Ignoring Claag, Jake continued his efforts to instill reason into everyone in the room.

"This is Hendrix's true appearance." Jake stripped Claag of the only remaining tap she had in their minds, which was the masking of her actual appearance.

INTROSPECTION: TRANSFORMATION

In an instant, Claag's appearance transformed from the projection of a somewhat attractive human woman in her early thirties to a mass of blue gas.

"This is just another one of your tricks. You want us to see what *you want us to see*," Emily rebutted.

As Jake suspected, this action had backfired, and he regretted going against his better judgment.

That was stupid. I knew I shouldn't have done that. That was stupid. What am I going to do? I don't know what to do.

"Accept it. It is hopeless. You are delaying the inevitable. What are you going to do?" Claag relayed to Jake in a taunting fashion.

Jake was showing moderately visible signs of breaking down. He was beginning to doubt himself and his ability to convince them of the truth. In addition to his self-confidence deteriorating, his stamina in insulating everyone in the room from Claag's desired actions was wavering.

"What can I do to prove to you what and who Hendrix and I are?" Jake said rhetorically to everyone in the room, somewhat in an act of desperation.

"How can you possibly think you can save the human race when you were unable to save your mother and brother?" Claag relayed to Jake. Claag then implanted an image of the crash site into Jake's mind. Rather than simply providing a stagnant view of his mother's and brother's dead bodies, Claag had them screaming for Jake, pleading for him to save them. Their fabricated loud cries reverberated in his head. Their bloody faces and bodies covered his eyes.

It was just too much for Jake to endure, and he instantly and reflexively relinquished his mental control over Claag due to the shock of what she'd relayed to him. Guilt that he had endured ever since the incident monopolized his thoughts and overcame him. Tears began forming in his eyes.

There was nothing I could do. There was nothing I could do. It all happened so fast. Before I knew it, the car exploded.

"That's what you humans do. You convince yourselves you did all you could when you fail. The greater the failure, the more self-convincing you perform. Pathetic," Claag said to Jake with growing vigor, recognizing her increased control over his will.

Noticing Jake's deteriorating confidence, strength, and overall condition, Claag increased the intensity of her will to kill everyone in the room. When undistracted, Claag's will was no match for Jake. But Jake was severely compromised, and his mind was fatigued.

In an instant, four people collapsed. It was as if Jake broke away from a trance, seeing these people collapse and realizing they were dead and that Claag had killed them.

I will not fail again. I will not let any more people die.

To Claag's disappointment, she recognized that killing those four people had only strengthened Jake's formerly eroding self-confidence and mental stamina. Jake recognized Claag's tactic and vowed not to allow her to compromise his focus again.

Everyone other than Jake, Claag, Emily, and Kent inexplicably raised from their seats, and without speaking a word, left the room. As they were departing, Emily and Kent inquired with raised voices why they were leaving and where they were going. In a trance, without response, they all filed out of the room.

"I'm becoming tired. While I have been communicating with you, I've also been fighting against Hendrix. She, Agent Hendrix, Claag, I mean the alien, has been trying to kill all of you. I lost my focus because of her psychologically manipulating me, and as you saw, she killed four people. I am compromised. My mind is not operating at its full potential. Having them leave was an act of trying to minimize the number of casualties if anyone else is going to die."

Scanning Kent's and Emily's reactions to his words, he knew he was finally getting through to them. Their growing doubt evidenced it, regarding whether Hendrix was indeed human.

"I want you to allow Hendrix to communicate openly with us," Emily insisted.

INTROSPECTION: TRANSFORMATION

"OK." And with that, Jake released his grip on Claag's mind, only allowing her to communicate with them.

"He is manipulating you. As you know, psychological manipulation is a tactic we have come to learn is prevalent among these aliens. You can't allow yourselves to succumb to his tactics," Hendrix said in a frenzy.

"Come with me," Kent whispered in Emily's ear.

"You two stay here. We'll return in a few," Kent said to Jake and Hendrix as he walked toward the door.

After closing the door behind him, Emily and Kent began conversing in the hallway.

"Aside from Jake's opening remarks, everything he has said has been focused on keeping all of us safe. The first time Hendrix was purportedly granted an opportunity by Jake to communicate with us, she focused on trying to discredit Jake. Is this what the mindset or actions of an FBI Analyst would be?" Kent asked.

"And Hendrix said that we determined psychological manipulation is a tactic that is employed by the aliens. This is the first I've heard of this," Kent continued.

Meanwhile, in the multi-purpose room, Claag was relentlessly bombarding Jake with nefarious thoughts.

"Stop," Jake shouted.

Claag was anguishing. She had never before experienced the sensation she was currently feeling. It was as if her brain was attempting to breathe while being suffocated. She was horrified to learn of yet another one of Jake's superior abilities. She was trying to appease him and convince him to stop hurting her, but Jake was overcome by pure fury; he was numb and deaf to all external stimuli.

An image then revealed itself in his mind via an intense shock to his brain. It was Langi in the same form of the elderly woman Jake encountered at Cherokee Park.

"This is not the way," she said. "Do not succumb to temptation. Do not do as Jarga would do. Have me not regret transferring my abilities and consciousness to you. Learn from our collective histories. The path to peace is not violence. There is another way."

Langi's consciousness was gone, and Jake instinctively released his telepathic grip over Claag. While Jake's mind and thoughts were cloudy, he heard an escalating sound, which soon became words coming from just outside one of the doors serving as an egress point for the multi-purpose room he was in.

Beginning from faint sounds and transitioning to loud audible shrieks, "Jayyysoooon. Jason. Jacoooob. Jacobssssss. Jacobssooooo. Kent. Kent. Open your eyes."

Jake transitioned his focus from Emily to Claag and scanned her mind. He was first overcome by sadness and then by severe remorse.

"You did it again. You allowed yet another person to die. How many more people are going to die because of you, because of your weakness?" Claag relayed to Jake. "It is hopeless. Succumb to the reality that you are a failure and that people will continue to die because of your powerlessness."

In spite of Claag's feeble attempt to further compromise Jake, at this moment, he found himself instilled with newfound strength. He resumed his grip over Claag's mind and barricaded the outside world from anything else she may wage upon it.

Acknowledging that defeat was likely imminent, Claag had felt that killing Kent was the worst thing she could do in that instant of opportunity. It was a tactic she'd hoped would distract the FBI from adequately preparing for Jarga's impending arrival, thereby simplifying their invasion.

FBI agents and other personnel swarmed around Emily as her tears poured onto Kent's lifeless face. Cradling Kent's head while working to stand up, she placed his head gently on the floor and then stormed back into the multi-purpose room.

"Why? Why?" Emily screamed at Jake, tears pouring down her face.

"I didn't do this. It was Hendrix...it was Claag. I'm so sorry. Please forgive m—"

"Bullshit. Own up to it. You senselessly murdered my partner...my lover...my best friend. And for what?"

"Please. Listen to m—"

"Why in the hell should I listen to you? Why should I even talk to you?" Emily asked in disgust while drawing her firearm and pointing it at Jake's face.

"Because if you don't, we'll have no chance. We'll lose everything."

"...everything he has said has been focused on keeping all of us safe," Kent's final words to Emily consumed her thoughts and reverberated like the beating of a healthy heart.

"...everything he has said has been focused on keeping all of us safe."

"OK. I'll listen," Emily replied, sounding as though the wind had been knocked out of her. She reluctantly returned her firearm to its holster. "You wouldn't let me discharge my weapon anyway."

Observing Jake's clarity and newfound strength, Claag had resigned to him and was content to await whatever her fate may be. However, she was still unwilling to reveal her alien appearance to Emily since doing so would substantiate Jake's earlier actions; it was her last hope that Jake would be unable to prove to them that she was an alien.

"I want you to draw and analyze our blood. You'll see I'm telling the truth once you do," Jake said calmly.

"How do I know you won't manipulate what follows?" Emily asked.

"Follow FBI protocols, and you'll know I didn't manipulate anything," Jake responded.

"What do we do with you two in the meantime?"

"Put us in whatever highly secured area you want, but you must keep me close to her so I can prevent her from doing what she did to Senior Master Sergeant Kent Jacobsen to anyone else. I cannot allow anyone else to die."

Acknowledging Jake's abilities, let alone Claag's potential abilities, Emily recognized the two of them were likely there of their own wills and that their physical restraints were pointless. Emily contacted the Pentagon Force Protection Agency (PFPA) using her mobile phone, and within moments, PFPA personnel rushed into the multi-purpose room.

"Take them to the 'dungeon,'" Emily instructed.

The dungeon was the most secure detention area in the country, located in the lowest floor within the Pentagon, the equivalent of many stories underground.

"And get them something to eat. Restraints won't be necessary."

The PFPA then motioned Jake and Claag to get up and accompany them to the dungeon. Because of Claag's unwillingness to cooperate, Jake forced her to comply. They both accompanied PFPA personnel to the dungeon and awaited the arrival of a medical technician to draw their blood.

As Jake anticipated, the medical technician arrived and drew blood via syringes equipped with traditional hypodermic needles for subsequent analysis. Jake conceived this plan since he knew a syringe equipped with a hypodermic needle would be incapable of extracting any of the gas comprising Claag's physical life form. And in the off-chance it did extract any gas, the alien substances would be easily detectable by those analyzing the results.

Just after Jake and Claag's departure, Emily called Dr. Agon and requested that he perform the analysis of the blood samples because of his familiarity with the extraterrestrial substance they had previously encountered. Emily acquired the blood samples from the medical technician and took them to the hospital in which Dr. Agon's research facility was located.

"I'm very sorry for your loss, Emily," Dr. Agon said as Emily entered into his office.

He walked to her and placed his right hand on her left shoulder.

"Thank you, Dr.—"

"Yash," he interjected.

INTROSPECTION: TRANSFORMATION

"The only way to preserve my sanity is to focus on the task at hand. Here are the blood samples. What the hell?"

With tears forming in her eyes, Emily looked down at the blood draw tubes in her hands and noticed one of them that had previously contained blood was empty.

"That is Hendrix's sample," she said. "This must be another one of Jake's tricks. Dammit."

Not understanding her comment about Jake, Dr. Agon took the blood samples from Emily.

"I'll personally analyze these samples immediately. Have a seat. I'll return in about an hour," he said as he left for his lab.

Emily's grief unexpectedly overtook her, and she began crying soon after Dr. Agon left his office. She was completely distraught and lost. Within a few minutes, her crying slowed until it came to a halt and she fell asleep.

Meanwhile, Jake and Claag were confined in adjacent isolated quarters in the dungeon. Unbeknownst to the FBI, the only reason they were able to confine Claag to her quarters was because of Jake's hold over her. He applied mental restraints on Claag, preventing her from doing anything but remaining completely idle mentally in her quarters. Despite Jake's concern that Emily may question the outcome of the analysis of Hendrix's 'blood sample,' he was hopeful that she would not suspect he was capable of manipulating anything she and anyone else involved in the blood testing effort saw. That is, he hoped Emily would not assume that he was able to force involved personnel to draw whatever conclusions he desired.

"I have the results, Emily," Dr. Agon said as he opened the door to his office without noticing Emily had been sleeping.

Reorienting herself as she awoke, Emily asked Dr. Agon about his findings.

"First of all, I confirmed there was nothing inside Hendrix's blood test tube. If possible, can you retrieve the hypodermic needle that was used to draw her blood? Perhaps there will be traces of blood on or inside the needle itself."

"Consider it done," she responded, although Emily was mystified about why the tube was empty when she'd seen that it contained blood as she left the Pentagon.

"What about the results of the other blood sample?"

"I correlated the DNA obtained from the sample to historical blood draw results dating back to when Jake Moore was born; there was a 100% match. I also compared Jake's DNA to that of his father and sister. I confirmed DNA sequences within Jake's DNA markers match those of his father and sister. The sample you provided and that I analyzed is undeniably tied to Mr. Moore's blood."

Emily then excused herself from Dr. Agon's office and contacted the medical technician, whose name she found out was Betsy, who'd performed the blood draw. Betsy indicated that the needle used to extract Hendrix's blood was disposed of in a biohazard waste disposal receptacle. She further explained that there was no way to know exactly which needle was used. The good news was the receptacles were sent to a third-party disposal service weekly, and it only had been a day since new receptacles were provided throughout the Pentagon's medical facilities.

Emily informed Dr. Agon she would pick up the entire biohazard waste disposal receptacle Betsy was certain she'd used when disposing of the needles used for the blood extractions and then return. Emily arrived at the Pentagon and decided to check up on Jake and Hendrix before picking up the receptacle.

"You hanging in there, Hendrix?" Emily inquired, noticing a blank look on her face as she peered through the small square of thick-paned glass that contrasted the steel door that served as the only egress for the quarters Hendrix was confined in.

"Hendrix?"

Hendrix was completely non-responsive.

"What in the hell did you do to her?" Emily inquired of Jake.

"You don't understand."

"Enlighten me."

I N T R O S P E C T I O N: TRANSFORMATION

"As I said before, what you think is human, I mean Hendrix, next to me is an alien. There is nothing that you can do to contain or restrain her. Everything she does is through her mind. I have to control her mind to contain her. And that's what I'm doing."

"Relinquish your control over her."

"The last time I did that, you saw what happened to Senior Master Sergeant Kent Jacobsen. I'm sorry, I must continue controlling her," Jake continued as he saw how heartbroken Emily became.

"I'm sorry. I was careless," Jake said softly as tears formed in his eyes.

Continuing in a soft-spoken voice and a somewhat winded demeanor, Jake said, "I will let Claag go once you provide me the results of the blood test."

Jake knew that the blood had not yet been analyzed by scanning Emily's thoughts. However, to maximize the likelihood of the blood being analyzed, he did not want Emily to know what he already knew.

"Enough of this 'Claag' business; her name is Hendrix," Emily responded. "Because of your damn tactics and theatrics, there was no blood in the sample tube, which has complicated matters. But I'll play along with your senseless game. We'll do what's necessary to obtain her blood, and then it'll be your ass on the line. It's only a matter of time."

Jake was relieved that Emily did not demand to be afforded the ability to interact with Hendrix; it was obvious her emotions were understandably influencing her. Not even four hours had elapsed since Claag mercilessly murdered Kent. Emily had not been afforded an opportunity to grieve his death sufficiently, and her intensifying grief was clouding her judgment fortuitously in Jake's favor.

Emily stormed out of the dungeon, obtained the receptacle from Betsy, and returned to Dr. Agon's office.

"Well, here it is Doctor, I mean, Yash."

"It's good you did not open the receptacle," Dr. Agon said as he took it from Emily.

He opened the box and estimated it contained approximately 30 hypodermic needles.

"Let me run these needles under my microscope; hopefully I'll be able to see traces of something that resembles the alien substance on one of them."

Dr. Agon observed each needle, one by one, until he proclaimed, "There it is," after the fourteenth needle. "This needle contains traces of the alien fluid."

Dr. Agon explained that the traces of alien material on the needle were consistent with what he would expect to encounter should the aliens' life form consist of a gas. He further explained that, contrary to the other thirteen needles he'd observed, which contained traces of blood both on the outside and inside of the needles, this was the only needle that solely contained traces of what appeared to be the alien substance, and it was present only on the outside of the needle with nothing contained within the needle.

Dr. Agon tested the liquid he could extract from the surface of the needle and confirmed it was identical to the alien fluid recovered at the Tranquility Airlines flight 2122 crash site and previously found by Kent and Emily at Theodore Roosevelt Island, thanks to the lead from police detective Billy Richmond.

Emily graciously thanked Dr. Agon for reorganizing his schedule to address her needs and then turned to leave promptly.

"I do not know where you are off to next, but I urge you to take it easy for the rest of the day; let work wait until tomorrow. I know your first instinct is to ignore my suggestion. However, I, too, have been enduring difficult times, and taking a much-needed break has served me well." Dr. Agon had not actually consciously or even willingly taken a break from his work, the 'break' he was referring to was his visit to the hospital. He realized both the treatment he'd received and his rest were instrumental in enabling him to recover his strength and rationally sort through his thoughts.

Emily heeded Dr. Agon's advice. She picked up some Chinese food and ate dinner at her home. She then resumed reading one of many classic science fiction novels written by John Scalzi until she fell asleep. She was exhausted.

Emily felt reenergized entirely when she woke up at 6 pm the following morning. However, her grief over losing Kent was ever-present.

If only at this moment I could wake up to realize everything that happened was simply a horrible nightmare. What am I going to do? How can I go on without him? He was the face of the Bureau I have come to know…and love. I am lost without him.

Unexpectedly, with tears running down her face, Emily was injected with a sense of duty and abruptly transitioned her thoughts to the matter at hand.

"What am I going to do about these results?" she said aloud.

She was perplexed regarding how she would confirm whether the alien sample was indeed extracted from Hendrix or from some other unknown alien that may be covertly involved with the FBI since Jake was conclusively ruled out by Dr. Agon's analysis of his blood sample. She sat on her sofa trying to formulate a means of confirming a correlation. What seemed like minutes were hours.

"I've got it," she screamed, noticing her clock read 2:30 pm.

"My god, where did the time go?" she asked herself, not realizing the hours that had elapsed while continuing to grieve Kent's death.

Emily took a shower and then went to the dungeon.

I don't know how this works. Read my thoughts. Please read my thoughts. Emily thought as she was looking Jake in the eyes through the thick-paned glass area within the steel door leading into his cell.

"I hear you," Jake responded telepathically, wondering where Emily was going with this.

"Your game is up. Your blood draw came back as expected," Emily said in a raised voice to Jake, ensuring Hendrix could hear her.

I know now you're not an alien. How far can I go away from you and still have you protect me?

"As far as necessary," Jake relayed to Emily.

Emily instructed the PFPA personnel accompanying her to remove Hendrix from her quarters. Hendrix waited for Emily to finish up with Jake so they could leave the dungeon together.

"You can't leave me here. You can't let her go. What are you doing?" Jake screamed, playing along with Emily's covert plan. He could sense Claag's pleasure witnessing him seemingly suffer.

Promise me you'll protect me, Jake. My life is in your hands now.

"I promise I won't let anything happen to you."

"I have a lot of questions for you, Jake, but Hendrix and I first need to help Luallen respond to the mass genocide that occurred at the museum. If I learn you played a role in that massacre, you'll likely never again see the light of day," Emily angrily exclaimed to Jake as she and Hendrix left the dungeon.

Emily requested Hendrix to accompany her to her cubicle to discuss the necessary assistance she required to support Luallen's crisis response efforts effectively. They both arrived at her cubicle, and just as they sat down, Emily flooded her thoughts with the knowledge that Hendrix, and not Jake, was the alien. Seconds, which seemed like minutes, elapsed with no reaction from Hendrix. Emily then decided to demonstrate visible discomfort, hoping that Hendrix would scan her thoughts.

Once again, Jake cautiously relinquished his telepathic grip over Claag's mind while carefully surveilling her every thought and action. Emily then screamed in agony as she clenched her temples with her hands. In an instant, the pain was gone.

"I've got you," Jake relayed.

Because he did not want to cause unnecessary commotion, Jake restrained Claag, yet allowed her to continue assuming the appearance she'd concocted for Hendrix's identity.

"Bring her back and then we'll decide what to do," he continued.

Emily was relieved not only because she was still alive, but also because she now knew that the outcome of Dr. Agon's analysis of the blood samples was correct. Her relief quickly transitioned to fury, knowing that Hendrix killed Kent.

INTROSPECTION: TRANSFORMATION

"You son of a bitch. *You* killed him."

"Since I have no idea how to kill you, I guess you're going to rot in here," she said to Hendrix hysterically.

Jake was forcefully escorting Claag back to the dungeon.

Emily called PFPA personnel to come and release Jake from his quarters and to confine Claag in her prior quarters. Unbeknownst to Emily, Jake subsequently suspended the PFPA personnel so he could have a difficult conversation with Emily.

"You need to know what these aliens look like," Jake said to Emily in a calm, eerie manner. "Look."

Emily turned to her right and saw a large mass of blue gas hovering approximately three feet off the ground next to her, just as she saw when Jake previously revealed Claag's life form in the multipurpose room.

Hendrix? This makes sense, Emily thought after comparing her true appearance to the alien substance she had previously recovered at multiple sites.

"Emily. We are in a tough situation. Restraining Hendrix, I mean Claag, all of this time has drained me. I'm exhausted. If we're going to have any shot at defending against the impending alien invasion, I can't be distracted by constantly restraining her," Jake said with a blank look on his face. "Everything you've seen...all that has occurred, it's only just the beginning. The aliens currently on Earth are just scouts inventorying our military defenses and intellectual capabilities. The rest, hundreds of thousands of aliens, are coming. If we don't prepare, we won't have a chance."

"You're suggesting we kill her?"

"I promise there is no other way. It's either restrain her and jeopardize all of us, or take her life, one alien life, to save billions of humans."

"How can you say that? You're just a kid," Emily exclaimed.

"I *used to be a kid*. That ended upon my alien encounter. I don't exactly know what I am now, but I know I'm no longer just a kid."

Seeing Emily's mystified facial expression, Jake concluded by saying, "I just can't explain."

"Can you show me?"

"I could try. But if I tried to show you, you still wouldn't fully comprehend what has happened to me. My new abilities. My new perspectives. My strong intellect."

An awkward silence followed for several minutes.

"There is another way. It would require a huge sacrifice from you, where life as you currently know it would forever change."

"What do I have to do?" Emily asked

"I could force everything Hendrix possesses into you, just like what happened to me from Langi...I mean, from the alien."

"OK, sure, let's do it."

"You need to think this through, Emily. Once the transfer occurs, it remains until you die. You will absorb her consciousness. There's no going back."

"I've lost the only love of my life. All I have left is my passion for helping people and for protecting my country. From what I've seen of your abilities, inheriting them myself will help me fulfill my life purpose. You have to let me do this, Jake."

"Even though I can use your help, and while it would be a huge relief to not be the only human with these abilities, this doesn't feel right to me, Emily."

"Do it. I need this," Emily insisted.

"Please forgive me," Jake telepathically relayed to Emily.

Jake implanted the thoughts and gesture necessary for Claag to accept and acknowledge the imminent end of her life. Seemingly to Claag, at her own will, she moved toward Emily and completely enclosed Emily within her. Upon initial contact, Emily instantly became unconscious. All of Claag's memories and experiences, both her own and those she'd absorbed from other aliens before her, were implanted into Emily's mind. Once the process was completed, both Emily and Claag fell to the floor.

INTROSPECTION: TRANSFORMATION

Observing this process revealed to Jake what had occurred during his alien encounter with Langi. Hours elapsed, and Emily was still unconscious, lying on the floor beside Claag's lifeless remains.

My god, what have I done? Jake thought, fearing the transfer was too much for Emily to endure.

To Jake's relief, he telepathically confirmed Emily was still alive, but he was concerned that she had not yet regained consciousness. Not knowing how much more time would be required, he relinquished his telepathic grip over PFPA and FBI personnel, yet prevented them from visiting the dungeon.

Days elapsed, and ice covered the surface of the floor, spanning throughout the entire corridor of the dungeon.

Something is wrong. There is too much strain on her mind and body. I don't think she's going to make it. I'm going to be all alone. What have I done? What am I going to do? Jake thought, pressing his back against the wall and sliding down until he hit the floor.

Bending his knees with his arms around them and his head tilted downward, he felt helpless.

*I can't do this by myself. I can't do this by myself. I can't do this by myself. I can't ...*Jake endlessly repeated.

Hours passed, and the entire corridor of the dungeon was filled with ice. Both Emily and Jake were engulfed by it. Jake was unconscious and violently convulsing. His skin throughout his entire body was a pale white, evidence that his entire system was shutting down.

Similar to a cardiac defibrillator administering shock to a patient who is not breathing, Jake instantly regained consciousness after hearing Emily yell, "Bullshit. It was all bullshit. There were so many signs. We could have stopped that alien bitch a long time ago."

"I'm not alone," Jake said faintly to Emily. "Finally, I'm not alone."

Emily could not move. Ice was everywhere.

"Hold on, Emily." In an instant, she watched Jake transform the ice into water, and then into gas.

227

Emily went to Jake, "Are you OK?"

"I'm fine, just exhausted. Can we stay here for a while?"

"Of course. Of course. I'm so sorry I ever doubted you, Jake. And I'm sorry you have to face this burden at such a young age."

Jake closed his eyes and fell asleep.